Outside In

Outside In

Courtney Thorne-Smith

BROADWAY BOOKS

New York

PUBLISHED BY BROADWAY BOOKS

Copyright © 2007 by Ernest, Inc.

All Rights Reserved

Published in the United States by Broadway Books, an imprint of The Doubleday
Broadway Publishing Group, a division of Random House, Inc., New York.
www.broadwaybooks.com

BROADWAY BOOKS and its logo, a letter B bisected on the diagonal, are
trademarks of Random House, Inc.

Library of Congress Cataloging-in-Publication Data
Thorne-Smith, Courtney.
Outside in / Courtney Thorne-Smith. — 1st ed.
p. cm.
1. Actresses—Fiction. 2. Fame—Fiction. 3. Hollywood (Los Angeles, Calif.)—
Fiction. I. Title.

PS3620.H77O87 2007
813'.6—dc22
2007008244

ISBN 978-0-7679-2749-9

PRINTED IN THE UNITED STATES OF AMERICA

1 3 5 7 9 10 8 6 4 2

First Edition

For Roger,
Above and beyond my wildest dreams.

Outside In

1

Kate stood frozen in her bathroom doorway, bracing herself for the inevitable, the unavoidable, the potentially painful moment dreaded by women everywhere: the morning weigh-in. Was it just her imagination or did the scale actually seem *mean* this morning, like the mechanical version of a popular yet cruel sixth-grade girl? Maybe it was the ungodly hour of the morning (four-thirty) or the fact that she hadn't had her coffee yet (the resultant weight-reducing "release"), but she could swear that the scale had seemed friendlier yesterday.

"For the love of god," she whispered to herself, "calm down. It is only a *scale*, only a silly number." Unfortunately, she had "only a lingerie scene" to shoot today and whatever the scale said would soon be reflected on camera and then on television screens across America for all of rerun eternity. Taking a deep breath and holding it in (in the faint hope of creating an "airier" self), Kate stepped onto the scale and watched as the small digital screen computed her weight, body fat, hydration level, and probably her credit score.

Oh shit.

Oh shit, *shit*.

Feeling dizzy, Kate braced herself on the edge of the sink. Her precoffee brain was having difficulty processing the information: how could she have *gained* five pounds? Stepping off the scale, she said a quick prayer to the god of arbitrary-numbers-upon-which-to-base-one's-self-esteem, removed her Cosabella thong panties (all of that lace must weigh a ton), and got back on the scale.

Oh shit.

"How's it looking?" Kate jumped as her husband, Hamilton, entered the bathroom—both because she was surprised to see anyone else in her bathroom at four-thirty a.m., and also because she wanted to create as much distance as possible between her body and the number shining up from the digital scale. He wasn't fooled.

"Oh, *Kate*," Hamilton groaned, somehow summoning the energy to accomplish the disappointment trifecta of head shake, eyebrow crease, and judgmental lip purse, all before his first cup of organic green tea. "How could you let this happen? You *know* how important this is, Katie. You *know* we need to show everyone how much better you are doing."

"Better," meaning *thinner*. Thinner than she had been three years ago, when her career had stalled after a promising start on a short-lived nighttime soap, when nights spent eating out with the proceeds from her first high-paying gig had added up to the Hollywood version of the freshman fifteen, complete with paparazzi shots and cruel nicknames in the tabloids. By the time Hamilton had approached her with the promise to reenergize her young career and rid her of "Katie the Cow" forever, she had been so grateful for the positive attention that she had quickly signed over the management of her career. Two months later, when the weight started to come off and the work offers began to come in, she'd happily signed over the management of the rest of her life when Hamilton surprised her with a proposal during her comeback appearance on *Regis and Kelly*. Three months later, in the wedding photos published in *People* magazine—not the cover, but a full two-page spread, nonetheless—Kate looked stunning in her (size 4!) Vera Wang gown, her curly brown hair streaked with copper highlights and painstakingly straightened as per Hamilton's detailed instructions. He wanted to model Kate's wedding-day look after Jennifer Aniston's ethereal beauty on the day she married Brad Pitt, even going so far as to hire Jennifer's hair and makeup team. The team had done their best, working their magic for four exhausting hours, but no amount of hair product or bronzer could change the freckled, fresh-faced, undeniably Irish Kate into a Greek goddess. Hamilton almost succeeded in covering his disappointment when she walked down the aisle, but Kate saw the flash of disillusionment in his eyes and silently vowed to do whatever it took to guarantee that Hamilton never again regretted his investment in what he lovingly referred to as his "chubby little has-been."

This morning, his tone made clear she had failed them both.

Kate hurried to wrap a towel around her traitorous body, feeling very small and hugely fat at the same time. "I know this looks bad," she stammered. "But, I mean, it's just five pounds. I mean, seriously, we're probably the only ones who will even notice . . . right?" She didn't believe the words as she said them, and she could tell by her husband's irritated sigh and the oh-so-subtle shake of his handsome head that he didn't believe them either.

"Sure, Katie," he said sarcastically. "I am sure no one will notice . . . just like they didn't notice before. I mean, who looks at actresses' bodies?" He turned to go but stopped at the door. When he spoke again, his voice was tinged with sadness. "I just don't understand, Katie. I really thought you understood how important this was . . . for both of us. But I guess all of the work I've put into rebuilding your career just doesn't mean that much to you." With that, he walked out of the room, leaving Kate alone with her shame.

She looked at the image in the bathroom mirror and watched dispassionately as a tear rolled down her cheek. She never looked quite real to herself. She often felt, when she saw her reflection, as if she were watching an actress in a movie. Today's movie was about a weak girl who couldn't control her appetite—a bad girl whose hunger was bigger than she was, bigger than the whole world.

The most frustrating part was that she had almost made it. She'd been good all week, sticking to Hamilton's "approved-food list": egg whites, chicken, low-sodium turkey breast. She had been losing weight, too, watching the numbers on the scale go down as her hip and cheekbones became more pronounced and, unfortunately, her mind became more and more preoccupied with food. She had tried to distract herself from both her hunger and her nervousness about being nearly naked on camera by watching television, but the commercials seemed designed to sabotage her diet with endless pictures of slim, happy, gorgeous women eating big, messy burgers while they laughed and fell in love with equally gorgeous, equally gluttonous guys. Fearing that hunger combined with the power of suggestion would propel her to the nearest drive-through, she forced her ravenous attention away from the television screen. Standing up, she gripped the edge of the couch to compensate for the dizziness that lately accompanied her every sudden move and made her way to the walk-in pantry. She was searching through Hamilton's impressive (girly?) supply of herbal teas that he swore were "just as satisfying as a snack" when her eye landed on a jar of honey-roasted peanuts, half hidden behind the fat-free mayonnaise.

Honey-roasted peanuts: sweet, salty, and creamy, all in one miraculous package. Kate found herself standing frozen, transfixed before the holy grail of caloric density. What harm could one or two peanuts do? In fact, she told herself, her metabolism was probably slowing down, starved as she was for fat and sugar calories. Two or three peanuts could be just what her body needed to kick it into calorie-burning overdrive. Feeling almost righteous, she reached for the jar and twisted off the lid, the pop and hiss of the vacuum seal releasing the familiar heavenly scent. She inhaled deeply and shook out three peanuts, closed the jar, and took her tiny bounty back to her spot on the couch in front of the television. She ate the nuts painstakingly slowly, enjoying each one as if it were the richest, most extraordinary piece of Godiva chocolate. *See?* she thought as she finished the last one. *No harm done.*

She was right, too. There had been no harm done by the first tiny handful of peanuts. But who had ever been able to stop at three honey-roasted peanuts? *Just three more can't hurt,* she told herself as she made her way back to the pantry, repeating the ritual of opening the jar, carefully shaking out three peanuts, and padding back to the couch.

And so the evening went, nut by nut, until Kate was shocked to find herself shaking out a handful of salt, sugar, and peanut dust. Hyperventilating from shame and the fear of being discovered, Kate hid the empty jar at the bottom of the recycling bin and went upstairs to brush the incriminating scent off her teeth and hide her disloyal body under Hamilton's bazillion-thread-count duvet. She clenched her eyes shut, trying to will herself to sleep before her husband came home from his business dinner, knowing that if he looked her in the eyes he would see her transgression immediately. He prided himself on his ability to "see right through her." When they first met, it had felt so much like love, like she was finally being "seen" by someone. His attention to her food, her clothes, and her career had felt so safe. When had it begun to feel so suffocating? *When I started hiding things from him,* she told herself, remembering what Hamilton's therapist, Penelope, had said when she complained about his control issues.

"It sounds to me like he is just trying to help you, Kate," the pink-clad, perfectly coiffed Penelope had said. "I wish *I* had someone who paid as much attention to me as Hamilton does to you. I mean, that is what you are saying, isn't it? That your husband pays *too much* attention to you?"

Kate had felt stupid—not to mention outnumbered—sitting in the corner of the therapist's extraordinarily feminine chintz couch and looking across at Hamilton and Penelope, who were both somehow perfectly color-coordinated with the beautifully decorated room, looking at her with expressions of pity mixed with indulgence as if she were a rather slow, rather spoiled child. Kate always felt like an interloper at these sessions, rather than a primary element in the marriage therapy process. She often got the sense that she was an intruder, interjecting herself inappropriately into her husband's primary intimate relationship: the one he had with Penelope. When she finally worked up the courage to bring these feelings into therapy—naively believing that she was following Penelope's directions to be as authentic as possible—she was met with matching sighs and a tag-team lecture from Penelope and Hamilton about how she was "projecting her own insecurity . . ." (Penelope) "We are in no way judging you . . ." (Hamilton) "It's just that introspection is so new and foreign to you . . ." (Penelope) ". . . that, of course, you are going to get . . ." (Hamilton) ". . . confused." The last word was said by both of them at the exact same time, eliciting identical giggles and smug smiles, which did absolutely nothing to alleviate Kate's feelings of alienation. She wanted to tell them how separate and alone their pathetic attempt to reassure her had made her feel, but, sadly, she had been too insecure.

"He's right, you know," she said now to her reflection, as more tears threatened to spill out of her brimming eyes. "Insecure *and* weak *and* indulgent *and* self-destructive, and now it's too damn late to fix it."

"Katie-Cow," called Hamilton from the bedroom, maybe even convincing himself that he was joking. "Isn't it time for you to get going? You don't want to make it worse by being late, do you?"

"No—I mean, yes, it is time for me to get going," said Kate, wiping her eyes as she reached out to turn on the shower. "You're right. I don't want to be late." *I don't want to go,* she thought as the tears forced their way back to the surface. But what she wanted had ceased to matter so long ago.

★　　★　　★

Twenty minutes later, driving her BMW M5 along the traffic-free Sunset Boulevard (one of the few benefits of a six a.m. call time), Kate strained to see the road through the frozen eye mask that Hamilton had forced on her so that her eyes "wouldn't be as swollen as her stomach." When her cell phone rang, filling the car with the theme song from *Jaws,* Kate answered with a forcedly cheerful "Hi, Mom."

"How did you know it was me?" asked her forever-caller-ID-mystified mother.

"Just psychic, I guess." *And who else is going to call me at five-thirty a.m.?*

"Well, anyhoo," said her mother, charging ahead in her coffee-induced morning list-making mode, "today is your great uncle Bert's birthday and I know it would mean a lot to him to hear from you."

"Uncle Bert? Do I have an Uncle Bert?"

"Of course you do, honey. He is Aunt Mary's new husband. You met him at their wedding."

"I didn't go to Aunt Mary's last wedding, Mom. I was working. Remember?"

"Well, be that as it may, it would be nice of you to call him and wish him a happy birthday."

"But, Mom," said Kate, wishing she had heeded her ring tone's warning, "I don't know him. Won't it be weird for him to get a call from a stranger?"

"You're not a stranger, you're family," said her mother. "And he's a big fan of your show."

Ah, the show. So it's not a call from his loving-although-unknown-niece Katie he is waiting for, but a special birthday greeting from Kate Keyes-Morgan, television star and pawn in her mother's bid for most loved and admired member of the large and *Generations*-obsessed McMannus/Keyes clan.

"Well, Mom, I'm driving right now, so I can't really write down a phone number. And I've got a pretty big day at work today, so why don't you just pass on my birthday wishes for me?"

"I'm sure you have three minutes for a phone call, Katie. I'll leave the number on your home phone and you can call in for it when you get a break." *Damn.* "So tell me, what 'big' thing is going on at work today?"

Going against years of experience and her inner voice that was screaming, *"Danger, Will Robinson!"* at great volume in her aching head, Kate decided to try for a little bit of unconditional motherly love and support. "Well, Mom, I have a lingerie scene today and I just don't feel great about my body. I know it's silly— I mean, I *hope* it's silly—but you know a few pounds of bloat can make you feel *huge,* even though you know no one else will even notice and you are just making yourself crazy for absolutely no reason," Kate said, talking faster and faster to cover the silence on the other end of the line. *Interrupt me, Mom. Tell me I am beautiful the way I am, at any weight, at any size . . .*

"What does Hamilton think?"

"What?" asked Kate, aghast but not totally surprised.

"What does Hamilton think? Does he think you are too heavy for your scene?" *Oh, that's right,* thought Kate. *I forgot that the unconditional love and devotion are reserved for men.*

"Well," she stammered, "he isn't thrilled, but you know what a perfectionist he is. I mean, he won't be happy until—"

"Until you achieve your true potential," interrupted her mother.

"I was going to say 'until I am a size zero.' "

"Well, there is no reason you couldn't be a size zero if you put your mind to it, dear. Hamilton is only trying to help you to be a success. I don't think any of us want to see you let it all slip away again, do we?"

"Certainly not—it would be such a disappointment to dear Uncle Bert."

"What's that, dear?"

"Nothing, Mom." Luckily, her mother's selective hearing

weeded out most sarcastic comments, especially when they smacked of the truth.

"Now, Katie, I'm worried about you."

"Oh, Mom, that's sweet," said Kate, surprised by her mother's sudden tenderness. "But I'll be—"

"I mean, really, what are we going to do about this bloat?" her mother interrupted, clearly excited to be talking about an area in which she had some real expertise: diuretics. "A seaweed wrap maybe? Or a sauna? I am afraid you have missed the window for a really good laxative, but maybe I could get you in for a cellulite treatment later today. Did you at least take a steam?"

"No, Mother," said Kate, adding shame about her lack of quick weight-loss tricks to the honey peanut/lack of willpower pile. "I didn't steam, and since I am on my way to work as we speak, my chances of sneaking in a cellulite treatment are pretty slim—pardon the pun."

"The pun? Oh, Katie, I hardly think this is a time for jokes, do you?"

"No, Mom, I don't think this is a time for jokes, but crying about my puffy belly will only create puffy eyes and then they'll only be able to shoot me from behind!"

"Oh, no we don't want that. Shooting you from behind has never been a good idea. Of course, I blame your father for that. Genetics can be cruel."

So can mothers, thought Kate as she begged off the call by pretending to be entering a bad cell zone. Her conversation with her mother had put *her* in a bad zone, but she knew it was her own fault. She had once again "gone to the hardware store for milk," which is what her makeup artist, Paige, called it whenever she tried to go to her mother for comfort and support. ("It's not her fault, Kate. Her shelves just aren't stocked with love and hugs. It's a hardware store, for God's sake. She's got hammers and nails and sandpaper. Just grab a helmet at the door and move fast.") *Just grab a helmet and move fast.* It was a good thing to keep in mind when navigating a conversation with her mother, and it applied just as well to navigating a day at work on her television show.

Kate covered the distance from her Pacific Palisades home to the Burbank soundstage where her television show filmed far too quickly. She pulled her car up in front of her trailer and steeled herself for the day's first encounter with the beautiful Sapphire Rose.

Sapphire Rose was what Paige referred to as a "piece of work." The tabloid press had dubbed her a "work of pieces" in honor of her myriad plastic surgeries. Whatever you called her, she made working on *Generations* feel like a Chinese torture chamber, complete with the subtle terror of never knowing what specific kind of pain lay in store each day. Some days, Sapphire would even be well prepared and pleasant, which really threw everybody off. Most days, though, she was raging, from either a fight with one of her young boyfriends, an unflattering photo in a magazine, or—even worse—no photo in a magazine.

At one point, she had been the "next big thing," with her face gracing the covers of magazines and movie offers coming in faster than she could read the scripts. Then one movie bombed, and then another, and very soon the movie offers dried up. Her agent had been able to turn the fumes of her movie stardom into a television deal, which eventually became *Generations*. The show, which followed the story of three generations of a wealthy Los Angeles family, was an instant hit, filling the nighttime soap opera void left by *Dallas* and *Melrose Place*. For many actresses, being the star of a hit show would be a victory to be celebrated, but for Sapphire it was merely a daily reminder of her failed film career. Even her yearly invite to the Golden Globes awards show was a source of pain rather than pleasure, due to the fact that the seating arrangement—movie stars in the center, television stars seated around them—served only to remind her of her former glory. In her mind, a TV show, even a hit, was a failure, and she seemed intent on making everyone around her pay for her disappointment.

"Good morning, Katie. Ready for another glorious day in New

Bedford?" Kate turned to see Sam, the show's production assistant, heading toward her car, his ubiquitous headset on and clipboard in hand. At twenty-two, he was the youngest member of the crew, and the most ambitious. He was 140 pounds of pure intelligence and drive. Although his job as production assistant made him the low man on the totem pole—the getter of coffee and runner of errands—Kate knew that someday very soon they would all be working for him. He opened her door with a comical flourish and a gallant "Is there anything I can carry for you, my lady?"

"With all of your free time?" Kate answered with a wink. Sam was by far the busiest person on the set—first to arrive, last to leave, and not a moment's rest in between. Everyone loved him and counted on him as the one person who could be trusted to get things done. Someday he would be running a studio, but today he was carrying her set bag to her trailer and schlepping coffee for spoiled thespians.

"I'm just on my way to make a Starbucks run for you-know-who. Do you want anything?"

"Oh yes, I would love a double cappucci—" *Lingerie scene, lingerie scene* . . . Hamilton's voice ran through her mind. "Black coffee. Black."

"Black coffee, black? As opposed to what? Black coffee, green?" teased Sam, putting her bag down on the couch in her trailer.

"As opposed to anything yummy, tasty, creamy, or in any way fattening or bloating, in honor of today's tiny costume," answered Kate, pointing to the minuscule lavender lace bra and panty set that taunted her from its seat of power, clinging to a hanger in her open closet. "How can anything so small make a grown woman feel so large?"

"*You? Large?*" asked Sam with disbelief. "No, you're crazy. In fact, you could use a few pounds—more than a few. At *least* four. I am going to get you the biggest, frothiest, most calorie-laden drink they sell."

"You know I won't drink it, Sam."

"Perhaps you won't, but I am going to get it for you anyway. Production is paying, and spending Jerry's money will bring me joy. It's not always about you, you know," he said with a smile and a wink. "When did you become such an *actress?*"

"*Me? An actress?*" Kate said, striking a dramatic pose, one hand on her thrust-out hip and the other stretched up toward the sky. "Darling, I am a *star.*"

"Be careful, star—you're going to pull a muscle standing like that if you're not careful," Sam said, laughing as he backed out of her trailer. "Now get thee into thy tiny costume and get thy ass into makeup, your star-ness. You don't want them to shoot your scene without you, do you?"

"Oh, Sam, you *know* I'd love nothing more, but I will pretend that I am a grown-up and go anyway. *Apparently,* they don't pay you if you don't do the work."

"Yes, they are snotty that way." He grinned. "Now stop stalling and get dressed. The sooner you start, the sooner you will be done and drinking your triple-cream vanilla caramel frappuccino." The door banged shut behind him with a tinny sound, and then there was just the hum of the generator and the internal buzz of Kate's insecurity. Sam was right about one thing: somewhere along the line she had become way too actressy. What happened to the strong, independent young woman who had come down to Los Angeles on her own at eighteen, full of dreams and feminist ideals? Her plan had been to be a *real* body doing *real* work representing *real* women. Of course, it is easier to embrace the reality of an eighteen-year-old body than that of a thirty-year-old. Maybe she could be a powerful feminist with a perfect body. After all, she told herself, it takes a lot of strength to starve day after day. Of course, it was not the sort of strength that adds anything to the world, except, of course, one more tiny body for other women to compare themselves to and come up lacking. Well, today she was five extra pounds of relatable. Granted, it was less "I am woman, hear me roar" and more "I am woman, watch me sneak food in shame," but if she was going to have a big belly with her lingerie, she may as well wear it with pride. It works for Jack Nicholson. Why shouldn't it work for her?

Yeah, *right.*

Kate sighed and dragged herself off the couch, trying not to think about how devastated she had felt when the press had turned on her before. She knew it didn't matter in any real way. This was her constant struggle: the part of her that knew it didn't really matter what anyone else thought, and the part of her that really wanted the affirmation anyway. She wanted to be strong, independent . . . and loved. She'd been dubbed too fat in the press while other actresses were criticized for being too thin. Was there a magic number, a secret "weight of universal love"? Maybe she had stumbled upon it by mistake and today would be the day that she hit body nirvana. Smiling at her own neuroses, she reached for the scrap of fabric that was pretending to be her costume, stepped into it, and turned toward the narrow full-length mirror on the back of the tiny bathroom door.

Big mistake.

Suddenly, her charming neuroses had morphed back into a big, fat belly. But *come on,* what was the problem with a slightly bigger body?

It made you a much bigger target. And Kate just didn't feel strong enough to field the blows.

Strong enough or not, however, it was time to head into the ring. Maybe—hopefully—it was all in her head. Yeah, Kate thought, if her head had migrated down to her stomach. Well, as Sam had said, one good thing about starting this scene is that it meant that it was almost over. Then, aside from being tortured by her bloated celluloid image in reruns for all eternity, she would never need to do it again. Different, more and/or less humiliating scenes, sure, but not *this exact one* ever again. She took a deep breath, reached into the closet for the terry-cloth robe that would be her cover-up and security blanket for the next few hours, and headed out into the early morning Los Angeles chill.

2

In her much larger trailer, exactly one hundred yards closer to the soundstage, Sapphire Rose was having her own wardrobe trauma. Sapphire's problem, however, was not her belly, but the *stupid* waistband on the *stupid* skirt that the impossibly *stupid* wardrobe girl had hung in her closet.

"*Goddamn it!*" Sapphire screamed, kicking the door of her closet, the base of her couch, and finally the front door until it swung open with a booming crash. "Where the *fuck* is the *fucking* wardrobe girl?" she yelled to the world at large, secure in the knowledge that someone would bring her the wardrobe girl (whose name was Karen, but Sapphire had stopped bothering to learn names long ago, preferring to use her memory for new diets and emergency contact numbers for her facialist and plastic surgeon).

"Is there a problem?" asked Sam, appearing at the foot of her trailer steps, Starbucks tray in hand, calm as always in the face of one of Sapphire's many storms.

"Yes, there is a *fucking problem*. It is the same *fucking* problem I have every *fucking* day. The *fucking* wardrobe idiot put the wrong *fucking* skirt in my *fucking* room and it doesn't *fucking fit!*"

"Wow," said Sam, "that is fucked."

"Yeah," said Sapphire, missing Sam's sarcasm completely, "and the day will be fucked if I don't get a costume that fits in the next thirty seconds."

"Thirty seconds. Wow. I better get right on that," said Sam, unflappable as ever as he handed her a triple-shot skinny caramel cappuccino and turned back toward the wardrobe trailer, wondering where they would find yet another set costumer to replace the one that Sapphire was about to get fired.

Sapphire slammed the door and struggled out of the too-tight skirt. Why did they do this to her? Why did they mess with her head like this? There was no way that this was the same skirt she had tried on last week. She had been on a raw-food diet for almost the whole weekend, so she clearly should have lost weight by now. *They're just jealous,* she thought, reaching for a raw seed and carrot muffin from the basket on her counter. *Jealous and incapable of the compassion and empathy needed to see how grueling it is to live with the constant pressure of my extraordinary talent.* Picking up her phone, she dialed her agent's number with one hand, using her other hand to open the door of her mini fridge and take out the raw butter and cheese that she had ordered her assistant to deliver before her 5:30 a.m. call time. Her assistant had also been ordered to clear out the remains of last week's Meaty Mediterranean Blood Type Diet. After five days of ground, broiled, and deep-fried lamb, Sapphire was more than ready to give raw food a try. After all, it had worked for Demi.

"Get me Michael," she barked at the nameless (to Sapphire, at least) assistant who answered the phone, reaching into the basket for another muffin and a handful of raw seed crackers. While she waited the interminable amount of time that it took for her agent to come to the phone (1.2 minutes), she broke off pieces of muffin and layered them with crackers and slices of raw cheese. *Dieting sucks,* she thought, realizing how much better a chocolate-chip muffin with peanut butter would taste. But she understood that dieting was simply the nature of the beast for a television star. She thought of the line from the Julia Roberts movie *Notting Hill* in which her character said she had been on a diet since she was four-teen. *Fourteen, my ass*, thought Sapphire. *My mother had me on my first diet at ten and I am still looking for the diet that will shrink that ass.* She was also looking for some raw honey, bending over her mini fridge and cussing out her assistant in absentia for not considering her sweet tooth. How was she supposed to lose weight without raw honey? Or a raw Snickers bar.

That was one thing she did miss about the Zone Diet: those Zone Bars had been the saving grace of the depressing home-delivered miniature meals. She'd had her assistant buy those bars by the case. But in spite of her discipline in limiting her snacking to the bars (the honey peanut really did taste like a Snickers) and the occasional chunk of cheese (or two), that diet hadn't worked for her either. She was coming to the realization that she had one of those elephant metabolisms: in the event of a famine, she would be one of the last ones standing, but until then she would just look fat.

Leaning into the fridge in search of more raw cheese, she caught sight of what looked like candy bars. She grabbed a hand-ful and read the label: Raw Bars. Thank God. She ripped open a package and bit off a chunk. Not bad. It tasted a little like the sesame candies she used to eat as a kid, the only remotely candy-like thing she could find at the health-food store where her mother did all of the family shopping. Sapphire had thought all grocery stores smelled like brewer's yeast until the glorious day that she went to the local supermarket with her neighbor's mom. While nice Mrs. Yeager piled her cart with boxes of Ho Hos, Twinkies, and brightly colored fruit-flavored juice drinks, Sapphire munched happily on the chocolate MoonPie she had been given to "tide her over." She felt as if she had stumbled upon a magical world of color, taste, and whole-body sensations. There were no bins of loose grains or baskets full of small, misshapen organic fruits. Instead, there were row upon row of boxes printed with rainbows and cartoon characters, beautifully arranged shiny apples, and perfect bunches of grapes. Chewing contentedly on her marshmallow patty, Sapphire looked longingly at the racks of candy at the checkout counter, knowing that soon she would be home, where the only after-school treat she was ever allowed was a piece of organic celery filled with oily natural peanut butter. Now, looking at the jar of raw almond butter her assistant had left on the counter next to the muffin basket, Sapphire was suddenly gripped by an overpowering craving for a MoonPie. Or two. After a day and a half of bean-sprout burger patties, she deserved it. She was about to dial her assistant's number when she heard her agent on the line.

"Sapphire Rose, my queen—how great to hear your voice! How's it hangin'?" *How's it hangin'?* thought Sapphire. *I have got to get an older agent.*

"Well, Michael, it is hanging like shit. That's why I am calling you at fucking early o'clock in the fucking morning."

"Okay, Sapphire, I can hear that you're upset. Did they move your trailer again? I made them swear it would be as close to the front door as humanly possible."

"No, it is not the fucking trailer. The fucking trailer is fine. It is the fucking *wardrobe* again. Why can't they just get clothes that fit me? I can't go through this every day, Michael. I just *can't*." Sapphire felt tears come to her eyes, threatening her newly applied eye makeup. Luckily, she was able to stem the tide of her emotions by stuffing her face with another muffin.

"Look, Sapphire, I am sure we can work this out. We always do," said Michael, trying to ignore the chewing and sniffling. "What exactly is wrong with your clothes?"

"THEY . . . DON'T . . . FUCKING . . . FIT!"

"I see," said Michael, lowering his voice to a near whisper and speaking in the very slow, measured rhythm he had learned from one of his mother's many therapists, a strategy that often came in handy when dealing with hysterical actresses. His entire childhood, peopled as it was with alcoholic, narcissistic parents, aunts, uncles, and assorted relatives, was like a preemptive graduate degree in dealing with highly emotional clients. "Is it possible someone has simply made an honest mistake?"

"An honest mistake? An *honest mistake?* What does that even *mean,* Michael? Is that a euphemism for *fucking incompetent*— for fucking with the head of the woman who has to go on camera and *shine* in *five fucking minutes?* I can't *shine* in clothes that don't fit, Michael! And if I don't shine, this show doesn't shine." Sapphire paused here for some well-placed sighs and sobs, which gave her time to reach into the back of the kitchenette cabinet for her emergency bag of miniature Snickers bars, hidden behind the super green phyto-juice packets and stay-slim protein powder. By balancing the phone between her shoulder and ear, she was able to perform the labor-intensive job of unwrapping enough bite-size candy bars to make an actual mouthful, all the while releasing one final, heart-wrenching sob and the plaintive sigh of wealthy, beautiful, spoiled women everywhere. "Why does no one understand how *hard* my life is?"

"I understand, Sapphire," said Michael so slowly that it sounded like *he* was on Thorazine, "and so do the people on your show. Everyone is working to make your life easier. Just last night I was talking to Bob Steinman about you and—"

"You were talking to Bob about me?" Sapphire broke in, her voice brightening and the chomping and chewing sounds stopping for one glorious moment at the mention of the president of Cutting Edge Pictures.

"Yes, I was," said Michael, altering his voice slightly to take on the affectedly cheery attitude of a parent helpfully (and hopefully) luring his three-year-old out of a tantrum. "I was going to tell you all about it just as soon as we got this wardrobe issue all figured out."

"What wardrobe issue?" Sapphire giggled, sensing that a much-desired treat was within reach. "I'm sure that the nice people here will find something for me to wear. I mean, we can't have me running around naked, can we?"

Dear God, no, thought Michael. "I don't think anyone wants that, Sapphire,"—as evidenced by the complete lack of argument over her no-nudity clause—"so why don't I make a couple of calls and get back to you when we have this whole thing worked out?"

"Call me back? You silly-willy, you know I won't be able to wait to hear about what you and that nice Bob Steinman were saying about me."

"And I can't wait to tell you all about it, just as soon as we get you all dressed and on set to start your day."

"I am on my way out right now. I'll just stop by the wardrobe trailer and ask those sweet wardrobe girls for some little thing to wear, and I'll call you just as soon as I finish this scene," she said, rooting around in her bag for a celebratory Snickers bar. Or three.

"I'll look forward to your call," said Michael, feeling anything but happy anticipation.

He knew he had to be crafty. The imagined conversation had to be promising enough to spark Sapphire's interest but vague enough to prevent her from checking up on it and catching him in a lie. The truth was that Sapphire Rose's attitude was finally catching up to her, and, in spite of the damage her unpopularity would cause his own wallet, Michael was finding some satisfaction in the fact that she was now persona non grata in project development meetings all over town. As much as he would miss the fat checks that her failing career generated, he wouldn't miss the endless, embarrassing phone calls he was forced to make on her behalf, complaining about everything from her wardrobe to the absence of lamb-based snacks on the craft services table. It was getting more and more difficult to generate the expected passion and vitriol when presenting his clients' ever more petty demands. Did it really matter whose trailer was a few yards closer to the soundstage? And yet, whenever he called a producer, he had to voice his clients' concerns as if he were reporting the need for an immediate heart-lung transplant for the leader of the free world. He tried to remind himself that it wasn't completely the fault of actors that they felt so ridiculously important. After all, the entire world treated them as if they were precious jewels, endlessly fascinating and worthy of being photographed and discussed, every tiny detail analyzed and appraised. Why did Sapphire think that the whole world cared what she wore and what she ate? Because enough of the world actually *did* care enough to buy the magazines and watch the innumerable celeb-reality television shows that seemed to be replacing real news.

Real news.

That had been his dream: to be a part of the world of "real news." He had grown up watching twenty-four-hour news shows. Michael and CNN had been his father's constant companions. His father had been his stability and his rock during the topsy-turvy years of Michael's mother's descent into mental illness, and the sound of the twenty-four-hour news channel had been Michael's lullaby. He would fall asleep to reports on the Gulf War, dreaming of one day being the reporter on the scene—barely flinching as bombs exploded all around him, putting forth a calm presence for the people at home, people such as a little boy with an erratic mother. But then his father had died of a heart attack during Michael's last year at USC. Between the pain of losing his father and that of his mother reentering the mental ward at UCLA Medical Center, Michael felt overwhelmed by the drama of his own life. So he had chosen an internship at super-agency BAM over the one he had been offered at CNN. The internship at the news giant would have been a step closer to his dream of being a reporter, but it was also two thousand miles away from his insti-tutionalized mother and his childhood home, which was the only place in the world where he still felt a connection to his father.

As time passed and he climbed the ladder at BAM, moving from intern to assistant and finally to agent, he told himself that *next year* he would move to Atlanta and start his "real life." But every year there was another raise, followed by a newer car, a bigger house, and a more beautiful (and thus more expensive) girl-friend. He joked with his fellow agents about the "golden hand-cuffs" that kept him bound to his childish clients and a job that they all agreed was shallow and soul killing. But his ability to be excited about the next model of BMW was fading, along with his ability to generate even phony interest in Sapphire Rose's latest diet or inane demand, leaving him increasingly depressed and dis-satisfied.

In other words, way too much like his mother.

3

Kate stepped up into the makeup trailer and was immediately enveloped in the homey smells of coffee, bacon, and hair-care products.

"Good morning, Herself," trilled Paige, Kate's makeup artist and main source of sanity on the *Generations* set. "What can I get for you, besides a larger costume and an apple fritter to help you fill it out?"

"Oh, I don't know," said Kate as she settled into the barbershop-style chair and sighed with pleasure as Paige pulled off her Ugg boots and worked her cold feet into a pair of electric warming booties. "Maybe an earthquake of some sort. Nothing major enough to hurt anyone, of course, just enough shaking to shut us down for a day or two to give me enough time to do a beet-juice colonic fast or get liposuction on my entire body."

"Well, I'm a little short on beet-juice colonics, but I can offer you coffee strong enough to create an earthquake in your bowels. Will that help?"

"Oh, yeah, that's a great idea. Nothing like a little liquid doody to really give a lingerie scene that extra juice—pardon the pun."

"Oh, that's lovely," said Paige, trying not to laugh coffee through her nose. "I swear I am going to call the *Enquirer* and tell them that their sweet little princess is a foulmouthed lunatic."

"Please do. I am so sick of seeing pictures of myself with the caption, 'The always adorable . . .' Of course, it still beats 'The always expanding . . .' "

"Oh please," scoffed Paige. "You were never fat. In fact, I know you don't want to hear this, but you actually looked much better then, much healthier. Truly, you look a little gaunt these days. I've stopped shading your cheekbones altogether, and I am seriously considering injecting some of my own fat into your cheeks if you continue to lose weight."

"Hey, speaking of fat cheeks, did you read that people are having *ass* implants?"

"I believe I did read that," said Paige, affecting a studious air. "It was in the *Financial Times*, was it not?"

"Oh, shut up," laughed Kate. "You know as well as I do that I probably didn't even *read* it at all. I probably saw it on E!, which, sadly, is where I get most of my news. But my ignorance is not the issue here."

"It's not?"

"No, it's *not*. The issue here is that women are now getting implants to imitate J. Lo's ass, when I have been starving myself in my effort to achieve the near asslessness of a young Greek boy."

"No, you wack job," said Paige, shaking her head and beginning to apply foundation to Kate's nearly perfect skin. "The issue here is neither your ignorance of world events—beyond the current trends in plastic surgery, of course—nor the size and shape of J. Lo's ass. The real issue is the fact that you think 'near asslessness' is a goal worth aspiring to."

"Well, I was going to save the world," answered Kate, enjoying the feel of the makeup sponge moving over her face, "but I was just so damn *hungry*."

"Ha ha," said Paige dryly. "You *think* you're joking, but there is more truth in what you say than you think there is. Come to think of it, judging by your weight right now, you probably aren't taking in anything I'm saying, are you?"

"Not really," admitted Kate. "Right now you just look like a big, fuzzy doughnut. You're probably better off waiting until after this scene to tell me anything important. Unless it is an important recipe of some sort, or a really detailed description of almost any carbohydrate-based food product, or—"

"Oh, shut *up,*" laughed Paige. "The only thing more boring than a do-gooder celebrity is a dieting celebrity. God forbid they combine and become the truly terrifying hybrid of the celebrity who is trying to do good by sharing her diet secrets. I do believe that is the first sign of the apocalypse."

"Do you think the apocalypse is imminent? Because then I could certainly have a cookie."

"If I thought it would make you eat more, I would call God personally and arrange it. I must say, the idea of watching you ingest a carbohydrate would *almost* be worth watching the world as we know it end. I wonder if I could have a cocktail on the eve of the apocalypse. The fires of hell would sure be a lot easier to bear if I could have a nice, big frozen margarita . . . or ten."

"Oh man, I would love to see you drunk," said Kate. "I bet you were a blast."

"Yeah, for a minute," said Paige. "Until the tears started flowing and I started vacillating wildly between proclaiming my undying love for you and screaming—well, scream-*slurring*—'You don't *know* me. You don't know me *at all.*' "

"I know you say that," said Kate, "but it is just so hard to picture you like that."

"Trust me, it wasn't pretty. Now, why don't you just relax so that I can get to work transforming you from a little Irish waif into America's favorite Waspy femme fatale."

"You're the best," sighed Kate, leaning back against the headrest.

"Thank you," said Paige, truly grateful for the compliment, because she so clearly remembered a time when the only thing she was the best at was ordering another drink.

The Paige that Kate and everyone else at work knew was the very definition of a "together woman": smart, responsible, upbeat, and charmingly self-deprecating. Just heavy enough to be non-threatening to women, but fit enough to be attractive to men. The Paige that they would have met ten years ago, however, was quite a different picture. Before she had been lucky enough to get "a nudge from the judge" in the form of ten court-ordered Alcoholics Anonymous meetings after her second DUI arrest, she had been a daily drinker on her way to becoming an every-single-minute-of-the-day drinker, having recently discovered the joys of the morning cocktail. In fact, she had been arrested first thing in the morning while on her way to work, which had turned out to be a plus. Even her well-honed denial couldn't rationalize a .05 alcohol level at seven-thirty in the morning as "normal drinking." Even so, if the Los Angeles court system hadn't insisted on her getting her court card signed at the end of every AA meeting she was forced to attend, she wouldn't have sat through a single one in its entirety. Her first meeting felt like the worst of high school assemblies, with all of the popular kids laughing and greeting one another while Paige stood alone feeling shy and insecure, still woefully ignorant of the rules of the popularity game. *This is precisely why I drink*, she had thought, standing at the door and trying to look like she *wanted* to be alone, that she had a very good—and very *cool*—reason to be hovering at the door looking lost, frightened, and pathetic.

"Hi, I'm Brad," said a voice to her left, startling her out of her self-pitying revelry. She turned to find a balding, middle-aged man standing next to her with a broad grin on his plain face and his right hand extended. Was she supposed to shake it? If she took his hand, did that mean they were going steady?

"Hel-*lo*," she answered in her best *I-am-not-available-and-*

even-if-I-were-I-wouldn't-choose-you voice, perfected through years of barroom exchanges with overly friendly guys just like this one. When paired with her standard pursed lips and haughty head turn, it was virtually guaranteed to get the because-I-am-too-good-for-you message across, without the need to exchange any actual, and possibly awkward, words.

"Yes, hel-*lo*," continued Brad, in an almost perfect imitation of her pseudogreeting, not only not taking the hint, but reintroducing his proffered hand and adding an indulgent chuckle to his silly grin. "And what is your name?"

Taken aback by his complete inability to understand when he was being blown off, Paige found herself taking his hand and telling him her name—her *real* name, even. She was that confused.

"Well, Paige, welcome. Is this your first meeting?"

Flustered further by his apparent ability to read her mind, Paige replied, "Yes, but I'm not really here—I mean, I am *here,* obviously, but not because I need to be—I mean, I need to be, but not because I have a problem with, you know . . ."

"Alcohol?" asked Brad, not unkindly.

"Right . . . alcohol. I mean, not *right* because I have a problem, but right because . . . well . . . never mind. The point is that I am here because I got a stupid DUI and I need to get this paper thingy signed." Paige rifled around in her oversized Le Sportsac handbag (decorated with countless colorful little martini glasses—in hindsight, perhaps not the best choice) until she found the narrow green card her lawyer had given her, along with instructions to have it signed at the end of ten different AA meetings. Thinking that maybe she could avoid ten wasted evenings, she held up her card and, treating Brad to her most winning smile, said, "Do you know where I go to get this silly thing signed?"

"As a matter of fact I do," said Brad, returning her smile.

"Really?" said Paige, leaning into him conspiratorially and actually beginning to enjoy both the flirtation and the promise of using this man's obvious attraction to her to her own advantage.

She might even let him kiss her. Buying her a drink was probably out of the question.

"Really," he said, once again matching her tone. "Come right this way." She allowed him to take her arm and lead her toward the front of the large auditorium, which was already three-quarters full with laughing, chatting, *way too happy* people. Were they going directly to the card-signing room? Excellent, she thought, she could be out of there in time for happy hour. "And here you are," he said, leaning over and grabbing a business card off a center-aisle front-row seat.

"Is this where I get my card signed?" she asked, beginning to panic as an attractively dressed blond woman behind a podium—a podium that stood roughly three feet in front of Paige—began to knock on its surface and call out, "Meeting time!" in a cheerful voice. If Paige didn't get her card signed and get out of there quick, she would be stuck.

"Yes, it is, and that woman right there is going to sign it for you."

"Great," said Paige, relieved, as she started toward the podium.

"Right after the meeting," said Brad as he pulled her gently back toward the chair he had cleared a moment ago. "Carolyn," he called up to the podium woman, "Paige here needs you to sign her court card for her *after* the meeting, okay?"

"Okay," answered Carolyn, smiling down at her with that same moony smile. "I'll sign it right after the meeting. You just sit tight."

Sit tight? Was this a meeting or was she getting a shot at the doctor's office? She did sit tight, though. What choice did she have?

The meeting went by in a blur of words, movement, and intermittent applause. Paige had trouble following the speaker, an older man whose tragic story of lost jobs, car wrecks, and a nearly broken marriage was met with laughter and nodding heads all around her. She was shocked that the audience wasn't treating his story with the gravity it deserved, but at the same time was envious of what seemed to be an easy camaraderie between the speaker and his audience and among the audience members.

After the speaker, Carolyn returned to the podium, looked pointedly at Paige, and asked if anyone who was "new to the program would like to stand up and introduce themselves?" *Introduce themselves? Whatever happened to Alcoholics Anonymous?* To her surprise, Paige heard the scraping of what sounded like a lot of chairs and turned around to see at least twenty people standing. One by one, they said their names followed by the phrase "and I am an alcoholic," which was then followed by applause and shouts of "Welcome" and "Keep coming back." The energy was infectious and Paige found herself wanting to leap up and proclaim herself a part of this happy club. Fear and insecurity held her to her chair, however, until an encouraging smile from Carolyn helped Paige gather enough courage to half stand on shaky legs and mumble, "Um, my name is Paige and I am . . . well . . . I don't know what I am." She held her breath, waiting to get thrown out for not following the rules, but instead felt warm hands patting her back and heard laughter, applause, and shouts of "You're in the right place, Paige!" and "If you find out, would you let me know?" which was followed by more laughter and a warm smile from Carolyn.

★ ★ ★

As Paige was putting the final touches on Kate's makeup, spot-covering her more insistent freckles and subtly overlining her lips to create the illusion of collagen without the danger of looking as if she'd been hit in the face with a two-by-four (although occasionally she did take it too far, eliciting cries of "Lucille Ball!

Lucille Ball!" from a clown-faced Kate), there was a rapping on the makeup trailer door, followed by Sam's head poking through.

"Thirty minutes," said Paige, before he could get a word out. "I still have to blow out her hair or America will think Melania got her finger stuck in a light socket."

"Hey!" said Kate.

"What?" asked Paige innocently. "It's my fault you come in here looking like a poodle?"

"Ladies," interrupted Sam. "Believe it or not, I did come all the way over here for a reason. Basically, thirty minutes is not going to be a problem. In fact, if you had an urge to do cornrows or hair extensions, now would be a good time."

"Oh shit," groaned Kate. "I have the sinking feeling that whatever you are going to tell me is bad news. Although I will say that whatever the sucky news is, the fact that it's coming from a guy who not only knows what hair extensions are but also how time-consuming they are to apply makes it a little easier to bear."

"Well then, let me start with this: eyelash extensions are the new hair extensions."

"Oh my," said Paige, fanning herself with a makeup brush and feigning a sexually charged swoon. "This must really be bad news. But on the upside, I think I just came."

"You're welcome," said Sam with a businesslike nod. "Now on to the less enjoyable reason for my visit: Sapphire is having the teensiest, tiniest little wardrobe issue and we may have a short delay."

"Oh, well, that doesn't sound so bad," said Kate, relieved that she would soon be on her way to doing—and finishing forever and ever—her dreaded scene. "It'll give me an extra twenty minutes to drop a few pounds."

"Very funny," said Sam, clearly not enjoying her joke. "Anyway, your own skinny-assed insanity aside, I said we *may* have a short delay. The other possibility is that we may have a *long* delay. We're already an hour behind schedule because of Sapphire's wardrobe dilemma, and if we don't get the scene *before* yours done by eleven o'clock, we are going to need to move outside to the restaurant scene because of the light. Then, and only then, will we know if we have enough time to come back here and get your scene done today, or if we will need to move it to tomorrow, or—don't hit me, I'm just the messenger—it may even need to be moved to next week sometime."

Kate's heart sank. As much as she had been dreading being filmed—and criticized—nearly naked, she had begun to see a light at the end of the tunnel. It was like dreading some sort of painful elective surgery for weeks and then, just as the gurney was being wheeled into the operating room, hearing that the surgeon had a very important golf game and the surgery was going to be postponed indefinitely. There would be relief, sure, but also a return to the hideous feeling of dreadful anticipation.

"Okay," said Kate, sighing and allowing just enough petulance into her voice to show that, although it wasn't really "okay," she would rise above it and be a good girl.

Sam looked at her for an extra beat, trying to figure out if she was really okay, before realizing that there was nothing any of them could do about it anyway. "Okay, then. I will find you and give you an update whenever I have one."

After the door slammed shut behind him, Paige turned to Kate. "Well, this sucks."

"Not really," said Kate dully. "Maybe it's just the universe's way of telling me I need more time to lose weight."

"Oh, *fuck me,*" shouted Paige, surprising both Kate and herself with her outburst. "I'm sorry, but if the universe is trying to tell you anything, it is to have a fucking snack and get your skinny ass into therapy."

"Yeah," said Kate, tears appearing in the corners of her eyes, "a snack is just what I need. Then I can be fat, lose my career altogether, and have nothing but time for getting to know the 'real me.' Well, I know the real me, Paige, and she is fat and lonely and even her mother doesn't want to be seen with her in public."

"Oh, honey," Paige said, enveloping her now weeping friend in a hug, wishing she could make her understand that the cure for her anxiety and emotionality wasn't *less* food. "Can we just get you some protein? Maybe an omelet?" Feeling Kate's back tense in panic and seeing the vehement shake of the head still buried deep in her shoulder, Paige reconsidered her attack. "How about some egg whites? What if we tell the caterer that we want egg whites in the exact caloric equivalent to what it takes to actually eat them?"

"Can I chew extra times to burn off the pepper calories?" asked Kate, lifting her face, exposing sad eyes and a mischievous smile.

"As long as you don't make any mouth noises or breathe your nasty eggs breath on me." Paige waited until Kate's smile reached her eyes and then pulled her out of her chair by the elbow. "Come on, my crazy friend, I'm not even going to talk to you until you have something in your system."

"Is that a threat?"

"No, it's a promise. The threat is therapy."

"I'm *in* therapy—with Hamilton and Penelo—"

"*Penelope?*" interrupted Paige. "Are you kidding me? That's not therapy, that's propaganda. She just wants you to go on *Jay Leno* and plug her stupid book, *Men Are in Charge and Women Should Shut Up and Take It in the Ass.*"

"Oh, be quiet," said Kate, laughing in earnest now. "It's called *Loving Our Men: The True Power of Women* and it's really good."

"It's really *bullshit*. Now, come on, getting some breakfast into you is the first step of your deprogramming. Once you come out of your hypoglycemic haze, then we start on the real work of getting you a hot, young boyfriend who wants you to have an ass that he can rest a place setting on. As it is, you'd be lucky to support one of those miniature souvenir spoons."

"Thank you," said Kate, with an exaggerated shake of her butt as she headed out the door.

"No, you idiot," shouted Paige. "That wasn't a compliment! It was a call to awareness!"

"Oh, well, in that case you should know that I don't take my own calls. All calls go through my manager. Would you like Hamilton's number?"

"You are hopeless," said Paige, catching up to her.

"Maybe so, but at least I'm married."

"As soon as I feed you I am going to kill you."

"Good, because I always feel like I want to die after I eat, anyway."

"Kate." Paige stopped dead in her tracks.

"Oh, lighten up," said Kate, shrugging off her friend's concern and heading toward the line of people waiting for their breakfast at the catering truck. "I'm kidding."

"I hope so," said Paige, but she knew she wasn't.

4

Twenty yards away, in the forty-foot-long semitrailer that had been outfitted with hanging clothing racks three levels high and two deep, Sapphire Rose was once again reduced to gulping, sobbing, tantrum-level tears.

"*Why are you doing this to me?*" she sobbed, as yet one more skirt didn't make it over her hips. "Why don't you buy any clothes that fit me? Do you hate me?"

Yes, thought Claire, the head costumer of *Generations. I do hate you, but that isn't why your clothes don't fit, you mean cow.* But of course she didn't—couldn't—say that. "Of *course* I don't hate you, sweetie. How could you even *think* that?"

"How could I even *think* that? How could I think anything else when every day of my life I put on my clothes and they don't fit? Do you know how hard it is to be Sapphire Rose, to be *People* magazine's second most favorite actress of 2003? It is a tremendous—a *tremendous*—amount of pressure to be looked up to by so many as a role model and a style icon. How can I be all that my millions of fans need me to be if my *clothes don't fit*?!" With that, Sapphire fell back onto the nearest folding chair and proceeded to completely ruin what was left of her makeup with more messy, snotty sobs.

Oh boy, here we go again, thought Claire, wondering where they were going to put yet another set of clothes for their shape-shifting star. As it was, two-thirds of the trailer (which was intended to hold the wardrobes of all ten of the principal actors, as well as extra clothes for scenes involving background artists) was now dedicated to holding row upon row of outfits for Sapphire, in graduating sizes. The most difficult part of Claire's job *should* have been the weekly challenge of choosing clothing for each individual character in that episode's script—clothing that not only suited each character's journey and each actor's personal preferences and creative vision, but also worked together as a whole with the set design and the ideas of the director and the producers. Sadly, most of her energy, and that of her five-person crew, was wasted on trying in vain to keep her star happy and well dressed, which involved the daily challenge of trying to judge her current size by sight and placing clothes in her trailer that either fit her or, barring that, were too large. The most recent diet debacle, the "Bah-Bah Thin Sheep" diet, had Sapphire eating nothing but incredibly pungent lamb kebabs, lamb stew, and the occasional King Henry the Eighth–style leg of lamb. She gained fifteen pounds in two weeks, which made the too-large option a practical impossibility, at least until Claire's assistant made it back from Bloomingdale's. Even then, with the clothes in hand, they would need time to replace all of the size tags in the new garments with the size 6 labels that Sapphire preferred.

"How could you let that horrible little assistant"—even Sapphire understood that whenever possible it was best to blame those lowest on the totem pole—"*continually* put clothes in my room that don't fit? Do you have any idea what that does to my self-esteem? I am an *artist.* I need to be taken care of like a flower, like a hothouse orchid, not squeezed into some polyester casing like a sausage!"

"Yes, Sapphire," sighed Claire, having learned long ago that trying to inject logic—or any level of objective reality—into a conversation such as this only prolonged the torture. "Of course you need to be handled with care. Don't we all?"

"Don't we all? *Don't we all?*" snapped Sapphire in a spiteful, mimicking tone. "What is that even supposed to *mean?* We *all* don't need to be on camera in five minutes. We *all* don't have the fate of this entire show resting on our shoulders *every single day of our lives!*" Collapsing once again in tears, the actress was barely able to summon the strength to reach into the candy jar on the counter and grab a handful of Jelly Bellies. "Why does no one understand how *hard* my life is?"

Because it is difficult to have compassion for a wealthy, child-like, mean-spirited, spoiled brat, thought Claire. But to the heaving, chewing mass of misplaced talent she said, "Oh, honey, I hate to see you so upset. I'm sure we will find you the perfect outfit. If we don't have it here, we'll just send someone out to find you something that you will feel comfortable in, okay?"

"*And* that looks good. It has to look good." Sapphire sniffed as she reached her damp, snotty hand back into the jar of jelly beans.

"Well, of course it will look good, darling—it will be on *you*, won't it?" Claire was rewarded with a small smile and, seeing her chance to get on with what was left of her morning, coaxed Sapphire out of her trailer by slowly backing toward the door with the now disgustingly sticky candy jar held suggestively in her hands. "Now, why don't you just take these over to Bruce's trailer and let him fix your beautiful face while I put together the most gorgeous outfit you have ever seen?"

"Okay." Sapphire sniffed again, taking the jar and explaining, "They're not for me, though. My new raw-food diet doesn't allow sugar, unless it's raw like honey or molasses or sugarcane in its—"

"Wow, isn't that *interesting,*" said Claire, ushering her out the door as quickly as possible without actually injuring her. "I can't wait to hear all about it just as soon as we get you all prettied up again and ready for your scene."

Always happier when groups of people rallied around the cause of beautifying her, Sapphire allowed herself to be aimed toward her personal makeup trailer and her very own team of ego boosters.

5

Driving home eight hours later, having finally been allowed to leave the set with the caveat to "stay close to the phone in case we need you," Kate felt better than she had in weeks. Maybe it was just the grounding feeling of having some food in her (Paige had somehow tricked her into eating lunch, too), or the relief of having her near-nude scene postponed. Her sense of well-being definitely *wasn't* the result of the six hours she had spent sitting in her dressing room, mindlessly flipping channels on her tiny television set.

First, the entire crew of 150 people was on hold for an hour and a half while they waited for Sapphire's new clothes to arrive from the local mall. Then they sat around for another several hours while her makeup was *re*-re-reapplied after the first two outfits she tried on proved to be too small, too, bringing on two more crying jags. The last one—lasting more than an hour—came complete with threats to quit the show and culminated with the star locking herself in her trailer and demanding a meeting with the producer, executive producer, and her agent. Thanks to the three men's combined and well-practiced ass-kissing skills, they were able to convince her that she was the most important, beautiful, and talented actress of her generation. *And* that her ass did not look fat in skirt number three. At that point, it was too late to film the scene in the outdoor restaurant because they had lost the light. This led to a brief—and terrifying—moment where it looked as if Kate would have to film her scene after all. Sam even told her to get dressed in her tiny costume and gave her a ten-minute warning—the entire thirty minutes of which she spent sitting on the edge of her hard little couch trying to keep herself from either hyperventilating or crying over the fact that she had allowed herself to eat two—*two*—meals and now she and her belly would soon be the target of the "Is She Expecting?" pages of *Star* magazine. Thankfully, just as her attempts at relaxing, meditative deep breathing were beginning to cause the decidedly unrelaxed feelings of dizziness and vertigo, Sam appeared at her door with a big smile on his face and the sign-out sheet in his hand. Sapphire, it seemed, didn't want her "time wasted" by being sent home without shooting a scene. In order to keep the fragile peace, the producer had found a short scene involving Sapphire sitting home alone, thus allowing the company to avoid another tantrum and finish the wasted day at a decent hour. They could then start extra early the next day, in the hopes of making up some of the time they had lost.

In the scene they ended up shooting, Sapphire was wearing a bathrobe.

Feeling like a death-row inmate who had been granted a last-minute reprieve and, miraculously, a BMW sports car in which to enjoy it, Kate drove along the Pacific Coast Highway, singing loudly and completely off-key with Sheryl Crow, "All I wanna do is have a little fun before I die. As she bopped her head from side to side, enjoying the view and her own terrible singing, Kate thought about how much she wanted to get back to being the person she used to be—the optimistic girl who had come to Los Angeles to become an actress because she loved the camaraderie of the stage. She loved that part of being an actor: being surrounded by imaginative, interesting people all working in tandem to piece together an entire world out of the combined energy of their collective pain, wisdom, and joy. The creative process was magical, spiritual. When had she made the shift from working to feed her soul to working for a paycheck, for the approval of a capricious press, for the validation of the masses? Somewhere along the way there had been a fork in the road and she had clearly turned down the wrong path. But maybe it was like Paige was always saying: it's never too late to start your day—or your life—over.

My life, thought Kate. *This is* my life.

She turned up the music on her car radio and a joyous white-girl-dancing grin spread across her face. She made the turn up Chautauqua Avenue, singing at the top of her lungs and waving at her fellow drivers, watching their judgmental stares turn into surprised waves and giggles when they recognized her as "that lady from TV." Or maybe they just couldn't believe that a driver in Los Angeles was being friendly. Either way, Kate felt like the whole world was smiling with her as she rounded the final corner before her house and made the turn into her wide, gated driveway. She punched in the gate code (Hamilton's birthday) and pulled up next to Hamilton's Porsche just as she and Sheryl were finishing their duet.

Getting out of her car, she took a moment to appreciate the perfection of the house she shared with her husband. She had to admit, Hamilton had done a wonderful job creating what he referred to as "the face we show the world." Even their cars were color-coordinated with the white and gray shades of the Cape Cod house and the pseudorandom English-garden landscaping. He had called in a decorator, a feng shui expert, and, of course, Penelope to collaborate on creating the perfect "power house." In fact, the only person whose opinion he hadn't solicited was Kate's, but her instinctive desire for a warm, tchotchke-filled space was so at odds with his vision that she (and Penelope) had decided it was in the best interest of her marriage to let him have free reign. His goal was to have their visitors enjoy an immediate feeling of warmth and welcome, but go home with a vague sense of inadequacy about their own imperfect sense of style. Judging by how Kate often felt in her own home, he had accomplished his mission.

Today, though, she was buzzing with positive energy as she danced through the side door into the granite and stainless-steel kitchen, looking forward to sharing her great mood with her husband.

"Honey, I'm ho-o-ome!" she called, taking off her shoes and placing them in their assigned basket next to the door. "Where are you?" She dropped her keys into the sterling silver key bowl that had been her Valentine's Day gift the previous year and headed through the house to look for Hamilton.

She found him in their backyard, sitting in one of their ecologically unsound but beautiful teak lounge chairs, talking into his telephone headset while typing expertly into his BlackBerry. She sometimes still felt a jolt when she saw him; his full head of thick, dark hair (expertly cut by Sally Hershberger to look as if he had just rolled out of bed—all for just five hundred dollars a pop), his square jaw (tanned to perfection from his weekly visits to Mystic Tan, ever since his cosmetic dermatologist had deemed exposure to the actual sun "poisonous"), his full lips (God given), and his gym- and Zone-toned body all worked together to turn her knees to jelly, just as they had on the first day they met. *Maybe a little lovin' before dinner,* thought Kate as she bounded into the yard. *Maybe even a little lovin' right here on this chaise.* But her happy plop onto the edge of his chair was met with annoyance and the always charming "back off" gesture, communicated with a dismissive flick of his right hand.

For once, Kate didn't get offended or hurt. Thanks to her good mood, she found only humor in the image of Fran Drescher doing "talk to the hand." Rather than lighten his mood, however, her giggle just seemed to annoy Hamilton. Adjusting his body so that he was now turned completely away from her, he curled his legs up in a decidedly girly way, forcing his arms into a cramped typing position. He looked exactly like a prissy schoolgirl writing a supersecret boyfriend note to her equally prissy BFF. Kate's giggle erupted into a full-blown laugh, and her pleasure—and her image of Hamilton as a love-struck teen—was not lessened by the snotty "Would you hold on one minute while I go somewhere *quiet?*" that he hissed into his silly headset. He glared at Kate with an exaggerated expression of disapproval, like a little girl imitating her mother's anger. That did it: Kate was now completely helpless with laughter, reduced to clutching her sides in happy pain. Hamilton leaped off the chaise and stormed into the house, pausing briefly at the door to nail her with yet another dirty look. Sadly, rather than looking menacing, he resembled Marcia Brady right after being hit in the face with her brothers' football. *I am so going to pay for this,* thought Kate, wiping tears from her eyes as she lay back on the chaise, exhausted and sated. *But it was so worth it.*

Forty minutes later, she was still waiting for Hamilton to come back outside and the few moments of giddy mirth began to feel a little less worth it. Was he mad at her? Or, even worse, hurt? As the minutes ticked by, Kate felt her light mood turn dark. Her heartbeat sped up as her dread began to mount. Even her breathing quickened as she tortured herself with thoughts of how she might have injured Hamilton's ego—and how he might react. *You know better than to make fun of him,* she scolded herself. Penelope's words rang in her ears. *A man is just an ego on two legs. Treat him like a king and he will take care of you like a princess.* How could she have forgotten? How could she have made such a basic, stupid mistake?

Kate jumped when she heard the sliding door open and found herself holding her breath, watching Hamilton walk toward her, a look of pained dignity on his face.

"Well, Kate," he said, sounding like a disappointed parent and perching primly on the edge of the chaise, "are you feeling better now?"

"Yes," she said, although in reality she was feeling monumentally worse. "Hamilton, I am so sorry. I don't know what got into me. I just . . ." Kate lost her train of thought when the hand she had laid on Hamilton's leg in the hopes of creating a loving connection was unceremoniously lifted up and dropped back beside her own leg.

"You know, Katie," he said without looking her in the eye, "I just don't want to hear it right now. I have had a very trying, very busy day, and the last thing I expected when I came home to my sanctuary—*my castle*—was to be the butt of some private joke of my wife's." He turned his head toward the garden, crossed his arms, and said, "Honestly, I just don't know who you are anymore."

Kate felt her world begin to spin. Had she screwed up that badly? Hurt him that deeply? She reached her hand out to touch his shoulder but he shrugged her off, turning farther away from her as if he couldn't stand to look at her. "Oh, Hamilton, I really am sorry. You know I would never hurt you on purpose." This was met with a loud "Tsk!" and a sad shake of his head, fueling Kate's panic that she had caused irreparable damage. "You do know that, don't you, Hamilton?"

"I thought I did, Katie. I thought this was a safe place for me, but now I'm not so sure. Maybe we need to do more work with Penelope or maybe you need to go see her on your own . . . I don't know. I just thought that we—that *you*—were further along than this. I really thought that we were at a place where I could begin to trust that my home is a respite from the jungle, a haven in this cold, hard world."

"Of course it's a safe place. *I* want to be your safe place." She scooted down closer to the edge of the chaise where Hamilton was perched so that she could wrap her arms around him, both to comfort him and to hold him in place. Hamilton allowed himself to be held for a moment, flooding her with a sense of relief—*he won't leave me today*—but then suddenly he was standing up and she was left leaning forward awkwardly, her arms held out as if awaiting a hug.

"I'm going out now," he said, smoothing the front of his Armani black-label slacks and carefully retucking his custom-made shirt. "My intention is to come home tonight, but I really can't be sure how I will feel. I may choose to stay at a hotel. Either way, I think it would be for the best if you called Penelope immediately and set up a series of appointments for yourself. You seem to have forgotten everything that she and I have worked so hard to teach you."

"Yes, of course," said Kate, feeling as though she were folding into herself, getting smaller and smaller, like an origami sculpture. "I'll call right away. And I am so sorry—"

"I know you are," he interrupted, clearly done with the conversation. "I just don't know if that's enough." With that, he walked across the yard and into the house, leaving Kate alone with the feeling of having chased away the one person she needed most in the world.

She heard the front door slam, then his car door, and finally the throaty growl of the Porsche's turbo engine fading to nothing as he drove away. Why had she laughed at him? *Stupid, stupid, stupid*, she berated herself.

Dragging herself off the chaise, she made her way into the kitchen on shaky legs and sat on an incredibly uncomfortable—albeit gorgeous—custom-made leather and steel bar stool while she flipped through their Rolodex in search of Penelope's phone number. She was embarrassed to call, embarrassed to admit that she was still making the same thoughtless mistakes. She could already hear Penelope's disappointed sigh, so much like Hamilton's. And it was no wonder that Penelope would be frustrated. After all, she and Hamilton had been trying to teach Kate how to have a healthy relationship since their third date. Instead of dinner and a movie, they had done dinner and therapy. At the time, Kate had been wary but flattered, since Hamilton had presented his unconventional courting method as a sign of his deepening commitment.

"You are a very cute girl, Kate," he had said as they drove to Penelope's office for the first time. "With the potential to be quite beautiful. But before I invest more time and energy into this relationship, I need to know that we are on the same page. I need to know that you will approach both our professional and personal relationships with a strong and disciplined work ethic."

"Of course," answered Kate, staring at his handsome profile and his strong hand resting on the gearshift. She was only too happy to accompany him to see his therapist. At this point, she would have happily followed him to the moon. And meeting Penelope felt like an important step, like meeting his mother.

"Did you read the book I had messengered over to you?"

"Of course I did," said Kate. In fact, she had been up reading until two a.m. in anticipation of that very question.

"That's my good girl." Hamilton reached over to pat her knee and Kate felt a happy blush burn her cheeks. "What did you think?"

"I thought it made a lot of sense," Kate said earnestly.

"Good," Hamilton said, "because if you don't understand Penelope's work, then you will not be able to be the partner I need you to be and we may as well stop right now."

Kate could tell by his tone that he meant every word he said, and she vowed in that moment to do everything within her power to become the partner that he wanted. In fact, she was thrilled to finally have a guidebook about relationships and a strong man who would define his expectations. She had always felt as though she'd been let loose in the romantic world without a map, left to fend for herself in the wilds of male/female interaction. In the company of this handsome man with his clear, unambiguous ideas about her life and career, Kate had felt safe for the first time in her life.

Now, staring at the phone and willing it to ring, she felt decid-edly unsafe.

Two long hours later, when the phone finally rang, Kate grabbed for it like a teenager awaiting an invitation to the prom.

"Hello?"

"Hello, Kate," said her mother. "What's wrong?" *How did she always know?*

"What? Nothing," lied Kate, hoping she sounded more con-vincing to her mother than she did to herself.

"Oh good," sighed her mother, not only convinced but clearly relieved. "I've been so worried about you."

"What? *Why?*" Kate felt as though she had been punched in the stomach. Had Hamilton called her mother? Warned her that her daughter might need help because of her impending breakup? *Oh God.* "What are you talking about, Mom?"

"Your scene, honey—I've been worried sick about it all day."

"My *what?*" Kate struggled to connect what she was feeling with the words coming out of her mother's mouth. Between her own panic and her mother's apparent insanity, she was having trouble following.

"Your *scene. Today.* At your *job,*" said her mother, now clearly annoyed at her daughter's denseness. "What is wrong with you? Have you been drinking?" The absurdity of this question—indeed, of this entire conversation—hit Kate and she burst out laughing. "Katherine, are you laughing? My God, you *have* been drinking. I just hope Hamilton isn't there to see you like this."

"Mom—"

"The last thing he needs after a hard day at work is to come home to find you—"

"Mother, listen to me—"

"—three sheets to the wind and acting like a stupid—"

"*MOM!*" shouted Kate, desperate to stop her mother before she was forced to listen to the specifics of her stupidity. "I am not drunk. When have you ever even seen me drunk?"

"I don't see any reason for you to use that tone with me, young lady," said her mother, clearly offended by Kate's response to her own apparently *in*offensive accusation of drunkenness. "I am not a stupid woman, and I am not someone who would just make something up. Frankly, I resent your implication."

"Oh, Mom," said Kate, abandoning her own anger as they entered the familiar territory of her mother's insecurity about her intelligence and Kate's lifetime appointment to the ego-boosting cabinet. "Of course you aren't stupid. You are very, very smart."

"Well, then, I just don't understand why you have to talk to me that way."

Physically cringing, Kate said, "I'm sorry, Mom. I really didn't mean to hurt your feelings."

"Yes, well, you did," said her mother calmly, having success-fully orchestrated her transition from villain to noble victim. "Now, why don't you tell me about your scene? Were they able to work around your weight gain? I was wondering if maybe they would shoot you behind a laundry basket or something, like they do for pregnant girls."

"Mom!" Kate was aghast. "First of all, I didn't have to do the scene today—it got rescheduled. But more to the point, I hardly look pregnant. I'm only five pounds up."

"Yes, but five pounds up from *what*, dear? Besides, five pounds is quite a lot on small frames like ours. You know, I only gained fifteen pounds total during my pregnancy."

"Yes, Mother, I believe you have mentioned that once or twice"—or thirty-seven thousand times—"but I am not preg-nant."

"No, dear, of course you aren't pregnant. This would not be a good time for a baby, what with your career finally back on track."

"Wait a minute—shouldn't you be pushing for a grandchild, pining for a little baby to spoil rotten?"

"Oh, Kate, I hardly have time to deal with a baby right now.

Your father and I have several trips planned and I have my book club. Besides, when the time is right for you and Hamilton to have a child, I really think it would be best for you to adopt, maybe from a foreign country. It's such good press, and it will allow you to keep your figure . . . such as it is." Kate briefly considered defending herself but decided she was just too tired. And fat. "Anyhoo," her mother went on, "I have got to run. I e-mailed you the number for Clean Colon, Happy Colon. I really think you should book a series of colonic irrigation treatments and get started on them as soon as possible. I think we can still hold out a faint hope that your belly bulge is nothing more than excess waste. Well, I've got to run now. Love you!"

"Yes," Kate said to the dial tone, "that couldn't be more apparent."

6

"Sapphire Rose on line three," said the little box on Michael's desk.

"Got it!" Michael yelled through his open office door. It made his assistant, Marjorie, crazy that he wouldn't talk into the box, but there were so few opportunities for fun during the day and watching her react when he didn't follow her obsessive idea of how things should be brought him far more joy than was probably warranted. He was determined to make her loosen up and relax her strict standards of behavior, but she was just as determined to convert him to the religion of "a place for everything and everything in its place." Their ongoing battle was just like the Crusades, except that they were battling over the importance of having a proper filing system instead of fighting for their eternal souls. Other than that, though, it was exactly the same.

"Hello, Sapphire," said Michael into the phone, feigning confusion when Marjorie gestured sternly at the intercom. "How did it go today after I left?"

"Well," said Sapphire, her tone making it clear that she was displeased but trying to rise above it. "Believe it or not, I am *just now* on my way home. I just can't get over how disorganized they are here. We never even got to that restaurant scene; we ended up just shooting me alone in my apartment—in my robe. Can you believe it? We didn't even *need* a skirt. I swear, it's a wonder they get anything done at all."

"Yes," said Michael, wondering less about production's disorganization and more about Sapphire's ability to completely rewrite history. Had she actually forgotten that he had been summoned to the *Generations* set this afternoon? That he had wasted his afternoon sitting in her trailer with the producer and executive producer trying to calm her down while she had held up production for no less than *six hours* with her endless tantrums? "It is certainly a wonder."

"It really is," said Sapphire.

"So . . . to what do I owe the pleasure of your call?" asked Michael, hoping against hope that she was not just looking for someone to talk to—or, rather, at—during the long ride out to her seven-million-dollar "cottage" in Malibu. He had to find her some friends. Too bad his mother wasn't alive.

"Michael, you *silly*—you *know* why I'm calling. You said you would tell me all about your little conversation with Bob Steinman, remember? You said you and he had had a conversation about me, and I just want to know if I need to start packing for my big location shoot in Paris."

Michael forced out a laugh, not because he found her comment about an imminent location shoot funny, but because he needed to buy himself some time. He had completely forgotten to make up a plausible story about his imaginary conversation, and now he had about thirty seconds to fabricate something that would fool Sapphire. Oh well, he was in the fantasy business, after all, and he was blessed with a completely delusional audience. "Right . . . That's right . . . I did say I would tell you about that conversation. But I believe I said that I would tell you *after* you completed the restaurant scene, which you still haven't finished. Isn't that right?"

"Don't you dare tease me like this, you bad boy. You tell me right now or I just might come over there and spank you," Sapphire cooed in what she thought was a sexy voice. Michael disagreed.

"Well, I guess I'll have to tell you, then, in order to avoid that spanking." Sapphire giggled girlishly. Michael choked back bile. "But first, I need to tell you that this is all *top secret*. I need to be able to trust you not to breathe a word of what I am about to tell you to anyone, not even Bob himself, or the whole deal could fall apart. Do you understand? If word gets out, there will be *no deal*." He emphasized "no deal" with roughly the same energy he would have put behind "the second coming of Christ," knowing that they shared similar levels of importance in Sapphire's consciousness.

"Yes, of course," she said, all whispery earnestness in deference to the sacred nature of a discussion about possible film work. "You know you can trust me, Michael."

Yes, just about as far as I can throw you, Michael thought, *but here goes nothing*. "There is a really big, really hush-hush project in the works about Vivien Leigh—"

"Oh! I have always related to her so much!" Sapphire squealed, thinking of the actress's beauty and talent.

"Yes, I can see why," said Michael, thinking of her well-known struggles with mental illness. "Anyway, it is in the works for, um . . ." Doing a quick calculation of how long he could keep her happy and docile with the promise of a possible film role and taking into consideration the emotional meltdown that would follow the unavoidable falling-through of the imaginary part in the imaginary film, while trying his best to contain the aforementioned meltdown within the confines of her hiatus from her real role on her real television show, he came up with a vague date several months in the future. ". . . Next fall . . . ish."

"Really? Wow, that is soon! Do you mean next fall as in the fall six months from now or eighteen months from now?"

Eighteen months from now? Could he really risk trying for

eighteen months of good behavior? "You know, that is a very good question. I can't believe I didn't clarify that for myself. Let me call Bob and get back to you in a few days, okay?" He needed time to do some more in-depth calculations. Agents should teach classes in emotional algebra.

"Yes, of course, take your time," said Sapphire brightly. "To be honest, I need all of the time I can get to do my research. I'll have my assistant start on that right away."

"Now, now," admonished Michael. "Didn't we promise to keep this a secret?"

"Oh, yes, of course—mum's the word. I won't tell her what it's for. I'll just tell her it is for a book I am writing. Did I tell you that I have decided to write a book?"

"No, you didn't," he said, surprised. "I didn't even know you wrote."

"Oh, sure, I write all the time. Well, I don't actually *write*—who has time for that? What I do is talk into a little bitty tape recorder and send it off to this lady, and she makes it into a book. You know, writing a book is so much easier than people make it out to be. I mean, I just talk about my day and all the deep thoughts I have and this lady—I think her name is Jane—or is it Joan?—whatever, it doesn't really matter. Anyway, she just takes what I tell her about my life—which is obviously so much more interesting than a normal person's life—and mixes it up and puts it back together into a story. It's what everyone is doing these days. I don't think anyone is actually sitting down in front of an actual computer anymore."

"Well, Jane Joan is," pointed out Michael.

"Well, duh, of course I know *she* is. She is a *writer*. That's her *job*," said Sapphire, as though Michael's statement was the stupidest thing she had ever heard. "What I meant is that none of the *authors* are writing. We don't have to, not with modern technology and all. I've done most of my book while getting my nails done. I mean, those girls don't speak English anyway, you know?"

"Yes, Sapphire, I know."

"So, it's not quite ready for you to sell it yet, mostly because June is so slow at typing it up. But as soon as she gets *An Enviable Life* back to me, I'll send it right to you so you can get it published. Should we talk about the book tour now? I want to wear mostly Versace."

"Right. Versace. You certainly have your finger on the pulse of the literary establishment," said Michael, suddenly exhausted and inexplicably sad. "Listen, I'm going to go put that call into Bob Steinman now. It could take a while for him to get back to me, what with pilot season and all, so don't worry if you don't hear from me for a few days, okay?"

"Okay. I'm heading into the tunnel so I'm going to lose you in a second. Bye-b—" The end of her sentence was cut off as she entered the tunnel that connected Malibu to the San Fernando Valley.

"Damn it," said Michael into the empty phone line, realizing she had succeeded in keeping him on the phone for her whole damn drive.

7

Kate woke with a start at six a.m., her body flooding with adrenaline. She struggled to remember what day it was, whether she was supposed to go to work today, whether, in fact, she was already late for work. She had fallen asleep on the couch—her anxiety over her fight with Hamilton finally exhausting her—before she had had a chance to call Sam to find out about her call time for today. She strained to remember what he had said when she'd left work last night. *Stay close to the phone.* Oh god, had they called last night? She tried to talk herself down as she picked up her phone, the beep-beep-beep of the voice-mail system telling her that there was a message. *It's okay,* she told herself, trying—but failing—to take a full breath, *it's probably not them. There are probably not a hundred and fifty crew members waiting for you to show up at work, expecting your car to pull in at any moment so that they can start their day.* She punched in her voice-mail code and waited the interminably long three and a half seconds for the irritatingly calm robotic voice (didn't she realize what was at stake here?) to tell her that she had received a call at 11:12 p.m. *Oh no.* "Hi, Kate, it's Sam." *Oh god.* "You're off the hook for tonight"—*thank god—*

"but in terms of tomorrow"—Kate felt as if her heart were going to pound right out of her chest while she awaited the verdict: good girl or bad girl?—"you are still on the hook." *What time? Get to the fucking time, Sam.* "I still don't have a time for you, but"—*but what? But what?*—"I can tell you it won't be early." Kate felt as if she were melting into the couch, both her held breath and her anxiety draining out of her. "Anyway, you are on a 'will notify' for tomorrow while we try to figure out what the day looks like. Apparently, Sapphire has a conflict of some sort tomorrow afternoon, so we need to do some shuffling around to find stuff to shoot without her. Our first choice would be to shoot the pool-boy scene, but the guy we hired to play the pool boy obviously wasn't expecting to work tomorrow, so we are waiting to hear if he can find an understudy to go on for him at his Chippendales show— do they really call them 'understudies' in male strip shows? Anyway, my point is that it doesn't look like we will get to you tomorrow, but I won't know until at least ten a.m., maybe as late as noon. You know the drill: wait by the phone, and if you go out make sure you have your cell with you. Sleep well."

Ironically, she had slept well, which wouldn't have been the case if she had heard the phone ring and had talked to Sam last night when she should have. She would have been too worried about her scene and too annoyed that her life was once again at the mercy of her erratic costar. What was it that made Sapphire feel that her personal schedule took precedence over those of almost two hundred co-workers? Kate would no sooner announce a "conflict of some sort" during a workday than she would, well, hold up the crew while she had her minions scour the ends of the earth for the world's most slimming skirt. For one thing, she didn't have any minions, and for another, she just couldn't imagine being that clueless about her effect on other people. Granted, she was lucky that her first and best acting teacher, Mr. Faldwell had drilled into his students that a piece of theater, whether on a stage or on a sound-stage, is a communal creation. "You may get treated differently because you are one of only a handful of actors, but you need to understand that you are, more importantly, a member of the crew. Get your own coffee; treat everyone with respect. It is far better to be in the trenches with a hundred friends than to be up in your ivory tower with only your royal ego to keep you company. Besides, when the chips are down, it is always the queen that gets beheaded first. Remember that." Kate had remembered, and it had kept her in good stead. Of course, she *could* call Sam back right now and say, "You know, I just remembered that I have a conflict, too. So, you see, I am just not available." Or, even better, what if she just never called at all, turned off her cell phone, and went to a spa?

Yeah, right.

She knew she would never leave her phone off, just as she would never put her own schedule ahead of production's. It just wasn't in her nature. She was a good girl through and through. So her time would be controlled and wasted by an insecure, immature actress. At least she could hang out with Paige and Sam while she waited.

While she waited . . .

Kate's heart sunk when she remembered that the reason she had fallen asleep on the couch was that she had been *waiting* for her husband to come home—waiting to find out if she still *had* a husband. Had he come home to make up with her, found the bed empty, and assumed that she had left? Had he come home at all? She jumped up and headed to the kitchen, hoping that he had somehow snuck past her. She paused when she got to the door, saying a quick prayer that she would find Hamilton sitting in "his" chair (the seat facing the view of the backyard) at their little table, having his daily breakfast of a single piece of low-carb toast with fat-free cream cheese and low-sugar strawberry jam and a cup of Splenda-sweetened green tea. When she opened the door, she was shocked to see that her prayer had been answered and braced herself for a continuation of last night's fight.

"Well, good morning, sleepyhead," said a very cheerful

Hamilton, jumping out of his seat and coming over to envelop Kate in an energetic hug. "I was beginning to think you were never going to get up. No work today?"

"Uh . . ." stammered Kate, trying to figure out what she had missed. Everything, apparently. "I'm on a will notify by ten a.m. When did you get home?"

"Oh, I don't know . . . midnight-ish. You were sound asleep on the couch, drooling away, just as cute as a bug in a rug." He gave her chin an affectionate little pinch and headed toward the counter. "What can I get you, my little princess? Tea? Decaf coffee? Wait a minute—your scene is done, isn't it? You could even have a piece of toast if you want. Shall we celebrate with a little sugar-free fruit spread? Yummy!"

Still trying to figure out how she had gone from the brink of divorce to being offered carbohydrates (well, carbohydratelike foodstuffs), Kate stepped gingerly into the minefield of communication with her husband. "Thank you, honey, that would be great. Although we didn't actually get to my scene yesterday. I didn't have time to tell you last night before—well . . . before you had to leave for your . . . thing, but yesterday was pretty much a waste of a day."

"Really?" Handing her a cup of tea and leading her to the table (apparently the toast offer was completly scene dependent), Hamilton was the picture of chivalry and husbandly concern. "Well, isn't that too bad? Why don't you sit right here and tell daddy what happened?"

"Well," said Kate, relaxing into his attentive mood, "it was just another high-drama day in the life of Sapphire Rose. Apparently, her new diet isn't working—*again*—so her skirt didn't fit—*again*—so we lost a whole day. Can you believe that?" Kate shook her head and grinned, ready to share a laugh with her husband at the absurdity of Sapphire's behavior. Instead, her grin was met with a very serious expression and a compassionate sigh.

"Poor Sapphire," said Hamilton, as if they had been discussing a dear friend who had just lost a parent to cancer. "It must be so difficult for her."

"What?" Kate was confused again. Was he kidding? Being sarcastic? Humor had never been Hamilton's strong suit, but maybe a sense of humor was part of his new, toast-offering personality.

"Well, I just think it must be difficult for her, being an artist in such a shallow medium. She is an artist surrounded by technicians. I bet it is lonely for her."

"Are you kidding?" Kate was hopeful, but her hope faded as Hamilton continued his ode to her tormentor.

"No, Katie-Cow, I am not kidding. I'm trying to help you understand what it must be like for Sapphire so that you can help her in her creative journey instead of focusing on how her struggles affect you and your little day."

She wanted to shake her head rapidly from side to side à la Scooby Doo, hoping to bring herself back from the alternate reality in which this conversation seemed to be taking place. Instead, she calmly said, "Honey, I understand the artistic temperament. I am an actress, too, you know."

"Oh, Katie . . . Katie, Katie, Katie." Hamilton placed his hand on top of hers where it rested on the table. "Of course I know you are an actress. I do your deals, don't I? I'm just saying that you are a different kind of actress than Sapphire, that's all."

"*A different kind of actress*? What does that even *mean*?"

"Now, let's not get all dramatic here." Kate's voice had been rising with the realization that he wasn't kidding, and Hamilton got up to get himself another cup of tea, clearly annoyed by her outburst. "There is nothing to get defensive about. The world needs technicians as well as artists. There is nothing wrong with what you do. You get paid quite well, for one thing, and for another, you get to work with one of the greats. I just don't understand what you think you have to complain about."

Too stunned to speak, Kate tried to process what her manager/husband was saying. Did he really believe that she was lucky to be in Sapphire's presence? That the spoiled star's tantrums were a sign of her artistic integrity and, as such, were to be honored and somehow admired instead of controlled? Kate didn't want to completely destroy their morning truce, so she concentrated on keeping her voice calm. "Hamilton, I can see that you admire Sapphire as an artist, but I really don't see how holding up an entire crew for eight hours because of a wardrobe issue has anything to do with the creative process."

"Of course you don't, darling, and I wouldn't expect you to. That is exactly my point."

"I don't even know what to say to that."

"That's the beauty part, isn't it, Katie? You don't have to talk. You can just sit there and look pretty."

Pinned to her chair by the blunt force of hearing her deepest fear spoken aloud, Kate was unable to talk, unable to stop the tears that filled her eyes.

"Oh, come on, enough of that, pretty girl," said Hamilton, pulling up a chair and taking her in his arms. "Is it so hard to be beautiful?" Lifting her chin with the forefinger of his right hand, he brought her eyes up to meet his. "You know the last thing in the world I would ever want to do is hurt you, don't you?" Kate nodded—whether it was of her own volition or powered by Hamilton's hand under her chin, she couldn't be sure. "Of course you do. So let's not get all teary about a simple fact of life: you are a gorgeous girl who looks great on camera and has created a career out of it. That is nothing to be ashamed of."

"Then why do I feel so ashamed?" Kate was barely able to manage through a fresh wave of tears.

"I don't know, baby. That's probably a good thing to bring up with Penelope. Did you call her yet?"

"Yes. She hasn't called back."

"Well, I'm sure she will. It's probably best if you stay home this morning and wait by the phone . . . with some cucumbers and tea bags over your eyes. We don't want you looking even puffier, do we?" asked Hamilton, giving her a kiss on the cheek before standing up and gathering the teacups and his toast plate. "So, you go ahead and set up a few appointments with her as soon as possible, and in the meantime, I will go by the *Generations* set and see what I can do to be of help to Sapphire."

"Help to *Sapphire?* What about me?" Kate knew she sounded desperate—probably because that's exactly how she felt.

"What about me," mimicked Hamilton, his patience wearing thin. "Oh, Kate, don't you see? This is *exactly* why you need help as soon as possible. You are obviously so threatened by Sapphire that you can't even see that she has been given a gift from God. All the rest of us can do—must do—is whatever we can to help her share that talent with the world. Now, I have to rush and get over to the gym in the next ten minutes or David Hasselhoff is going to horn in on my training time with Thor again. I really hope that by the time I get back you will have spoken with Penelope. And get those tea bags on your eyes immediately." Hamilton looked closely at her face for a moment, clearly not happy with what he was seeing. "Actually, a steam wouldn't hurt either. Of course, that might dry out the skin around your eyes." Noticing the clock on the wall behind Kate's head, Hamilton jumped up, grabbed his keys, and headed toward the door, talking rapid-fire over his shoulder. "I don't have time to figure *this* out for you, too. Just get rid of the water weight in your face and belly while trying to keep some semblance of moisture in your skin—and *go see Penelope.*"

With that, he was out the door to meet his trainer, leaving Kate feeling puffy, dry, and bloated . . . and ashamed of it all.

8

Standing in line at the Pacific Palisades Starbucks, Michael felt as if he had been dropped into a twenty-first-century remake of *Leave It to Beaver* that featured only extraordinarily wealthy, attractive, and slim families. He occasionally stopped here on his way to work, when the traffic on the Pacific Coast Highway forced him to take the Sunset Boulevard route to his office in Beverly Hills. He was struck every single time by the seemingly contradictory feelings that, on the one hand, he was in the only real neighborhood in Los Angeles, while at the same time, the entire town felt as if it were actually nothing more than an elaborate movie set, the people too damn gorgeous and too well dressed to be real. He often fantasized about living here with his own family one day, wondering idly if his future wife and children would make it through the rigorous Pacific Palisades casting process or if they would all be gently directed over the hill toward the Valley.

"You're next," said a quiet voice at his left elbow, waking him from his reverie.

"Oh, right, I'm sorry," he said, intending to turn and place his order but finding himself frozen, looking into the cutest face he had ever seen, surrounded by a mop of wet hair, tendrils falling haphazardly from a tortoiseshell hair clip.

"Sir?" The clear-skinned teenager behind the counter was trying to move the amusement park–size line along as best he could. "Sir, would you like to order?"

"What? Oh, yes, I would like to order." Michael tore his eyes away from the freckle-faced vision on his left and ordered. "Coffee, please."

"Just *coffee*? Don't you want a triple-caf decaf mocha frappe superdoody?" The girl grinned up at him, treating him to a view of her greenish blue eyes. Well, greenish blue–reddish eyes. Had she been crying? Stepping past him she smiled at the teenager clerk and said, "Decaf soy latte, please. The big one."

"Venti," said Michael, trying desperately to think of something clever or charming to say to keep this girl near him, to keep her talking to him.

"Right, *venti*," she said. She accepted her change from the counter girl, dropping a dollar into the tip jar. "Of course, tomorrow I'll be right back to saying 'the big one.' "

"Yeah, you'd think they'd learn and just start calling it that." *Damn it*, Michael chided himself, *charming and clever, not inane and redundant*.

"Yeah, you'd think," she said, with a smile that didn't quite reach her eyes. She grabbed her drink off the counter. "Well, have a good day."

"I'll try," he said, trying to figure out if her smile meant she was interested or if she was just being kind to the sad inarticulate man. "In fact, I may even go for a *venti* day." At this she laughed— victory!—but did not slow her fast walk toward the front door. He did get one more knee-buckling smile, though, as she turned to let someone enter. *Man, is she cute*, thought Michael. *And there's something about her . . . She looks familiar*.

He was still smiling thirty minutes later, in spite of the bumper-to-bumper traffic on Sunset Boulevard. If anything would make him leave Los Angeles one day, it would be the suffocating traffic. Unless, of course, his soy-latte-ordering future wife wanted to stay in Los Angeles to raise their beautiful, well-behaved children near the Starbucks where they met and began their fairy-tale life. *First you need to get her number, numnuts*, Michael berated himself, but even his own self-flagellation couldn't dampen his spirits. After all, she had told him that she would ask for "the big one" again *tomorrow,* meaning that she was a daily user. Thus, Michael need only go back to the scene of the crime and wait for his angel to appear. And if she didn't appear, he would simply go back the next day and the next, ad infinitum, until her need for a soy latte drove her into his arms—or at least close enough to his arms so that he could get her number. Granted, his repertoire of charming repartee would need to expand past the current variations of descriptive words for big cups of coffee, but he had at least a day before there was the possibility of seeing her again and a long drive with nothing to do but plan spontaneous witticisms.

He was still thinking about his mystery girl when he pulled up to the *Generations* soundstage. He had been called back to the set for a meeting organized, apparently, by the agent of one of the other actresses on the show, to discuss "ways to make the days go smoother." Michael knew that was code for "ways to control Sapphire," and he also knew that he probably should have felt threatened by the fact that someone else was taking the reigns on an issue involving *his* star client's star vehicle, but he just couldn't work up any substantial give-a-shit anymore. Even the worst-case scenario—the other agent stealing Sapphire right out from under him—didn't sound so bad. In fact, it was almost as seductive a fantasy as his coffee-shop girl.

"Michael, you're here!" Walking toward him at a fast clip, with a nervous smile plastered across his desperately pleasant face, was Jerry Smith. Jerry was *Generations*'s line producer. As such, he was in charge of the show's budget, which made him the go-to guy for most problems on the set. It was his job to make sure everything stayed on track. It was the ideal job for a tough, disciplined, Doberman pinscher sort of a guy. Unfortunately, Jerry was more of a chocolate lab, all needy good humor and physical awkwardness. "I'm so glad you made it!" he exclaimed, grabbing Michael's hand and pulling him into an awkward half hug.

"Yup, I made it." Michael took a step backward to distance himself from Jerry's breath, which was a nauseating combination of stale coffee and fear. "Who else is coming to our little summit?"

"Little summit—HA! HA! HA!" *Even his laugh is needy,* thought Michael, trying his best to hold his ground against the double whammy of Jerry's excessive volume and the expulsion of rancid air. "That's a good one."

"Yes, I've been working on it all morning."

"Right, well, time well spent," said Jerry, completely missing Michael's sarcasm. In fact, he probably added "spend more time preparing witty comments" to his mental calendar. "Anyhoo, I don't think this will be too bad, do you? I mean, it's just a catch-up-and-chat, right? I probably have nothing to worry about, but, you know, worrying is my job. I'm so gosh-darn used to worrying that I even worry when there's nothing to worry about, like today, right? I mean, she's not mad at me, is she? Is there something that you think I should know before we head into her trailer?"

"No, Jerry, she loves you." *In the condescending, impersonal way that all queens love their obsequious subjects.* "I think we can believe what we have been told—that we are all here to brainstorm ways to make Sapphire's life easier. And, really, who doesn't want to spend their limited time on this earth doing that?"

"Oh, *I* do. Of course I do," said Jerry, still completely oblivious to Michael's sarcasm and now visibly relieved that he probably wasn't about to lose his job. "I think that's uppermost in all of our hearts and minds. Although it is a little weird that Hamilton Morgan called the meeting, isn't it? I mean, he's not even Sapphire's manager, he's Ka—" He stopped himself midsentence as if only then remembering he was speaking to the person whose job might really be on the line and placed a clammy hand on Michael's shoulder. "I'm sure you're right. I'm sure we're all just here to help our special girl."

"Yes, our special girl," said Michael, mirroring Jerry's intensely concerned expression and tone, purely for his own amusement. "Why don't we go and see if the short bus has arrived with our special girl, shall we?"

By the time the two men had walked the one hundred yards to the door of Sapphire's trailer, Michael had had to extricate himself from the "comforting" arm Jerry kept throwing over his shoulder no fewer than three times. Although not remotely comforting, Jerry's needy groping did distract Michael from his resentment about having been called to this meeting in the first place. So at least it was a fresh, new annoyance.

"*I got it,*" Michael snapped at Jerry, whose ill-timed attempt to reach around him to open the trailer door had almost knocked him off the rickety steps.

"Oh, right, right, of course. My bad," said Jerry, quickly pulling back his hand and dropping his head to his chest, as if Michael's impatient tone had been a rolled-up newspaper aimed at his nose.

When they finally succeeded in opening the door, they were met with quite a cozy little tableau: Sapphire and Hamilton sitting together on the couch, his arm over her shoulder, her head resting on his chest, a Kleenex clutched in her hand to stem the tide of tears that ran down her face. They didn't bother to pull apart at the interruption, but instead looked up calmly as if their being intertwined were the most natural thing in the world.

"Hello, Sapphire," said Michael, stepping up into the tiny living room and trying to clear enough space for Jerry to enter, as much out of a desire to have another witness to the scene as out of politeness.

"Hel—*oh!*" Not surprisingly, Jerry was completely unable to hide his shock. Michael did a quick check of the carpet under-neath Jerry's feet to make sure his excitement hadn't caused him to piddle.

Slowly removing himself from his embrace with Sapphire, clucking words of comfort and flattery along the way, Hamilton stood and held out his hand toward Michael. "Hello. You must be Michael. I'm Hamilton Morgan. I hope you don't feel like I am stepping on your toes by calling this meeting."

"No, I don't feel like you are stepping on my toes," said Michael. *My livelihood, perhaps.*

"Good, good," said Hamilton, settling back down on the couch next to Sapphire and gesturing toward two empty chairs. "Please, gentlemen, have a seat. Let's get down to the business of helping our star shine, shall we?"

Jerry didn't even make it the foot and a half to his seat before blurting out, "Well, I, for one, think it would be difficult to make her shine any brighter than she already does!"

"Thank you, Jerry," cooed Sapphire, dabbing at her dry eyes to remind everyone that sometime in the very recent past she had been injured to the point of tears.

"I'm merely stating a fact," said Jerry earnestly.

"Yes, well, be that as it may," said Michael in an attempt to interrupt the spontaneous honorarium, "I think it is important that we clarify exactly what we hope to accomplish here today." As he spoke, he watched with fascination as Hamilton's arm made its way to the back of the couch behind Sapphire, like a high school suitor staking his claim. "Also, I find myself a little bit curi-ous about how you two kids came to plan this little meeting in the first place."

"Oh, Michael, I'm hardly a kid," giggled Sapphire, throwing a coquettish look toward Hamilton, who smiled at her indulgently before taking over the job of fielding Michael's questions.

"I would agree with Sapphire on one point; she's not a kid—

although she certainly looks like she could be." Sapphire actually batted her eyelashes. Michael felt his stomach turn. "What she *is* is an artist, and she needs to be treated as such."

"Right," said Michael. "I understand that she is an artist—an artiste, if I may—but I still don't understand why I, her agent, am here at a meeting called by you, *not* her agent."

"Yes, we understand how that might feel awkward for you," said Hamilton, allowing his hand to drop off the back of the couch and rest gently on Sapphire's shoulder. "Originally, I reached out to Sapphire on the behalf of my client, who was frankly too intimidated to come to her on her own, which I think is easy to understand. Sapphire is, after all, a legend—deservedly so, I think we can all agree."

"Oh, absolutely!" chimed Jerry.

"Yes, I think we can all agree on Sapphire's legend-osity," said Michael, growing more annoyed by the minute. "Now, can we move on to the purpose of this meeting?"

"I know why *I'm* here! I'm here to help our star shine!" exclaimed Jerry, adding *redundant* to his list of annoying personality traits.

"Down, boy," said Michael under his breath.

"What?"

"I said, 'Let's get *down* to business,' " said Michael. "We are *all* here to make Sapphire's life easier. I spend the better part of my day on efforts geared toward making Sapphire's life easier. This meeting, in fact, is taking valuable time away from that, my primary purpose, so let's get to it and get on our way, shall we?"

"Yes, absolutely," said Hamilton, maturing from smitten schoolboy to businesslike agent before their eyes. "We need to change the focus of this set. This is not an ensemble drama, it is a star vehicle. The problems that arise do so because of the schism between what this show actually is—the Sapphire Rose show—and what it has been run as—the aforementioned ensemble drama."

"Absolutely! I couldn't agree with you more completely," chimed in Jerry, all but licking Hamilton's hand.

"Okay, I've got to admit, I'm a little confused," said Michael.

"Confused? What is there to be confused about?" asked Sapphire, clearly baffled that anyone would fail to see the simple, unarguable truth of Hamilton's sentence.

"Well, Hamilton, I am confused as to why you are in here basically working *against* your own client. Don't get me wrong—I am all for other people doing my work for me, but I have to ask—what does your client think of what you are doing? Who is your client, by the way?"

"Kate Keyes-Morgan."

"Oh, right. Keyes-*Morgan?*"

"Yes, she is my wife as well as my client, so that should give you extra assurance that I am trying to do only what is best for everyone."

Or that you are an even bigger asshole than I'd thought you were, thought Michael, but he said, "Yes, of course—how could anyone doubt your sincerity?" *Unless they saw you and Sapphire sitting so close together on the couch that it looks as if you had a glue-gun accident.*

"I sure don't doubt it!" piped in Jerry. "In fact, I am going to go out there right now and get to work on this right away, making sure that all of Sapphire's scenes are up first so we can get her home lickety-split to get her beauty sleep—not that she needs any, of course."

"I think that's a great start," said Hamilton.

"I agree," added Sapphire.

"Hold on!" snapped Michael, causing Sapphire and the two stooges of ass kissing to turn and glare at him at once. "Don't you think this is a little bit, I don't know . . . inconsiderate to the rest of the actors on the show?"

Sapphire gasped. "Whose side are you on, Michael?"

"I'm on your side, Sapphire, as always, which is why I would be remiss if I didn't point out that if you, as the highest-paid person on this set, inconvenience everyone else who works here for the sole purpose of making your life a little bit easier, well, it might not seem altogether fair."

Sapphire stared at him blankly. "What does fair have to do with it? Is everyone else the star of the show?"

"No, of course not, but everyone else is a *part* of the show, and you don't want them feeling that you don't respect their time, do you?"

Sapphire continued to stare at him as if he were speaking a foreign language. Finally, Hamilton spoke up. "I see your point, Michael, and it is certainly admirable, but I think you underestimate the esteem that your client engenders."

"I'll say!" Jerry piped up.

"See what I mean, Michael? These are people who want to make Sapphire's life easier, because they all know that without her, there is no show. Take my wife, for example. She was inconvenienced yesterday when the wardrobe department hit its little snafu, but she understands that it is not all about her schedule, that the privilege of working with and learning from one of the greats is a reward unto itself."

"That is so true," said Jerry, nodding earnestly.

"It really is," agreed Sapphire.

"Fine," sighed Michael, realizing he was fighting a losing battle. "Let's go ahead and try a scheduling change, but please be subtle about it, Jerry. And I think we need to be prepared for the possibility of some sort of fallout from the rest of the cast."

"They'll be fine," said Hamilton.

"They'll be happy to help," guaranteed Jerry.

"Who cares?" asked Sapphire.

★ ★ ★

Two minutes later, Michael and Jerry stood outside of Sapphire's trailer.

"Wow, that went really well, don't you think? I mean, really, this has always been Sapphire's show anyway, so it's sort of like we're just making it official, right? I think this is just going to be great for everyone, don't you?"

"I don't know," said Michael. "I'm not sure that everyone else is going to be quite as excited about this as, say, you and Sapphire are. I mean, how must this feel for that guy's poor wife? Do you think she really knows that he's here doing this?" *And probably doing Sapphire,* Michael added silently.

"Oh, I'm sure she does. Kate is a real team player. Have you ever met her? She's a real doll."

"No, I really haven't met most of the cast. Sapphire keeps me pretty busy."

"Yes, I can imagine. It is God's work, though, isn't it?"

Michael waited for a smile, a laugh—anything to show that Jerry was kidding—but it never came. Michael would never stop being blown away by the hypnotic power of celebrity. "On that note, I am going to be on my way."

"Good idea. You start working on your end, and I'll get right to work here on mine." Jerry leaned in, treating Michael to another dose of his sickening fear breath. "I don't mind telling you now that I was a little scared back there. I'm thinking we both dodged a bullet, you know?"

"*You?* Scared? Wow, I'm floored. You seemed like the picture of self-contained confidence." Leaving his sarcasm-resistant colleague outside of Sapphire's trailer, Michael headed toward his car, thinking of the bullet that Jerry had dodged.

It was now heading straight at him.

9

"So, what do you think?" Paige was facing Kate in the makeup chair, brushes primed and ready for action.

"Oh, I don't know. Do you think it's worth it?"

"Well, which is worse: getting your makeup done for no reason, or getting called to set and trying to do a thirty-minute makeup in two minutes?"

"Skip it, then?" asked Kate, lifting herself out of her seat as if she were going to head out and get on with her day.

"You wish." Paige laughed, pushing Kate back down into the chair and turning to finish setting up her makeup, laying out base, blush, powder, and eye shadow in neat rows like a surgeon's tools. "Now, just sit back and relax. This won't hurt a bit."

"That's what my high school boyfriend said—and he was lying, too."

"Yes," said Paige, holding up the makeup brush that she had just dipped into Kate's foundation. "The difference is that I really am just going to use the tip."

Kate laughed and said, "Oh, thank God for you. I don't think

I could do this job if you weren't here saying inappropriate, semi-offensive things to me every day."

"Right back at ya," said Paige. "It's all about you and the free bacon for me."

"Not necessarily in that order?"

"Kate, how could you even *say* that?" asked Paige in mock horror. "Of *course* not in that order. You know how I feel about my bacon."

"I do. In fact, I have seriously been considering an intervention. Is there a twelve-step program for bacon?"

"I can stop whenever I feel like it . . . I just don't feel like it. It is getting awkward, though, lying to waiters about the big bacon party I'm throwing later to try to cover up how much fried pork I am ordering for myself."

"*Big bacon party?* Good cover. I can't imagine anyone seeing through that clever ruse."

"Exactly," said Paige. "Now shut up and hold still so that I can waste both of our time getting you ready for a scene that they will never shoot. Did Sam give you any sort of an idea of timing?"

"Not really. He just said that they needed me here 'on deck' while they wait to see what the outcome of Sapphire's emergency meeting is."

"Sapphire called an emergency meeting? What is *that* about?"

"I don't know," Kate said into her lap, not wanting to lie straight to Paige's face.

"I hope she's not meeting with craft services about that new diet she's on. The stage still smells like lamb from her last insane food plan, and I heard her new thing is raw food. Can you imagine what it will smell like around here if she insists on sashimi for breakfast?"

"Maybe you'll luck out and it will be a raw-bacon diet."

"Ugh! I think you may have just stumbled upon the one and only way I will pass up a piece of bacon. Suddenly I feel strangely noble, like a pillar of discipline."

"The question is, do you feel disciplined enough to actually stop talking and do my makeup?"

"I will do your makeup, but I have no intention of not talking. In fact, I intend to talk the entire time, starting with my earliest childhood memory and working my way slowly and painstakingly through my comically awkward adolescence, all the way to my eventual transformation into the beautiful—albeit *fluffy*—swan you see before you today. They may even be ready for your scene by the time I am done with my fascinating monologue, which should be sometime next week."

"By all means, carry on," said Kate, relaxing back into her chair and closing her eyes. "If you hear a sort of snoring sound, it just means that I am listening extra hard."

"Of course," said Paige, clipping Kate's bangs back with a gentle sweep of her hand. "I wouldn't take it any other way. So, it all began thirty-five-ish years ago in lovely Berkeley, California . . ."

Kate allowed herself to drift off to the comforting sound of Paige's voice. She loved listening to her, loved her self-deprecating humor and her honesty. Paige was usually the person in the room who said what everyone else was thinking but was afraid to say out loud, and Kate envied her that freedom. She felt so restricted, so bound, by her fear of saying the wrong thing or, even if it was the right thing, that it would somehow be misquoted and used against her later. Hamilton was constantly reminding her that her conversations (with anyone other than him) were really *currency* for other people, whether they simply repeated what she said at a party to look popular and important or if they actually called a tabloid and traded her confidences for cold, hard cash. The scary part about the tabloids wasn't how much they made up but how much they got right. And they were famous for getting their most accurate information from "on-set sources," which meant that during her fourteen- to sixteen-hour workdays, Kate felt as if she were living in enemy territory, always wondering which one of her "friends" was actually a spy. She wanted desperately to believe that she could trust Paige, that their relationship could grow into a real friendship, but she had gotten so hurt during the "Katie the Cow" days when so much of what she had shared with people she thought she could trust had turned up on the front pages of the rags, always accompanied by an unflattering picture of her taken first thing in the morning, squinting into the harsh morning sun as she squatted down to pick up her newspaper, wearing an ugly, bulky robe or oversized sweatpants. Either that or the photo was an extreme close-up of her taking a bite of food at an outdoor restaurant. Never mind that the bite was usually just lettuce with no dressing—the close angle and the "Mooooooooooore food for Katie" caption created the illusion that she was an out-of-control glutton. She had solved that problem by choosing to embrace her hunger rather than food. She would never again be photographed eating outside, because she no longer met friends for lunch. She avoided being photographed when eating by *not* eating, and she avoided being misquoted by not sharing anything real with anyone. So she had won, and outside of the extreme emotional and physical deprivation, her victory was sweet indeed.

She was startled out of her daze by a sharp knock on the door and Sam's voice saying, "Coming up!" He opened the door and made his way up the rickety steps of the makeup trailer and balanced his metal clipboard, a Starbucks tray, and a paper plate overflowing with bacon, struggling to close the door behind him without dropping everything or interrupting the conversation he was engaged in on his headset. "Yes, I am here with her now . . . Yes, I will tell her . . . Yes . . . Right . . . Got it . . ." He rolled his eyes and smiled at the ladies, nodding from them back to the tray and the bacon to clear up any nonexistent mystery about whom the treats were for. With one more "Right . . . Got it!" he plunked the trays down onto the counter next to Paige and Kate and fell back into an empty chair with an exasperated sigh. "Is it just me or is everyone crazy?"

"Well," said Paige, "it's both, really. Everyone is crazy *including* you."

"Oh, thank god. Does that mean I get a two-week vacation to the loony bin?"

"Well, yes, it does," added Kate with the exaggerated enthusiasm of a game-show host. "And the best part is that you are already here! *This* is your loony bin!"

"Noooooooooooooooo," whined Sam. "I want the box with the sandy beaches and mai tais!"

"Then you should have taken that job on *Lost*."

"And give up being abused by you two every day? Never!"

"Uh-huh," said Paige, unconvinced. "That and the fact that they never offered you a job."

"Yeah, I guess it's mostly that. On a brighter note, I did bring bacon."

"Yes, I did notice that," said Paige, picking up two pieces and taking a healthy bite. "I can't help but think this means bad news."

"*And* Starbucks," he said, taking two cups out of the tray and handing one to each of the ladies.

"*Really* bad news," said Kate, accepting the cup and immediately looking under the lid for any signs of cream or anything else remotely tasty and, by definition, fattening.

"How could more time together be bad news?"

"Sam!" said the women together, both ready for the anticipation to be over and for the actual pain to begin.

"Okay, okay," said Sam, pushing himself up out of his chair and, backing toward the door, clearly preparing for a quick exit should bacon start flying at his head. "There has been another change of plans."

"Uuuuuuuuuuuuugh," groaned both women simultaneously.

"I couldn't agree with you more, and all of our combined agreement gets us a whole bunch of diddly-squat. So here is where we stand: we are going to start with Sapphire's scenes to get her out early, and then we hope to get to your scene before the end of the day today."

"And if not today, it will be the first scene up tomorrow?" asked Kate hopefully, afraid that her growing anxiety over the endlessly rescheduled lingerie scene was in danger of leading her smack into the middle of a fear-numbing—and figure-killing—Krispy Kreme doughnut binge.

"Well, yes and no," hedged Sam. "Your scene will be first up—right after Sapphire's scenes. The new world order here on the ever-crazier *Generations* set is that her scenes will be done first, with all other work for the day scheduled after hers are completed."

"What? Do we even get to know *why*?" asked Paige, through a mouthful of pork.

"I would tell you if I knew. All I know is that this is what was decided in this morning's meeting with all of the brass." He looked pointedly at Kate. "Your husband was there. You might want to ask him."

"Yeah, I'll do that," said Kate in a near whisper, feeling suddenly nauseous.

"Oh, there is one more thing," said Sam over his shoulder as he headed out the door. "There's sashimi at craft services if you want any."

★　　★　　★

Driving home seven hours later, Kate tried to decide if her headache and nausea were the symptoms of a burgeoning flu, the result of her frustration over being sent home yet again without completing her much-dreaded (and ever-elusive) near-nude scene, or the fact that her husband had apparently just sold her down the river. Paige had been admirably restrained; she didn't ask Kate for any insider information about the secret meeting, which was a tremendous relief because Kate didn't have any. She had expected—and been promised—a full report from Hamilton as soon as the meeting ended. What she had gotten instead was a hastily scrawled note on the door of her trailer, saying that Hamilton had looked everywhere but couldn't find her," and he had "to dash over the hill for a meeting" and would call from the road. He hadn't called. In fact, her phone didn't ring for the rest of the day. The day had dragged on, Kate checking her phone repeatedly (even calling the phone company to make sure that her phone was able to receive incoming calls) and feeling more and more like a rejected one-night stand. She had spent the remainder of the afternoon holed up in her trailer, embarrassed to show her face outside, sure that everyone could see through her robe to the silent cell phone in her pocket.

A television or film set was just like high school, with clearly defined cliques and a carefully orchestrated hierarchy. The only thing that crossed freely over all of the social dividing lines was gossip, and a piece of information as hot as a secret meeting with one of the show's stars orchestrated by the husband of another of the show's stars, but *excluding* that second star, was sure to spread like wildfire. By now, Kate was sure that everyone knew all about the scheduling mandate, and even if they didn't know for a fact that it had been Hamilton's idea (even Kate didn't know who had said what during the actual meeting), it was quite clear that no one had put up much of a fight in her defense—or in defense of any of the other actors, for that matter. But that was really the whole point, wasn't it? Sapphire Rose was the homecoming queen and everyone else was just lucky to have been granted a spot in the marching band.

But why is my husband in her court? wondered Kate, feeling the knot in her stomach twist and grow as she turned into her driveway and spotted Hamilton's car.

Kate walked in the front door and called out a tentative "Hello?" hating how unsure she sounded in her own home.

"Katie!" boomed Hamilton's voice from down the hall. "I'm so glad you're home!"

"You are?" asked Kate, startled first by Hamilton's enthusiastic tone and then by the bear hug he gave her when he bounded into the entryway seconds later.

"Of course I am! Why wouldn't I be, you silly goose?"

"Well, I didn't hear from you all day, and you didn't come by to see me at work, so I guess I just wondered what—"

"Didn't you get my note?" interrupted Hamilton, extricating himself from the hug and moving to the console to tidy the already perfectly tidy mail tray.

"Yes, I got it. I guess I just thought it was weird that you didn't try to find me to say good-bye."

"Katie, don't start this," said Hamilton, turning back to her. "You know that I am a very busy man."

"I know that, but it just seems to me like you could have taken five minutes to come to the makeup trailer and say good-bye."

"And it just seems to me that you could take that same five minutes and try to be a little less self-centered and overly sensitive."

"What? I don't think . . . I mean, I'm just asking why you left without saying good-bye to me, your wife," said Kate, rapidly going over the events of the day in her head, trying to see where she might be overreacting. "I don't think that makes me overly sensitive."

"Of course you don't, darling," said Hamilton, taking her by the hand and leading her down the hall toward their bedroom. "That's why it is so lucky that I am here to set you straight. Now, come with me to the bedroom and help me pick out a tie."

"Are we going out?" asked Kate, feeling more and more like Ingrid Bergman's character in the movie *Gaslight*.

"No, sweetie, *I* am going out. I have a very important business meeting with none other than your friend Sapphire Rose, to discuss the possibility of representation. Apparently, she has been considering taking on a manager for quite some time, and after today's meeting, she feels I just might be her guy." Hamilton sat Kate down on the edge of their bed and headed over to the vanity and his extensive collection of hair-care products.

"You just might be *her guy?*"

"Yes, that's what she said. Isn't that exciting?" Hamilton said, sounding like a cheerleader who had just secured a date with the star quarterback.

"Well, I guess so . . . but isn't that a conflict of interest?"

"A conflict of interest? With whom?"

"With *whom?* With me!"

Hamilton stopped primping long enough to treat her to a patronizing smile. "Now, Katie, we mustn't let petty jealousy get in the way of our future. Sapphire Rose is going to have a long and profitable career, and we want to be a part of that, don't we?"

Kate sat on the bed gripping the duvet with trembling fingers, watching the room spin along with Hamilton's version of reality. Attempting to keep her voice calm, Kate said, "It just seems to me that it might be difficult to service two clients on the same show at the same time. Like today, when you had that meeting on the set—"

"*Damn it, Kate!*" The sound of his Mason Pearson hairbrush crashing into the bottles and jars on the vanity was almost as shocking as his harsh tone. "Do you have to ruin everything with your fucking narcissistic insecurity?" He turned and moved toward her purposefully, stopping directly in front of her and waving a pointed finger inches from her nose. "I have one shot—*one shot*—at working with one of the greats, and you can't see beyond your spoiled little nose to give me the *minuscule* amount of support I need to show that you are capable of caring about anyone besides yourself!"

Kate was speechless for a few moments before finally finding the strength to say in a small voice, "I'm sorry, Hamilton. You know I would never do anything to stand in the way of your success."

"Oh, Kate," said Hamilton, turning away in disgust and throwing himself dramatically onto the Eames chair next to the vanity. "That is the saddest part. I do know that you would never stand in my way . . . intentionally."

"Or unintentionally," argued Kate.

Hamilton dropped his head into his hands with an audible sigh of frustration. "Oh, Katie-Cow, that is exactly the problem, don't you see? You don't even have the self-awareness to *know* what you are doing, so I can't even talk to you about it. Did you ever make an appointment with Penelope?"

"I've been trying to reach her and I will make one, I promise. But I'm here right now. Talk to me." Kate moved over to where Hamilton was perched and kneeled in front of him, trying to get him to look her in the eye. "Tell me what I am doing wrong."

Hamilton sighed deeply, as if debating whether she was worth talking to at all, then said, "You are allowing your jealousy and insecurity to get in the way of my happiness, which is the epitome of 'lower consciousness' behavior. You need to reread pages fifty-seven to fifty-nine in Penelope's book. In fact, you should probably reread the whole book, because you seem to be backsliding quite severely. The only way for *you* to be happy is for *me* to be happy, and the only way for me to be happy is to be allowed to follow my bliss. And right now my bliss is Sapphire Rose."

"Your bliss is Sapphire Rose?" Kate demanded in disbelief. "Do you hear how that sounds?"

"Do you hear how you sound, Katie? Whiny and insecure." He got up, grabbed his jacket from the back of the chair, and headed toward the door.

"Hamilton, wait," said Kate, still kneeling on the floor, having a hard time processing what she was hearing and standing up at the same time. "You know I love you."

"Yes, Katie, I know you love me." He continued to head toward the door, pausing one last time to turn and add, "But that's not really the point, is it?"

With that, he left the room, and, moments later, Kate heard his Porsche starting up and the familiar sound of the turbo engine driving away.

She didn't sleep at all that night. Her mind was racing with all of the things she would say to Hamilton when he came home—if he came home. She would try harder, be better, be *more* for him— or less. Or *both:* she needed to be more of the good, pretty parts and less of the ugly, needy parts. How had she forgotten so much of what Penelope had taught her? She knew better, damn it. She knew that she had been beyond lucky to find such a handsome, successful man to take care of her and that her only job—*her only job*—was to look beautiful and treat him like a king. How had she forgotten something so simple? How had she let her petty insecurities ruin his day *again* and threaten the health of her relationship? The relationship was her domain, her responsibility, and she had let it slide. What Hamilton really needed was for her to support and adore him—what *she* really needed was for him to love her. And not leave her. She couldn't go back to the way she had been before he came into her life. She couldn't stand the thought of being Katie the Cow again, of moving out of this beautiful house and being alone, of losing the security of being Mrs. Morgan. Mostly, she couldn't stand the thought of telling her mother.

Oh god.

What would she say to her mother? She would be so disappointed. Kate knew that in her mother's eyes there were two Kates: the fat, unemployable embarrassment that she had been before Hamilton, and the beautiful swan he had created. Her mother much preferred the Kate she could brag about to her book club to the one who sat in her old bedroom all day, crying and eating Kraft macaroni and cheese. At the time of her very public humiliation, she had looked to her mother for the oft-advertised unconditional love that a mother is supposed to shower on her children like a broken water main, but had found only drops of tolerance, tinged with impatience and disappointment.

Conditional as it may have been, her mother's loving admiration of the past two years had felt so affirming. With her handsome husband and her "pretty girl" role on a television show, Kate was finally the daughter her mother could be proud of. Now she was in danger of losing that, too. She couldn't stand the thought of once again seeing her own self-hatred reflected in her mother's eyes. "How could you let this happen?" her mother would ask, just as Kate was torturing herself with the same question. That was the problem, in a nutshell: When she was with her mother, it was two against one. There was no one on Kate's side.

10

"Michael, you're late," scolded Marjorie when Michael passed her desk on his way into his office.

"Late for what?" asked Michael.

"Late for *work!*" said Marjorie, saying the word "work" with the same energy with which one might say "life, liberty, and the pursuit of happiness!"—which, for Marjorie, could all be found in an organized work space.

"Yes, I see your point," said Michael. "Unfortunately, work seems to get in the way of my wasting an inordinate amount of time hanging out in overpriced coffee shops. I'm sure you can see my dilemma."

"No, I cannot," answered Marjorie primly. "There is perfectly good coffee here that you can drink at your desk while you start on returning your calls. The phone has been ringing off the hook and I am quite out of excuses for you."

"A: I love that you just used the word 'quite,' and B: you don't have to make excuses for me, Marjorie. I'm a grown-up." Michael picked up the stack of phone sheets and started to head into his office.

"Oh, I see—was there a very important meeting of the top secret grown-ups club at Starbucks this morning?"

Stopping in his tracks, Michael turned to her with a big grin and said, "Why, Marjorie, was that a joke?"

Embarrassed, Marjorie pretended to look for something in a pile of papers and said, "No, just a question."

"And quite a funny and charming one at that." Leaving a blushing and smiling Marjorie at her desk, he headed into his office and closed the door behind him.

He *was* late—late and disappointed. He had spent the morning at Starbucks, pretending to work on his laptop but really just surfing the Internet while hoping to see his mystery girl. Two hours of sitting and drinking coffee had left him jittery and frustrated, but no closer to a dinner date.

For the first half hour, he had jerked his head up every time he heard the door open, expecting to see her face. After the first thirty-seven or so times in a row that it was *not* her, he found himself creating superstitions: if he didn't look up for thirty seconds, it would be her; if he waited until he heard the counter person say, "Welcome to Starbucks," it would be her; and finally, if he held his breath and counted to fifty before looking up, then it would *definitely* be her. In spite of his efforts, she never showed up. He left at ten a.m. feeling hurt and a little angry, as if he had been stood up on a date.

"Snap out of it—you don't even know this girl," he said to himself. He was sitting behind his desk, staring at the stack of phone messages but seeing only her face. He knew intellectually that his crush was ridiculous and based on absolutely nothing beyond a fantasy created by hormones and projection, but that knowledge did nothing to dim his ardor. After all, isn't that what love at first sight really was—projection and imagination? He felt he deserved a little slack. What was so strange about the fact that he was sitting at his desk, literally surrounded by scripts he needed to read and phone messages he had to return, unable to get started on any of it because he was too busy daydreaming about a future with someone he didn't actually know? What was really wrong with spending his mornings sitting in a coffeehouse hoping against hope to catch a glimpse of a girl he had met once for all of thirty seconds?

"Because it is *stalking,* you idiot," he said aloud, forcing his attention back to his paperwork.

Unless . . . The scraps of colored message paper faded again into the background as his mind took off once more. Unless . . . he was destined to be with the soy latte girl, but circumstances beyond the control of the universe had cut their initial meeting short, and it was up to him to reconnect with her so that they could marry and create—out of their extraordinarily passionate and satisfying physical union—the singularly exceptional (and cute) child who was destined to grow up and save the world. If that were the case—and who was to say it wasn't—then he was much less of a stalker and way more of a hero. Surely, if the *fate of the world* rested on his ability to get the phone number of the cute girl with the coffee-ordering problem, then he had no choice but to sit in Starbucks every morning for as long as it took to complete his mission.

"See?" he said to himself, finally able to turn his attention to his work now that he had a really solid plan in place. "That's not the least bit crazy."

"Hamilton Morgan on two," squawked the black box on his desk.

"*Got it!*" he yelled through his closed door, smiling at Marjorie's frustration and annoyance and wondering idly if that joke would ever stop being funny. He quickly decided it would not and turned to the far less joyful task of picking up Hamilton's call.

"Hamilton, how are you?" asked Michael, adding for his own entertainment, "And what fresh hell do you have for me today?"

"What fresh *what?*" stammered Hamilton, either genuinely not understanding or taken aback by the truth inherent in Michael's question. "Oh! What fresh hell! Ha ha! That's good—I'm gonna have to use that!"

"Yes, you do that," said Michael, a little disappointed that his barb had been deflected so easily. "Seriously, though, Hamilton, to what do I owe the pleasure of this call?"

"Great news, my friend—*great news!* We are going to be working together!"

"We are?" asked Michael warily.

"Yes, we are. Your favorite client and I had a very successful dinner last night, and I am pleased to say that she now has twice as many good men in her corner. I think you probably know what I'm getting at here, don't you, my friend?"

"I think I do, my friend, but why don't you tell me anyway?" said Michael, wanting to hold on to his denial for one more brief, heavenly moment.

"The lovely Sapphire Rose has asked me to work as her manager—with you staying on as her agent, of course. She is fiercely loyal to you, Michael, and I want you to know that I intend to work *with* you, not against you."

"Why would I think anything else?" asked Michael, wondering if Hamilton actually believed that the underhanded stunt he had pulled yesterday with his "secret meeting" counted as teamwork.

"Well, you wouldn't—and that is exactly my point!"

"Oh good," said Michael. "I was hoping you would have a point."

"Well, I think we both have a point," said Hamilton, suddenly serious. "We have a point of *focus*—a point of energetic coming together, if you will—and that point is Sapphire Rose. I want *you* to understand that *I* understand that you have had the pleasure of working with her for some time now and that you and she probably have a way of working with which you are both comfortable. I want you to know that I have no intention of changing that—at least not the parts that are working. I think we will all get a clearer sense of our collective direction as we get deeper into our weekly work sessions."

"Our weekly *what?*"

"Oh, right! I forgot to mention to you one of the great ideas that Saph and I came up with last night. First of all, I want to make clear that what I am about to say is in no way a criticism of the way you have been conducting your business."

"Of course," said Michael, knowing full well that people only say that right before they criticize the way you conduct your business.

"Well, Sapphire has been feeling that she hasn't been getting quite enough attention. Again—I don't blame you, Michael. I realize that it is the nature of the *agenting biz* that the sheer number of clients which you are required to service at any one time cannot help but interfere with your ability to give real quality time to any one person. Obviously, that's where I come in. I make it a policy to take on no more than five clients at any one time, so each one gets plenty of individual attention. You see, what makes my side of the business different—"

"Right, Hamilton—I do have a fairly good working knowledge of how the *managing biz* works. In fact, I am thrilled and delighted that Sapphire has someone else on her team to work toward giving her all of the attention she wants."

"The attention she *deserves*, Michael."

"Yes, Hamilton, let's hope we *all* get what we deserve."

"Amen, my friend." Hamilton paused for a moment to highlight the profundity of their shared mission and then continued. "So, it works better for our girl if we meet her at work for our little weekly powwow. That way, if there is anything we need to address with anyone on her behalf, we can do it immediately. How are Mondays at six a.m. for you?"

"*Six a.m.?* In the *morning?*"

"Unless you know of a six a.m. in the evening." Hamilton chuckled at his own joke, then switched gears as if to signal the end of a shared amusement. "Seriously, though, I realize it is early, but Sapphire gets to work that early almost every day and she has felt alone in that for far too long. We all benefit from her efforts, and I—well, she and I—feel that having that kind of support at the very start of her week will go a long way toward making her feel that we are really on her team."

Michael debated the merits of arguing with Hamilton about his ridiculous plan but decided that he just didn't have the time, energy, or interest. The truth was, he didn't see himself as a part of this dysfunctional little ménage à trois for very long anyway—threesomes so rarely worked out in the long run—so he decided he might as well ride it out for the sheer entertainment value. Besides, the early hour would allow him the double benefit of missing traffic and making it back to Starbucks in time for his stalking—um, *coffee*.

11

Kate stood in the doorway of her home gym and stared at the treadmill. Her head was so foggy from the stress of another sleepless night spent waiting for Hamilton to come home that she was having trouble remembering how to work the damn thing—or why she had ever even cared in the first place. When her phone had rung at two a.m., she had jumped at it, hoping it was Hamilton calling to apologize and tell her that he was on his way home, but the voice on the other end of the line had been Sam's, letting her know that she would finally be given the dubious honor of showing her ass to the world. Her call time was two p.m., which meant that the actual ass showing could happen anytime between then and the anticipated wrap time of two a.m. the following morning.

So here she stood, trying to communicate to limbs that were weighed down with the heaviness of depression that it was imperative that they get on the scary-looking machine and walk miles to nowhere on the rotating belt. Her limbs weren't buying it. Somehow her legs knew what her brain was refusing to compute: something bad was happening.

Kate leaned against the doorjamb and allowed herself to slide down the edge until she was sitting on the floor, her coffee cup cradled in both hands for warmth and security. She felt adrift and confused. Hamilton hadn't called or come home last night, and her anxiety had morphed into a profound ache deep in her belly. For most of the night she had been as jumpy as a cat, trying unsuccessfully to stay a step ahead of her fear with manic tidying of her already immaculate house, carrying the portable phone with her from room to room so that it was never farther than arm's length away, running to the front window each of the countless times that she thought she heard Hamilton's car driving up.

"No wonder you are tired, you idiot," she said out loud into the oppressively empty house, letting her head fall back against the doorjamb. "You probably covered ten miles last night."

Normally, covering ten miles on an empty stomach would have been cause for celebration and a sanguine trip to the bathroom scale, but this morning, Kate was having trouble remembering why being weak from overexertion constituted a victory.

"Maybe because Hamilton isn't here to remind me," she said again aloud, eliciting a tiny chuckle of recognition, which far too quickly evolved into tears. *Hamilton isn't here to remind me. Hamilton isn't here.* Kate put her coffee cup down on the floor next to her, its weight too much to bear. How was she ever going to perform today? How was she going to *stand up,* much less work out, take a shower, drive to the studio, and stop crying long enough to do her scene? She certainly didn't possess the strength required to hold in her stomach and position her legs in such a way that her cellulite didn't show. Maybe they could just use a mannequin—or better yet, maybe they could get a body double with rock-hard abs and legs, and then she could get a spokesperson contract for a fat-burning diet pill and do countless interviews about how she eats like a pig and doesn't exercise "but still, the weight just falls off!" *Without Hamilton here to guide your career, you'll be lucky to get that,* Kate reminded herself—on the off chance that her marriage crashing to a halt wasn't enough to sustain her depression.

"You know what? You're probably just overreacting," Kate said, gathering the superhuman strength required to lift her coffee cup, hoping that if she could just get a little bit of the caffeine into her system, it would give her the unimaginable amount of extra strength required to actually stand up. "Of course, overreacting or no, you have now officially become the crazy lady who sits on her floor and talks to herself." That, combined with the image of Hamilton's face should he come home to see her like this—slumped on the floor in her ratty sweats, teeth and hair unbrushed—gave her the impetus she needed to force herself into some semblance of action. No workout, perhaps, but at this point, getting herself into the shower was an inspirational accomplishment.

When she dragged herself into the makeup trailer a few hours later, she could tell by the look on Paige's face that the undereye concealer and fake smile she had painted on before getting out of her car weren't fooling anyone.

"*Oh shit,*" said Paige, rushing down the trailer's narrow pathway and pulling out a chair for Kate as if she were an ailing elderly person in the grips of a fainting spell. "What happened to you?"

"Nothing."

"Nothing, huh? Then why do you look like your dog just died? Oh god—your dog didn't die, did it?"

"I don't have a dog."

"Oh, thank god," said Paige, sinking into the chair that she had pulled out for Kate. "It sucks when your dog dies."

"Did your dog die?"

"Yes, when I was ten years old, and I am nowhere near over it."

"I'm sorry," Kate said, enjoying her crazy friend and her first authentic smile of the day.

"*Oh no, you don't,*" Paige said, sitting up and pointing an accusatory finger at Kate. "You are not distracting me from finding out what has turned your beautiful face into a swollen tear duct."

"It's nothing. I just didn't sleep last night." Kate hated to lie, but what was she going to say? That her husband *may* have left her for the crazy woman in the next trailer? That even if he hadn't actually left her, he had taken time out of his busy schedule to let her know that said crazy woman was far more talented and economically viable than she was? That would be great. And the capper would be when she asked Paige not to share with anyone what was arguably the juiciest piece of gossip of the year (well, maybe of the week, this being Hollywood and all). It wasn't that she didn't trust Paige, she just didn't trust herself to know what to say in a way that wouldn't come back to haunt her. "Seriously, I'm fine."

"You're not fine, but I'm not going to push it. I mean, seriously, if I were you I would have lost it a hundred times already over all of this ridiculous Sapphire scheduling bullshit, so I'm just going to pretend that *that's* the problem, and I am going to shut up and do your makeup."

"Thank you."

"You are welcome," said Paige, pulling a frozen eye mask out of the mini fridge behind her and placing it over Kate's face. "You do know that I am lying, right?"

"Yes . . . and thank you," said Kate, concentrating on keeping her mouth shut, as Paige's kindness and genuine concern threatened her resolve to keep all of her pain to herself.

"Coming up!" called Sam, opening the door and stepping into the trailer. "We need an estimate on Kate. We're gonna be ready on set in fifteen."

"I just got her in my chair," protested Paige.

"I'm not even due in for fifteen more minutes," added Kate, taking off her eye mask and pointing to the wall clock.

"I hear you, and everything you say is true," conceded Sam. "It is also true that we finished the last scene sooner than we expected and if we don't get you prettied up and out there in thirty, they are going to skip your scene and move on to the next one. Is that what you want?"

"What I want is the standard hour I get to do Kate's makeup."

"And I want a pony, but we don't always get what we want, Paige."

"Don't be a wiseass, Sam."

"Don't be a prima donna, Paige. We need her in thirty. Yes or no?"

"Thirty isn't enough time. Whose ass is on the line if she doesn't look good?"

"Well, actually, it is my ass on the line," said Kate, beginning to feel like a kid caught between fighting parents. "Today it is quite *literally* my ass, so, theoretically at least, no one will be looking at my face anyway. What if we put my hair up, do a quick face paint, and send me on my way?"

"Great," said Sam.

"Wait!" said Paige. "Kate, you have a right to take the time you need to be comfortable, you know. They'll wait for you."

"No, they won't."

"Sam! You're not helping."

"I'm trying to, believe it or not. The new scheduling mandate is making everyone crazy, and we need to get done what we need to get done. No exceptions."

"Unless you are Sapphire Rose."

"*Now* you're catching on." Sam held up a finger to pause the conversation while he listened to his headset for a moment. "Got it . . . I'm with them now . . . Yes, she's in the chair . . . Twenty-five minutes to camera?" He said the last bit into his mouthpiece, but he looked toward Kate with raised eyebrows that said "Are you in?" Shrugging her apologies to Paige, Kate nodded to Sam, who said, "We're good here," and headed out the door.

Paige shook her head but went to work anyway, quickly pinning Kate's hair in a tousled updo and applying her makeup in record speed.

"What?" asked Kate when Paige had gone twenty minutes without saying a word.

"Nothing," said Paige.

"Bullshit."

"Bullshit? *You* got to say 'nothing.' "

"Yes, because nothing was wrong with me."

"Bullshit."

"Be that as it may, you are chomping at the bit to tell me what is on your mind."

Paige paused for the briefest of moments. "*Damn it!* Damn me and my inability to have a private thought. Here is the deal, Kate: I can't stand to see how they are treating you. You have more power here than you think."

"I don't want power, Paige. I just want to get this scene done and go home and crawl into bed."

"Kate, you can still crawl into bed, after you—"

"Paige, *please* . . ."

Paige inhaled deeply, as if readying herself for a standard women-in-power diatribe, but the tired pleading in Kate's eyes stopped her. "Okay, enough said—for today."

Just then there was a knock on the door and they heard Sam's voice call, "They're ready for you!"

"She's coming," called Paige, handing Kate her lip pencil. "They can wait two minutes for you to look less like the undead."

"Less like the undead, huh?" said Kate, quickly coloring in her mouth. "You make me feel like a pretty, pretty princess."

"I'm just doing my job, Your Highness."

Kate handed back the pencil. "Seriously," she said, "thank you."

"Seriously," Paige answered, "you're welcome. Now go get dressed—I mean, undressed—and I'll meet you on set."

Kate was laughing as she headed out the door.

★   ★   ★

Kate's laughter stopped abruptly when she turned the corner and almost collided with Hamilton as he exited the trailer closest to the set—Sapphire Rose's trailer.

"Kate!" Hamilton exclaimed, as if he were surprised to see her there—on the set of *her* television show.

"Hamilton," Kate said, somehow able to keep her voice relatively calm, although inside her head there was a screaming cacophony of pain, blame, and unanswered questions.

"I am so glad to run into you here," he said, taking her by the arm and steering her away from Sapphire's door and toward her own trailer. "I was worried about you. You didn't answer any of my messages."

"You didn't *leave* me any messages," Kate said definitively, for once sure of her position. "I had the phone right next to me all night."

"You did? How sweet." Hamilton kissed her on the cheek as he opened her trailer door for her and followed her inside. "Were you worried about our little tiff?"

"Hamilton, it was more than a tiff. You didn't come home last night—and you didn't call."

"Sweetheart, of course I didn't call. I didn't want to wake you. I e-mailed you several times, though, so that you wouldn't worry."

"E-mail? I don't even know how to check my e-mail unless you are there to set it up for me!"

"Really? Oh, darling, you are so endearingly technologically ignorant."

"Hamilton!" Kate was rapidly losing her cool. "Where the *fuck* were you last night?"

"Kate, I don't think it's necessary for you to use that tone. I, for one, am doing my best to stay calm, even though you are clearly losing control."

They were interrupted by a knock on the door and Sam's voice calling, "We're ready for you, Kate."

"Getting dressed!" she called back, and immediately began rushing around her room, grabbing bits and pieces of her costume (which was quite literally made up of bits and pieces) and working her way into them as she tried to get some sort of straight answer from Hamilton. "Okay, Hamilton, I am calm. I hear you that you tried to reach me. I didn't get the messages. Please tell me where you were."

"I don't know if this is really the time to discuss this, Kate. You have to go to work, and you clearly have some feelings that you need to work through before you can hear my news in a way that will be satisfying for me."

"Hamilton," said Kate, keeping her voice exaggeratedly calm and taking the time to pull him down to sit with her on the sofa, even though she absolutely, positively needed to get to set immediately. She knew she wouldn't be able to work without getting some sort of answer from him, and she knew he wouldn't share anything with her unless he felt he had her full, undivided attention. "I do want to hear your news. You and your news are my top priorities."

"Well, sometimes it just doesn't feel that way."

Oh god, thought Kate, *I don't have time for pouting.* "I'm sorry, honey—I shouldn't have snapped at you about the phone thing. It's my fault for not checking the e-mail."

"Yes, exactly," said Hamilton, brightening a little as he sensed the tide turning in his favor.

"Kate! We really need you!" Sam's voice was developing a definite edge. Kate knew she couldn't stall anymore.

"Right away!" she called, getting up from the couch and surrendering her dream of going into her scene free of the feeling that her entire life was falling apart. "I guess this will just have to wait until tonight, then."

"Okay, darling," said Hamilton, opening the door for her. "But don't forget to say hello to your husband's second favorite client when you pass her trailer!"

"What?"

"Sapphire has agreed to join our little management family! Isn't that great?"

If it hadn't been for Sam reaching up and placing a steadying hand on her elbow, Kate felt sure she would have passed out.

"Isn't that *great*?" repeated Hamilton.

Knowing that Hamilton wouldn't be happy until he got the answer he wanted, she forced out a weakly cheerful "Yeah . . . great" and allowed Sam to lead her down the rickety stairs.

"Oh, and honey?" Hamilton called, causing Kate to stop in her tracks and Sam to elicit an audible sigh of impatience. "You really aren't looking well. I hate to say it, but honestly? You are looking a little *bony*. It is just not a good look. Make sure they do what they can to help you with the lighting. We don't want you showing up in an article about scrawny actresses, now, do we?"

★   ★   ★

By the time Kate made it to the set, her head was spinning. Her thoughts, dominated for so long by her neurotic fear of looking fat in the scene that she was finally about to shoot, now turned to the novel fear of appearing too thin and the very real fear of losing her husband to her costar. *Don't be ridiculous*, she told herself silently. *Everyone knows that in Hollywood you can't be too rich or too thin.* She tried not to think about the other truism about Hollywood: you most certainly *can* lose your husband to your costar.

"Katie, good, you made it," said Jimmy, the director for the current episode, walking efficiently toward her with his assistant, Pearl, fast on his heels. When he reached her, he threw an arm over her shoulder, turned abruptly to the left toward where the cameras were set up, and continued his brisk pace, with Kate now attached to his side. "I'm sorry to rush you, Katie, but this new scheduling crap is making everyone crazy around here, and I'd hate to have to send you home again without finishing this damn scene."

"It's no problem."

"I knew it wouldn't be for you. You're a trouper. Okay, I think you know what this scene is about, don't you, darlin'?" Jimmy had been a television star in his own right in a short-lived but popular Western drama called *The Cowboys,* and although he had been born and raised in Michigan, his speech was peppered with endearments from the Hollywood version of the cowboy vernacular.

"Yeah, I think so. Is there somewhere specific you need me to start?"

"Yeah, actually, start *and* finish. Because of the time crunch, we had to go on ahead and work this old dawg out with second team while we were waitin' on you. I'll call Mary over to show you what we worked out."

"Oh, okay . . . but—" Before Kate could finish, Jimmy was out of earshot, moving quickly back toward where the directors' chairs were set up, talking rapid-fire to his note-taking assistant the whole time. What Kate had intended to tell him was that she had a few ideas about how she wanted to play the scene. It was a short scene, but it was important in that her character had to make an emotional transition, which Kate had to show solely through her movement and expression. Her character, Melania, realizes that she is no longer in love with her wealthy husband (with whom she just made love) but is in fact falling for the gardener, Gunther (who the audience knows is actually an Eastern

European prince in hiding from his enemies). In a previously shot scene, Melania had woken up in the bed she shared with her husband, Paul, and exited the room. Today's scene picked up as she exited her bedroom and walked across the living room to stand at the window in the predawn light, watching Gunther as he unloaded his truck in front of her house. Knowing that in the following scene she had to be madly in love with Gunther and full of loathing for her husband, Kate had spent quite a bit of time working on ways to illustrate Melania's state of mind: first, she envisioned herself spending a few moments looking at the stiffly posed family photos on the mantel as a way of representing the years of unhappiness with Paul; then she had seen herself moving toward the piano and briefly touching the decanter of whiskey that rested on its surface to remind the audience of the pain caused by his drinking problem; and finally she would move toward the small table next to the window where she wanted to place the book that Gunther had given her (a worn but beautiful copy of her favorite novel, *Anna Karenina,* that Gunther claimed to have found in one of the yards he worked on but that the audience knew was a very rare and expensive first edition). Only then would Melania look up to see her soon-to-be lover outside her window and realize her true feelings.

"Hey," said Kate's stand-in, Mary, as she approached. "Let me show you what he wants. Basically, you walk from the door to this mark at the window. That's it. Pretty simple."

"Oh," said Kate, trying to figure out how she was going to communicate Melania's life-altering realization in a three-yard walk. "Is there room for me to stop at the piano or go to the mantel?"

"You know, you're gonna have to ask Jimmy, but he is superstressed and Jerry is totally breathing down his neck about getting to the next scene before lunch, so my guess is that there's not a lot of room for change. Knock yourself out, though."

"Oh, *bite me.*"

Mary stopped and looked at Kate closely. "Hey, are you okay?"

"Yeah, I just had some ideas about the scene."

"No, not about the scene. Are *you* okay? You don't look like yourself."

Before Kate could answer, she heard Jimmy yell, "Okay, people, we have got to go! What's the holdup?"

"We're good," Mary called back, moving quickly out of the way, knowing that if her conversation with Kate was targeted as a waste of time, it would be *her* head on the chopping block.

"Let's go then, people!"

"Right!" shouted Rick, the first assistant director, through his bullhorn. "Let's do this! Final touches!"

"Final touches" was the signal for the beauty squad to descend on Kate. Paige came rushing in, lip gloss and powder at the ready, and Gladys, the on-set costumer, followed close behind to take Kate's robe and slippers. Primped and near naked in her lavender lingerie, Kate moved to her starting position and took some deep breaths, trying to work her way into Melania's mind-set. She briefly debated calling Jimmy over to discuss her ideas for the scene, but he seemed so stressed—everyone seemed so stressed—that she decided to make do with the simple action the director had worked out for her. Hopefully, the audience would fill in the blanks.

"*Aaaand* action!" called Rick, and Kate began her slow walk across the room, trying to replace the *actual* reality that she was an actress in her underwear in front of hundreds (soon to be millions) of people with the *imagined* reality that she was a real woman having a private emotional moment in her very private home. She got about halfway across the living room set, lost in her inner monologue of lustful thoughts about Gunther and hoping that she wasn't pushing too hard to show the audience the intensity of Melania's feelings (she had learned from painful experience that even love can look like constipation if the actor is trying too hard to illustrate the emotion through facial expressions alone). Her intense fantasizing was interrupted by Jimmy's voice yelling, "CUT!" followed by a sudden swell of activity as assistant directors whispered frantically into walkie-talkies and various crew members hurried over to confer with the director.

"I need wardrobe and makeup at the monitor!" Rick called out, causing a flurry of movement in the dark corner where Paige and Gladys had put their portable set chairs. Paige's knitting and Gladys's Treo went flying as the two women grabbed their overstuffed set bags and hurried over to find out what was going on.

Kate was left alone and confused in the middle of the set. Had she suddenly sprouted a cystic pimple that was somehow catching the light and creating a distracting shadow that fell across her face? Or—god forbid—did she have some sort of hideously humiliating wardrobe malfunction that the director was too embarrassed to tell her about? Just last week, Gladys had told her about a time she had been asked by several crew members to bring underwear to the set for an actress who liked to practice high kicks while wearing short skirts sans panties. Kate did a quick and (she hoped) subtle check of her costume, making sure that all of her delicate bits were covered. Everything seemed okay, so unless she had gotten her period (in which case she would simply kill herself right there), there was nothing to do but stand alone like the cheese in the children's game and wait for the other kids to come and get her.

Finally, Paige and Gladys broke away from the group and walked toward her, both sporting pained smiles. Paige spoke first: "Well, the good news is that they don't think you look too fat."

"Okay," said Kate, steeling herself. "I'm assuming there is also bad news."

"Well," said Gladys, looking to Paige for support, "bad-*ish*."

"For the love of god," said Kate, "I am standing here in my underwear. Would you please just spit it out?"

"They're afraid you look too thin," said Gladys.

"And tired," added Paige.

"Are you *serious?*" Kate could hardly believe her ears.

"They want you to wear a robe."

"And, apparently, take a nap," said Paige.

"They want me to *take a nap?*"

"No, but they want me to make you look rested, and I can do only so much with a tube of concealer."

Kate was staring at Paige blankly. She was simply too tired and too hungry to keep up. *Too thin? A nap?*

"Kate, I'm kidding," Paige continued, bringing her out of her confusion. "Well, not about the robe part, but they would *never* stop production for you to take a nap." Kate managed a small smile as Paige whipped out her magical makeup bag and Gladys walked back to the director to figure out where they would place the robe on the set so that Kate could slip it on at the beginning of the scene, creating a transition from the scene they had already shot in the bedroom, which showed her wearing just her lingerie.

Kate sat on Paige's tiny foldout set chair and watched as the entire crew ran around trying to find a way to deal with her inadequacy. She desperately wanted to sneak back to her trailer—or even better, to her house—for just a moment of privacy in which to process her humiliation, but, as Jimmy said, she was a trouper, which meant that she would bury her own feelings for as long as was needed to get the day's work done. She would smile gamely at the myriad crew members who passed her chair and do her best to make light of her mortifying embarrassment, because that was what everyone expected of her. They counted on her to step up and make everyone feel comfortable, no matter how unfairly she was treated or how badly she felt. They counted on her to be a good girl.

Finally, after thirty minutes of frantic activity and intense conversations involving much pointing at Kate and aggravated head shaking, it was time for Kate to play the scene. The dreaded underwear was covered by a silk robe, the bags under her eyes masked with a thick layer of concealer. When, after two takes of the scene, the director of photography was still not happy with how she looked, he resorted to blasting Kate's face with direct light from a large handheld bulb, in an attempt to camouflage her apparently hideously tired appearance. Kate could hope only that her squinty eyes would be read as overwhelming passion.

★   ★   ★

Kate's car limped along Sunset Boulevard, the lethargic pace of the traffic matching her mood. She looked around listlessly, vaguely taking in the seemingly endless array of fast-food restaurants. For once, her mind didn't scroll through the menu of each restaurant in a hunger-fueled fantasy of forbidden foods. The irony of her situation hadn't escaped her: she had been ordered by her boss—a Hollywood producer, for god's sake—to put on weight, but she had no appetite. It was as though if she took in food she would have to take in everything else that was happening in her life, and if felt as if the pain of that could kill her. Of course, starvation would eventually kill her, too. She numbly searched her soul for the part that cared but came up empty.

The turnoff for her street arrived way too soon, and before she knew it, she was pulling into her beautifully landscaped driveway. She was surprised to see Hamilton's Porsche there and even more surprised to see a cherry red Mercedes convertible parked next to it. Oh lovely, he was having a meeting with his new star client in Kate's home. How . . . homey.

She quickly glanced into her rearview mirror and flinched. When had she aged ten years? Apparently, it had been an even longer drive than it had felt like . . . through the desert . . . with leeches sucking all of the moisture from her body while an evil facialist applied a drying clay mask. At least the red in her eyes set off the blue of her irises nicely. There was something to be said for looking so absolutely terrible, though: when there was no hope for meaningful, immediate improvement, there was no need to try. Forgoing even the standard undereye mascara–removing hand wipe, Kate grabbed her purse and, with a groan of effort, dragged her uncooperative body out of the car and through the front door of her house.

"Hello!" Kate called, surprised to see her living room empty. "Hamilton, I'm home!"

When no one answered, she began a quick sweep of the house. Kitchen: empty. Patio: empty. Screening room: empty. She made her way down the hallway and heard music coming from the bedroom—was it Prince? As she got closer, she could tell that, yes, it was definitely Prince. In fact, it was the *Purple Rain* sound track— otherwise known as the sexiest album ever produced. She found herself frozen at her bedroom door, her hand centimeters from the doorknob, unsure whether she wanted to see what was on the other side. She leaned into the door to see if she could hear anything over the pulsating rhythm of the music. Was that groaning? Yes, there was groaning—there was *definitely* groaning—but was it part of the song? She tried to remember that song where Prince meets a girl named Nikki—was there a lot of groan-filled sex? Nikki *was* a sex fiend, that much Kate remembered, but she couldn't get clear on whether there was any actual bumping and grinding. When the song ended and the groaning did not, Kate got her answer. Well, part of her answer. She still needed to open the door to find out the rest. Taking a deep breath and saying a short prayer to the god of don't-let-it-be-what-I-think-it-is, Kate threw open the door and turned toward the bed.

The *empty* bed.

Still confused, Kate heard the opening strains of "When Doves Cry" coming from the closed door to her home gym, attached to the bedroom. Images of Hamilton and Sapphire entwined on the weight bench, gyrating in sync to Kate's favorite song, flashed through her mind, making her dizzy with dread and rage. She grabbed the doorknob, took a few steadying deep breaths, and flung the door open to reveal Hamilton, drenched in sweat, leaning over a woman who was—just like in Kate's nightmare—lying on the weight bench. Unlike the image in her fantasy, however, this woman was lifting weights. And groaning.

Groaning from the strain of *lifting weights*.

Hamilton stood and turned at the sound of the door opening. So did a pink spandex–clad Sapphire Rose.

"Hey, Kate," said Hamilton, acting as if his wife walking in on him and her costar, drenched in sweat and groaning away, was the most natural thing in the world. "You're home early."

"Not really," said Kate, picking up the remote and turning down the music. "It's six o'clock."

"Six o'clock!" exclaimed Sapphire, sitting up and playfully slapping Hamilton with a towel. "You rascal. You told me it was five o'clock."

"It was, the last time I checked. Is it my fault that time flies when you're having fun?"

"Excuse me," Kate said, interrupting their lively banter. "Hamilton, could I talk to you?"

"Sure." Hamilton plopped down next to Sapphire on the bench and began massaging her shoulders. "What's up?"

"Alone?"

Sapphire turned her head to look at Hamilton, and they exchanged a knowing glance before Hamilton deigned to answer his wife with a curt "Fine." With one final sensual squeeze of Sapphire's shoulders, he followed Kate back into their shared bedroom. "Okay, Kate, here we are, all alone. What is it?"

"Exactly," said Kate, closing the gym door. "What is it?"

"What is what?"

"What is going on?"

Hamilton sat down on the bed with an exasperated sigh.

"What is going on is that I am working out with my client. Exactly how I work out with *all* of my clients."

"You have only two."

Hamilton froze, his eyes locked on hers. "Nice, Katie. Really nice. I've spent the last three years of my life and career completely focused on you and bringing your career back from absolute disaster, and now you are trying to punish me for my sacrifice."

"No, I'm not trying to punish you. I appreciate what you did for me, it's just—"

"Just that you can't get over your own petty jealousy and insecurity to support me in *one one-hundredth* of the way that I have supported you." Hamilton got up from the bed and crossed back to the gym door, turning back to Kate before going in. "It is astonishing to me that you can't see that *everything* I do, I do for you—for *us*. I am going to go back in to my client now, and I am going to finish her workout, and then I am going to take her out for a postworkout dinner. We were going to invite you, but now I can see that you're not ready to behave like a grown-up. Perhaps you should just stay in and have some strained carrots and peas. Lord knows you need to eat something. You look awful."

Kate stood stunned as the door closed behind Hamilton. She heard Hamilton mumble something she couldn't quite make out, followed by a full-voiced Sapphire saying, "Well, if that's what working out gets you, I'll take my big ass any day." Then Hamilton mumbled something else, and Kate walked out of the room to the discordant music of her husband and Sapphire's shared laughter.

12

9:15.

9:30.

Michael's mornings now passed in fifteen-minute intervals. He had created a game for himself where he was allowed to look up from his computer every quarter of an hour. He was allowed to check the door, the coffee-ordering line, and the neighboring tables for no more than one minute, then he forced his attention back to his writing.

His *writing*.

The first two days of what he privately referred to as his "Starbucks-girl stakeout," he had sat alone at a table facing the door, with only his BlackBerry for company. But he had found that he was envious of the people around him, typing away on their laptops. He'd often wondered about people who sat with their computers in coffee shops: didn't these losers have homes? But his mornings spent stalking—*waiting*—had changed his perspective. The place that used to be nothing more than a quick caffeine stop at the beginning of his hectic business day now felt more like a creative community, and he wanted membership. He wanted to be one of the losers, one of the coffee-shop writers who didn't know one another by name but nodded over their cappuccinos when they looked up to ponder a new sentence or celebrate the successful completion of a good paragraph.

The sad truth was, he'd all but given up on finding his dream girl. He still played the fifteen-minute game with himself, but it had become more of a writing ritual than a girl hunt, a moment's pause to search for a word or to think about the structure of a particular sentence. As his stories took shape, he found himself amazed by how quickly the mornings passed and how difficult it was to tear himself away from what he still thought of as his "silly hobby" to make his way across town to his real job. He hadn't told anyone about his mornings spent chipping away at short stories—*short stories,* for god's sake. He would have been more willing to admit to the stalking, or, if forced under torture to explain why he was typing so many words in a row, he could see himself admitting to writing something more acceptable—a screenplay for a big-budget action movie, say, or a nice masculine nonfiction book about something really important, such as making money. Writing short stories in a town where one was hard-pressed to find anyone who reads much beyond scripts (and the occasional popular novel—but only to find out if it is worth optioning as a screenplay) was folly at best, career damaging at worst. If word got out that Michael was spending so much of his time doing something that had very little chance of generating income or getting him closer to people who could generate income for his company (clubbing being a far better use of his time than creating), he would be dubbed "artistic" and promptly lose his status as a serious player. So he sat in his little corner of Starbucks and worked away on his computer, secure in the knowledge that if someone from work should happen upon him, he could quickly close his writing program and pull up something more acceptable . . . such as porn.

As he was completing his 10:45 sweep of the shop, searching for the proper word to describe the nosy neighbor in his story, his eye caught sight of a familiar mop of curly hair at the exact

moment that his mind caught the word that he had been struggling to find (*invasive*). Torn between getting the word down and
getting down with the girl, he panicked and yelled, "Invasive!" in
her general direction. Every head in the coffeehouse turned to look
at him, including the one with the curly hair, whom he now *definitely* identified as the girl he had spent the last week (his whole
life?) looking for. Sadly, she now probably identified him as the
crazy man who had yelled "Invasive!" for no apparent reason.

Surprisingly, she smiled at him. Out of pity, maybe, but crazy
men who yell in crowded places can't be choosy about other people's motivations, so Michael decided to interpret the smile as an
invitation and walked over to where she was standing at the end
of the long ordering line. The good thing about being thought of
as crazy, Michael noticed, was that people tended to give you a
wide berth, so his path to "his" girl was cleared as people all but
leaped out of his way.

"Hi," he said, trying to look sane, which unfortunately trans-
lated into a stiff grimace of a smile.

"Hello," said the girl, subtly taking a step back and glancing
toward the nearest exit.

"Listen," Michael began, leaning in to whisper to her but
pulling back when he noticed her recoiling. "Okay . . . I know that
must have seemed odd." Michael tried a charming giggle, which
only seemed to scare her more. He felt his time with her slipping
away as the line moved forward and decided that his only option
was full speed ahead. "Okay, um, here's the thing: I am a writer
and I got excited because I found the perfect word to complete a
difficult sentence and in my excitement I yelled and I scared you
and I am sorry and can I buy you a cup of coffee to apologize?"

Time stopped for a moment (an hour?). She watched him carefully, perhaps looking for any telltale tics or growls that would
negate his story and support her original analysis of him as a wacko.

"It's just a cup of coffee," he said, using instincts honed over
years of closing deals for his clients. "Seriously, if you don't let me

apologize to you over a cup of coffee, my neurotic writer's brain will obsess over how I frightened some poor girl by yelling 'Invasive!' for no apparent reason, and I won't be able to write at all for the rest of the day, and my poor, sick mother won't get her medication."

"Your mother won't get her medication?"

"No. Not unless you let me buy you a cup of coffee." She smiled. She *smiled*. Michael held steady, willing his legs to stand firm rather than break into a victory jig.

"So, just so I'm clear . . ." she began.

"Yes?" They were next up to order, and Michael knew that the deal would close or fold in the next thirty seconds.

"You yelled 'Invasive' because you are a writer who found the perfect word, not because you were warning the rest of us of an alien invasion. Is that right?"

"Yes."

"Huh." She took the final step up to the counter to place her order. "Decaf soy latte."

"That'll be three sixty-seven," said the counter guy. Michael held his breath, not wanting to push his luck but unsure of his next move.

"He's paying," she said, brushing by him with a sly smile and heading over to wait for her drink.

"Oh, right!" Michael fumbled with his wallet, handed the counter guy a five-dollar bill, and told him to keep the change in his hurry to follow his girl.

"Thanks, man!" said the guy to Michael's back. "That'll be right up, Kate," he called to the girl.

Kate. *Her name is Kate*, thought Michael as he closed the distance between them. *Why does that sound familiar? Why does she look familiar? Kate . . . Kate . . . Kate!* He worked to hide his shock at the realization that his girl was actually Hamilton Morgan's girl. *His* Kate was Kate Keyes-Morgan.

"Where are you sitting?" she asked, her voice calling him back to the present moment. "I'll just doctor up my coffee and meet you over there."

"Oh, right," he stumbled, conscious of not wanting to lose his hard-earned uncrazy status by looking too shell-shocked. "I'm right over there by that laptop."

"Great, I'll meet you there," she said as she took her coffee from the counter and headed over to the condiment station.

Watching her walk away, Michael could now clearly see that she was indeed his client's costar. He should have seen it sooner. After all, he was an agent, for god's sake—he knew all about covering freckles and straightening hair and how much smaller stars always appeared in real life. How had he missed it with Kate? Usually he could spot an actress a mile off: the need to be the center of attention, the furtive glances around the room to make sure that she was being noticed. As he watched Kate patiently wait her turn at the condiment station, bending over twice to pick up a napkin and a straw that other customers dropped and taking the time to wipe up the drops of milk that she herself spilled, he understood his mistake. She had fooled him by acting like a real person.

Her coffee doctored, she turned around and scanned the room, looking for him. He waved and she smiled, an ear-to-ear grin on her makeup-free, freckly face. Damn it, she wasn't acting. She was real and she was undeniably charming. Unfortunately, she was also undeniably married. Granted, her husband was a world-class prick who clearly didn't deserve her and was probably sleeping with Michael's own client, but she was married to him nonetheless. Pursuing a relationship with her would be morally wrong.

"Hey," she said, sitting down opposite him.

"Hey," he said back, losing himself in her greenish blue eyes and realizing that he was a far less moral man than he liked to think.

"I'm still not convinced that you're not crazy."

"Good," said Michael, mirroring her smile. "That is the first thing we have in common."

She laughed. Michael thought it was the sweetest sound he had ever heard.

13

Kate was at loose ends. She stood on the corner of Swarthmore and Sunset, contemplating her next move and coming up blank. She knew she had to pick a direction quickly or risk looking strange to her new "friend," Michael, who could probably see her through the window. Unfortunately, she didn't really have anywhere to go. She didn't want to go home to her empty house— well, she assumed it was empty. It had certainly been empty when she had left this morning, after another sleepless night spent waiting for her husband to come home. He hadn't. He also hadn't called or e-mailed (this time she had checked), so she could only assume that he had spent the night with Sapphire. Or that he had died in a fiery car wreck. Secretly, she hoped for the latter—it was so much more attractive to be a widow than a dumpee.

When the light changed, Kate crossed the street, trying to look purposeful despite her absolute purposelessness. She wondered if Michael was watching her. She was a little bit surprised to realize that she *wanted* him to be watching her. Her hour with him had been a wonderful, bright spot in her otherwise horrible week. He had made her laugh, and he, in turn, had laughed at everything she had said. She had forgotten how good it felt to really connect with a man like that—if, in fact, she had ever felt it before. Michael made her feel funny and smart and interesting. It had been years (three, in fact) since she had been with a man who made her feel like a whole person instead of a pet project. And it was the first conversation she had had in a long time with someone who knew her as simply "Kate," without the baggage of "Kate Keyes-Morgan, television star." The joy of having an actual conversation with someone without her persona interfering made her realize how deeply flawed her fantasy of fame had been.

She remembered the exact moment that she had decided she wanted to be famous. She had been in the sixth grade, sitting home alone in front of the television, eating the standard parents' night-out dinner of Kraft macaroni and cheese, and watching Olivia Newton-John in *Grease*. She had felt so much genuine love and admiration for the gorgeous actress that she was sure that Olivia could feel it through the screen. *I want that*, she thought. *I want to be loved that much*. Twenty years later, Kate *was* the woman on the screen and, for all she knew, there were little girls out there right now who actually loved her like that, who sat in front of the television when their parents were out and fantasized about how great it would be to have her as a friend/confidante/mother. What she now knew for sure was that actors can't feel the love through the screen. The great irony was that the more popular she had become as an actress, the more alone she had felt. In fact, rather than heal the self-conscious anxiety of adolescence and quell the fear that strangers were staring at her and judging her every move, fame had exacerbated those feelings . . . and added unflattering photographs with snotty captions.

It wasn't that Kate didn't appreciate her fans. In fact, people were extraordinarily pleasant to her, but their loving attitudes often came with a price. Her first show, *Girl Time*, followed the loves and lives of four young women sharing an apartment in San Francisco while they worked the long hours of interns in a busy emergency room. It had been a huge hit right out of the gate. As the four insecure, overwhelmed young actresses made the rounds of the talk shows, awards banquets, and photo shoots that crowded their every spare evening and weekend, Kate noticed something: somewhere along the line people had stopped asking "How are you?" and had instead started conversations with "You must be so happy!" and "You are so lucky!" She was happy . . . sometimes, and she felt lucky, too . . . most of the time. The few times, however, that she answered honestly, voicing her true feelings of confusion or ambivalence, she was met with such profound disappointment that she stopped trying to be real and began utilizing the tried and true method of popular girls everywhere: tell people what they want to hear. Kate acted happy no matter what she was feeling inside, which supported their fantasies of how wonderful it must feel to be famous, which, in turn, allowed Kate to avoid her deepest fear: disappointing people. Outside of the overwhelming isolation and loneliness caused by her inauthenticity, the plan worked really well for everyone.

Well, everyone *else*.

Right now, what Kate needed was a plan for today. Having successfully crossed the street and marched a few hundred yards up Swarthmore Avenue in her bid to look busy and important to Michael, she was now faced with the reality that she had nowhere she needed to be. It was Saturday, so there was no work; she had already worked out (making sure not to touch any towels that may have touched Sapphire's pink-clad, sweat-soaked body); and she had just finished her Starbucks run, leaving her with fifteen-sixteenths of a day to fill. It was days like this that she wished she had learned how to knit. Or fly a plane. She had never been a "life is too short" type of person. Life to her, even at the relatively young age of thirty, felt incredibly long. Her days had always stretched out before her, with endless hours spent waiting: waiting for her mother to come home; waiting for Hamilton to come and rescue her; waiting for Sam to come and get her for her next scene;

waiting for someone—anyone—to tell her who they needed her to be and what they needed her to do. Her life often felt like a series of scenes from the children's book *Are You My Mother?* where a baby bird approaches a bunch of different animals, hoping one of them is the mother whom he is searching for. Luckily, Hollywood was full of animals.

Kate heard some movement behind her and turned around to see a group of giggling preteen girls hiding behind some bushes and pointing at her. It was hard to have a private, emotional moment when the rest of the world saw you as an exhibit in a zoo. The monkey at the San Francisco Zoo used to throw his feces at the crowds that gathered to stare and point at him. Dismissing that as a response *almost* immediately, Kate chose instead to smile at the girls, eliciting squeals, more giggles, and one "Oh my god!" before the girls fell into the bushes in paroxysms of laughter. Kate found herself laughing, too. She then turned around and headed toward her car, knowing that a nice, anonymous emotional meltdown on a street corner simply wasn't an option for her. She would have to have her breakdown in the privacy of her own home.

When Kate pulled up to her house and saw the shiny, red Mercedes convertible parked next to Hamilton's Porsche, she realized that her private breakdown would have to wait for another day. She considered turning her car around and driving away, but she still had nowhere else to go, so she parked her car next to Sapphire's and headed into the house.

The scene that greeted her in the kitchen was not the hideous debauchery she had feared. It was, in fact, a scene that could be described only as domestic bliss. Hamilton sat at the kitchen table reading his newspaper, basking in the glow of the late morning sun and the attentions of Sapphire, who was serving him piping hot scrambled eggs out of a skillet. They were so lost in their happy tableau that they didn't hear Kate come in. Kate was forced to clear her throat no fewer than three times before they noticed her standing in the middle of the kitchen. Hamilton didn't even have the good grace to look embarrassed, greeting her instead with a hearty "Good morning!"

"Good morning," said Kate tentatively, feeling like an outsider in her own kitchen.

"Would you like some eggs?" offered Sapphire. "I think I could find one or two more in the fridge, although to tell you the truth, it is not very well stocked."

Was she actually being scolded for not stocking the fridge? "No, thank you. To be honest, I really don't have much of an appetite."

"Yes, that is quite apparent," said Hamilton. "You know, Kate, you really should eat something. The big head/small body lollipop look is so last year."

"You know, Kate, he's right," Sapphire interjected. "No man wants to cuddle up at night with a bag of bones."

"Excuse me?!?"

"I'm just saying—as a friend—that you might want to put on a few pounds before you head back out there."

"Before I head back out there? What is *that* supposed to mean?" Kate couldn't believe her ears. Was her dear "friend" Sapphire actually giving her dating advice in front of her husband?

"Okay, Katie, I think you need to sit down and take a deep breath," said Hamilton, gesturing to the chair across from him as he lovingly pulled Sapphire down into the one at his side. "Sapphire and I have something we need to talk to you about."

Kate obediently took her seat. "Okay."

"I think it is fairly obvious what is happening here." Hamilton looked toward Sapphire, who placed her hand gently over his and looked up at him adoringly.

"Well, it's not obvious to me," Kate lied, trying desperately to stall the inevitable.

"Sapphire and I have fallen in love." With that, they both looked toward Kate as if awaiting her blessing.

"Are you *fucking* kidding me?" Kate's pain and disbelief propelled her up to a standing position.

"Oh dear," said Sapphire, moving closer to Hamilton, who placed a protective arm over her shoulders as if to shield her from Kate's bad breeding.

"Now, Katie, I don't think that sort of language is necessary, do you? I was sincerely hopeful that we could all discuss this like the evolved adults we are—well, that some of us are and some of us are striving to become." He smiled condescendingly at Kate, as one would smile at the village simpleton.

The room had started to spin. Kate saw bits and pieces of Hamilton's and Sapphire's smug faces as they came in and out of focus, but mostly what she saw was her own rage and confusion. She needed them to know how much pain they were causing her— how wrong, cruel, and misguided they were—but all she seemed to be able to manage was another strained "Are you *fucking kidding* me?"

"Oh, Katie," said Hamilton, shaking his head in pity and disappointment. "I can see we are not going to get anywhere with you right now. You are clearly too upset to have a rational conversation. As usual, you are letting your emotions run away with you."

"*Letting my emotions run away with me?*" Kate stammered. "What reaction should I have, Hamilton? Should I give you my *fucking blessing?*"

"That would be lovely, Kate, but I honestly don't think that you are up to it quite yet. I think that would be a great area to discuss with Penelope when—"

"*Fuck* Penelope!"

Hamilton gasped at this blasphemy.

"Oh dear," Sapphire simpered; moving even closer to him.

"I have no interest in sitting here watching you throw a tantrum, Kate," Hamilton said, maintaining his affectation of patience. "Nor do I wish to drag Sapphire into your little drama."

"My little drama? You two are having an affair!"

"See, Kate, that is exactly what I am talking about—that kind of dramatic, accusatory language. Sapphire and I are not having an *affair,* we are in love. Frankly, you know as well as I do that you and I have been growing apart for some time."

"No," said Kate, the reality of the situation finally beginning to sink in. "I did not know that."

"Well then, you were the only one. Penelope and I have been discussing it for months."

"Discussing you and Sapphire?"

"No, of course not. What has happened between me and Sapphire is, well, a happy surprise."

"Not for everyone," Kate snapped.

"There is no need to be rude, but I see that you just can't help yourself. I really think it would be best if you left before you say something that you regret."

Kate couldn't believe her ears. "Are you kicking me out of my own house?"

"Oh, come on, Katie, was it ever really *your* house?"

Kate sank back down into the nearest chair. Her legs had turned to jelly, so she was really left with no other choice.

"Sapphire and I have decided that we want to live together," Hamilton went on, "and we think that living together in this house makes the most sense for us."

"But . . . what about me?" Kate hated how pathetic she sounded, but she just felt so darn . . . pathetic.

Sapphire leaned into Hamilton and, in a stage whisper that could have been heard across a football field, said, "It's just like you said. She is totally making it all about her."

"I know, baby," said Hamilton, planting a kiss on her surgically miniaturized nose. Turning to Kate, he said, "If you could just try to stop being so overly emotional and see this situation objectively, you would see that it is best for everyone. Sapphire and I are two people, so we need the space this house affords, and—let's be realistic here, Kate—the only thing in this house that is really *yours* is your wardrobe . . . such as it is."

Kate opened her mouth to protest, but before she could utter a word, she was struck dumb by the realization that what he said was true. Hamilton had chosen the house without her input while she was spending a month at the Ultimate Health spa preparing for their wedding with a month-long liquid diet. By the time they got back from their honeymoon, the house had been completely furnished. The truth was, most of her clothes had been bought by a stylist, so they didn't really have much to do with her, either . . . such as they were.

Kate sat silently for a moment, then made a painful admission: "I don't know where to go."

"Oh, Kate, do you really think I would ever put you out on the street?" asked Hamilton, kind again now that he sensed he was going to get his way. "Haven't I always taken care of you?" Kate admitted to herself that, yes, he always had taken care of her, and she began to relax into her habitual response of letting him do so.

"Yes, you have."

"Exactly, and I am not going to stop now." He smiled at her. "Now, you'd better go start getting your things together, okay?"

"Okay," said Kate dully, standing up on numb legs and turning to go.

"Your mother is expecting you."

14

Kate stood on her mother's doorstep willing her finger to ring the doorbell. She knew in her heart of hearts that this was a terrible mistake, but Hamilton had convinced her that this was the safest place for her to be. "The hotels are crawling with paparazzi, Kate. Do you really want to deal with that right now?" And just like that, he had gotten his way again. *Maybe this is for the best anyway*, thought Kate. *Maybe this is the time that my mom will step up and be there for me.*

Then her mother opened the door.

"Hello, Kate," she said coolly, making no move to welcome her into the house.

"Hi, Mom."

"Well, I guess you should come in." Her mother stepped backward in the marble entryway, opening the door just wide enough for Kate to step through. "How long do you think you will be staying with us?"

Kate bristled. "I don't know, Mom. What's standard for women who have been dumped by their husbands?"

"Oh, Katie, do you really think it is necessary to talk like that?" Kate had forgotten that, to her mother, any sentence that contained both "dump" and "husband" was profanity.

"I'm sorry, Mom, but it's true."

"I know it's true, dear, but that doesn't mean we have to *talk* about it."

"What would you like to talk about, Mom?"

"Honestly, Kate," sighed her mother, "I don't have time to talk. Your father and I have an event at the club and then we have a dinner to attend, so I won't have time to talk to you at all until tomorrow."

"Should I have my people call your people to book an appointment?"

"Oh, there it is again. Do you really think sarcasm becomes you? You know, Katherine, no man wants to come home to that sort of attitude."

"Hamilton isn't breaking up with me because of my sarcasm, Mom."

"No," conceded her mother. "Not *just* your sarcasm." She turned on her heels and headed down the hallway, leaving a shell-shocked Kate standing in the open door. "Well, are you coming, dear? I barely have time to show you to your room before I need to get your father ready for our party."

"Yes, I'm coming," answered Kate, collecting herself and following her mother through the unfamiliar house.

Kate's parents, Henry and Marcia, had moved out of her childhood home the day Kate graduated from kindergarten and relocated several times, following their hobbies from condo to condo. First they had moved into a two-bedroom unit in Marina to try their hand at boating. When they realized they didn't especially like the water, they decided to try their hand at horseback riding and bought a large three-bedroom near the equestrian center in Studio City. They soon found that, although they loved horses, they couldn't take the heat of the valley in the summer, so they bought a town house on the Mountaingate Country Club property in Bel Air and took up golf. In each home, Kate's designated space got smaller and smaller. It wasn't due to lack of room. In their current home, Henry and Marcia had four bedrooms, but each one served a more important function than welcoming their daughter. They each had their own office (for what, Kate never understood), and the only other spare room was their designated junk room. Or, as Kate would be calling it for the foreseeable future, *home*.

Struggling with the foldout cot, Kate could hear her parents getting ready in the room next door. More accurately, she could hear her mother directing her father's attempt to get dressed. "Oh, Henry, you can't be serious. You can't wear *that*. Just put on what I laid on the bed." Then there was her father's familiar mumble, followed by her mother: "How could you not see it? It's right there on the bed. I swear to god, Henry, you better pray I don't pass on before you do or you'll die of starvation." Mumble. "Why? Because you won't be able to find the refrigerator, that's why." Mumble . . . mumble . . . *squeal!* "Oh, Henry, you stop that right now. You're going to mess up my makeup." Giggle . . . mumble . . . giggle.

Kate went out to sit in her car.

Fighting or fucking. That was her parents in a nutshell. And there just wasn't room in their little shell for Kate. She often wondered why they had decided to have a child, finally coming to the conclusion that they had simply wanted to see what a child born of their love and exceptional DNA would look like. Once they got a good look, they seemed to lose interest.

Kate rolled down her car windows to avoid suffocation and wondered how long it would take her parents to notice that she had left the house.

Ha.

When she was nine years old, one of her little girlfriends had asked her, "You know how when you're really mad at your mom and dad? And you hide from them and then they can't find you?

And then they get really worried and your mom cries and everything? And then they find you under the sink and they are all happy and everything and then they give you ice cream?"

"Yeah," said Kate, even though the one time she had hidden from her mom (under the bed, since her mother used Kate's bathroom cabinet to store her extra makeup), she had woken up in her hiding place the next morning. The note her parents left for her on the kitchen counter said they had gone out for breakfast.

"Of course, I would probably get arrested for sleeping in my car in this neighborhood," Kate said to her rearview mirror. "And Lord only knows if my parents could fit bailing me out of jail into their busy social calendar."

She sat in her car until she saw her parents' pink Buick pull out of the garage. Henry never complained about driving a car that was the exact shade of Pepto-Bismol, his pride in his wife's Mary Kay cosmetics success blinding him to his emasculation. Kate waved as they drove by, even though she knew that her wave would go unanswered. Her mother would never take her eyes off the vanity mirror, and her father would never take his eyes off her mother.

Unobserved pouting was just as unsatisfying at thirty years old as it had been at six, so Kate decided to surrender to the fact that she would be spending her first night as an abandoned woman alone in a strange condo. Dragging her bags down the long hallway to the junk room, Kate realized that, in spite of the thirty years of evidence to the contrary, she had somehow imagined that she would spend this evening being comforted by her mother. How could she have forgotten that her mother viewed pain as a contagious disease, particularly when caused by something humiliating or embarrassing? The simple truth was that Marcia was not a fan of *anything* that made one less attractive. Cancer was always bad because of the hair loss, but anorexia was a negative only in extreme cases. Kate secretly believed that her mother was disappointed that she'd never been featured in any "Scary Skinny!"

magazine photo spreads. Looking down at her jutting hip bones, she thought that perhaps her mother would finally be proud of her—until she remembered that she'd just been dumped.

Skinny and dumped.

Marcia would never be able to compute such an oxymoron. Kate pictured her mother, arms flailing wildly as her body spun around in circles, repeating, "Does not compute, does not compute," until her head finally popped off from the strain.

The sound of Kate's laughter echoed back to her through the empty house. Was there anything sadder than a woman laughing alone? Or, more to the point, was there anyone *crazier* than a lone laugher? *Or,* thought Kate, *is there anything sadder, crazier, or more pathetic than a woman wondering whether her pathetic life is more sad or crazy?*

"No," Kate said aloud. "Except maybe talking to yourself."

She considered trying to squeeze herself into the space under the bathroom sink but shuffled into the family room instead and settled into her father's La-Z-Boy recliner. If she was going to die of loneliness, she would breathe her last breath while watching E!

When she woke up at dawn the next morning, she found a note from her parents. They hadn't gone out for breakfast without her.

They had gone to Palm Springs.

This called for a full-fat latte.

15

Michael wondered if arriving at Starbucks before it opened was a new low or a new level of accomplishment. When he had woken up at four-thirty a.m., his mind had been racing with story ideas. He couldn't wait to get up and start writing, but when he sat down in front of his computer his mind went blank. He looked around his carefully decorated condo. The black leather couches and glass coffee table belonged to "Michael the agent." In spite of the beautiful ocean views, this was a place for quick catnaps squeezed in between business dinners and breakfast meetings, not a place that welcomed a day spent in creative pursuits. Like so many of the accoutrements of his glamorous life, his home didn't seem to fit him anymore. Maybe it never had. Now, standing outside of Starbucks at five a.m., chatting with his fellow laptop-clutching insomniacs, Michael felt as though he had discovered something that he suspected the members of his high school's marching band had known all along: nerds have more fun.

When the doors finally opened at five-thirty, the teenager who stepped aside to let the line move inside shook his head indulgently at his crazy regulars. He had to be up at this hour or he would be fired. The fact that these loonies chose to be here, looking as happy as Michael did, was just plain wrong.

"Good morning, Chad!"

"You do know that it is annoying to be so chipper this close to dawn, don't you?" growled the hungover teenager.

"Annoying, Chad? Or charming?" Michael all but skipped over to "his" table to put down his computer before taking his place in the line that would be only this blissfully short until the rush began at six a.m.

"Annoying," said Chad, settling in behind the counter.

Michael laughed and considered where a cranky barista could fit into his new story.

Since he had begun writing in earnest, he found his life much less annoying. Almost anything—or anyone—was fodder for one of his stories. Even Sapphire Rose had graduated from being a constant source of irritation and frustration to being a wellspring of material for a modern fairy tale he was writing about a wicked stepmother who tortured her beautiful and kind stepdaughter by forcing her to undergo experimental plastic-surgery procedures that she was considering for herself. He hadn't figured out how the story would end yet, but he was thoroughly enjoying the process of transferring his ridiculous experiences with Sapphire onto the page. He was also enjoying writing about the beautiful stepdaughter. He called her "Cat." At some point, Cat would be rescued by a handsome prince. Michael thought he might call him something along the lines of "Michael."

Looking around the quiet coffeehouse, Michael reminded himself that 5:45 a.m. was probably too early to realistically expect to see Kate. He was still buzzing from their conversation the day before. She seemed to like him, too, even though she thought he was just a struggling writer. In fact, they had chatted for an hour and she hadn't even asked him what kind of car he drove, which had to be some sort of record for the Los Angeles dating scene. They really hadn't had time to talk about cars, though. They'd talked about the horrors of sixth grade and the escape they had both found in books. They'd talked about the difficulty of staying sane and grounded while negotiating the drama of West Los Angeles. And they'd spent quite a long time trading mother stories. They had talked like old friends.

Not really what Michael was shooting for, but it was a start.

He heard the front door open and glanced up casually, expecting another one of his fellow insomniacs. He was happily surprised to see Kate. He was a little less than happy to see that she looked as if she hadn't slept all night. She seemed downright fragile, her velour sweat suit hanging off her like hand-me-downs from a much larger (albeit fashionable) cousin. She didn't see him right away because her head was down, her eyes fixed on her Uggs-clad feet as she slouched to the counter. She managed a wan smile for Chad as she placed her order, then moved slowly over to the other side of the shop to wait for her coffee, all but disappearing into the nook between the wall and the condiment table.

Michael considered leaving her alone with her thoughts but decided against it when he realized that would mean that he wouldn't be able to talk to her. He would compromise by holding off on a hug . . . for now.

Kate didn't see him until he was directly in front of her and even then only mumbled, "Excuse me," to his feet as she tucked herself even deeper into the corner, trying to clear the way for him to get to the milk and sugar.

"Kate?" Michael spoke softly to avoid drawing attention.

When she finally looked up, her eyes were red and swollen, and it took a few moments for recognition to register. "Michael. Hi." Her hands fluttered around her face, briefly touched her hair where it had escaped from her black baseball cap, and then settled in front of her mouth, as though she was trying to hide.

She looked like a frightened animal. Michael wondered if her disheveled state had anything to do with Hamilton. If so, he might very well need to kill the bastard. *Then Kate would be single,*

Michael thought brightly. *Of course, you would be in jail, so it wouldn't do you any good.* He noticed Kate's eyes beginning to tear up. He reached up and gently moved her hands away from her face so that he could see her better. "Hey, are you okay?"

"Yeah, I'm fine," she said, her chin trembling.

Michael grabbed some napkins off the counter and wiped the tears off her cheeks. "Do you want to come over and sit down?"

"I can't," she sniffled.

"Why not?" asked Michael, fearing that she was about to bolt.

"Because," Kate barely managed to choke out, taking the napkins from him as her tears began to flow in earnest, "I have to wait for my coffee."

Michael couldn't help it. He laughed. Thankfully, so did Kate.

"Okay," said Michael, gently leading her to his table. "How about this crazy plan: I could get your coffee and bring it to you."

"I don't know," said Kate. "It's very heavy. I got whole milk today."

"Good. You need it." Michael pulled out a chair. "Now sit."

She sat.

16

Hamilton and Sapphire woke up together on their first morning as an official cohabiting couple and, as soul mates are wont to do, spoke at the exact same time: "When should we put out a press release?"

"Jinx!" they trilled in unison, collapsing into laughter and falling together into an embrace, each privately thinking how great they must look tangled up in the Frette sheets.

Hamilton pulled back and regarded Sapphire with a serious expression. "We do have other things to consider before we go to the press, darling."

"Are you worried about hurting Kate?" asked Sapphire in a rare moment of sensitivity.

"No," said Hamilton, true to form. "I was talking about figuring out the proper timing for our debut. Although we do need to consider Kate:—if she plays the victim card, it could impact public opinion of our union."

"But I am far better suited to you than she ever was." Sapphire pouted.

"Yes," said Hamilton. "But as unfair as it may seem—indeed, as unfair as it *is*—Kate's status as the abandoned woman may generate public compassion and support. I know this is difficult for you to understand, but there are many women out there who have been in Kate's shoes and might see our love as something untoward."

"But that's so unfair. Can't you just tell them that she brought this on herself by refusing to wear high heels and proper lingerie?"

"I wish I could, darling. The fact that it's all so obvious to you is one of the many reasons why you are such an extraordinary woman." Hamilton kissed her forehead and Sapphire adjusted her position to avoid the unflattering, harsh morning sun coming through the bedroom window. "But, believe it or not," he went on, "there are women all over the world who believe that they can wear flat shoes and cotton underwear and still have a loving relationship with a man."

"Not a *real* man."

"No, of course not, but they don't know any better. It is sad, really, because they could learn so much from you, but their minds have been poisoned by the wrong influences—feminists and the like."

"Evil feminazis!"

"Yes," agreed Hamilton somberly. "All we can hope for is to be a beacon of sanity in this crazy, crazy world."

"Oh, Hamilton, I do love you."

"And I love you. Now, how long do you think it will take you to get ready to go out and grab a quick bite?"

"No time at all," said Sapphire, sitting up in a way that she knew flattered her Mystic-Tanned back. "I just need to take a quick shower, do my hair, and put my face on, and I am good to go. Should we say an hour?"

"An hour it is." Hamilton knew it would be closer to ninety minutes, and the fact that she was willing—no, *eager*—to spend an hour and a half making herself attractive for him made him feel ten feet tall. Kate had always prided herself on being showered and out the door in twenty minutes, which he took as a personal affront to his masculinity. Why did some women believe it was okay to leave the house without makeup? Or stay *in* with no makeup, for that matter? "And you are worth every second, my pretty, pretty princess." Sapphire smiled at him beatifically over her shoulder as she slipped into her pink silk robe and kitten-heeled slippers and headed for the bathroom.

Hamilton watched her walk to the bathroom, swinging her ample bottom from side to side, and thought about the wonderful turn his life had taken. Finally, he had a woman who shared his vision, who really, *really* wanted a private jet. When he had met Kate three years ago, he had thought that she shared his values and goals and that she had the potential to help him achieve them. True, she had been a bit chunky and her haircut was abysmal, but he thought he saw in her enough raw materials to create a profitable business out of the scrap heap she had made of her career. For that first year, they seemed to be on the same page, both of them focused on her diet and on rehabilitating her broken sense of style. She had followed his advice to the letter, eating only from his list of "allowed" foods, working out with his trainer, and wearing only clothes chosen by his stylist, Armand. He and Armand were happy with what they were seeing, and so were the casting agents who began to open their doors to the remade Katie the Cow. Hollywood loved a comeback almost as much as it loved watching a successful career come crashing down, and with Kate, they had both. It wasn't long before Hamilton got her a small part on the pilot for *Generations,* which became the surprise hit of the season. Hamilton thought his dreams were finally coming true, but his dreams soon became a nightmare. His young wife, once so adoring and obedient, began to use volatile words and phrases such as "respect" and "feeling heard." He had so hoped that Penelope would help Kate to see the value of surrendering to her proper role in their relationship. Tragically, Kate continued to blather on about her feelings and, even worse, her *thoughts.* She even began choosing some of her own clothes, often showing her disrespect for

Hamilton by choosing comfort over sexiness. From there, it was only a matter of time before Hamilton was forced to look elsewhere for the constant stroking that his male ego required. He felt no guilt about ending his marriage with Kate, just the frustration and disappointment that came from working so diligently to try to help someone, only to have that help refused. He didn't look forward to watching Kate's inevitable decline: any satisfaction he would gain from being proven right would surely be lessened by how her failure would impact his piece of her future earnings.

Whatever he lost out on with Kate, however, he was sure to make up for with Sapphire Rose. Sapphire was a real woman. Well, maybe not *technically* real—she had been completely up-front about the chest, cheek (all four), and lip implants—but real in all the ways that mattered. He had given her Penelope's book to read after their first meeting in her trailer, when he'd first felt their extraordinary chemistry and sensed that they might have a future together. She accepted it with the graciousness due any gift from a man but admitted that she was not much of a reader and asked Hamilton to tell her about the book instead. She'd listened raptly as he espoused Penelope's teachings, nodding excitedly as he told her that in exchange for her unquestioning support and adoration he would treat her like a princess—which included regular gifts of jewelry and lingerie.

"Oh my god," she had gasped, placing her hand on her overflowing bosom in the general area where her heart might also be found. "It's like you are reading my mind. I am *all* about jewelry and not questioning *anything!*"

Looking into her sapphire blue eyes (her stage name had been chosen immediately after settling on the perfect shade of colored contacts; she came very close to being called "Ocean Waves"), Hamilton knew they had a future. He also knew that her contract would soon be up for renewal, and he was confident that he could negotiate a very bright, very financially solvent future for both of them.

And what was more romantic than that?

17

By the time Michael made it back with her coffee, Kate had pulled it together a little bit and was looking more embarrassed than distraught.

"Sorry about that," she said, reaching up for her coffee. "And thank you for this."

"You don't have to thank me. You paid for it."

"Yeah, what is *that* about?" She grinned. Michael melted.

He pulled out the chair across from her and sat down. It seemed too early in their friendship to sit right next to her, with their thighs firmly pressed against each other. Maybe after their second cup of coffee. "So, do you want to talk about what has you so upset at this ridiculous hour of the morning? I mean, besides the fact that you had to pay for your own coffee."

"Well, it's mostly that."

"Kate."

"*Partly* that?"

"Fine. I will accept that *part* of your pain is due to the three seventy-five you spent on your latte. I just sense that there *may* be something else." *And I so hope that something else is an impending divorce . . .*

"It's my mother." *Damn.*

"What about your mother?"

"Well, I'm staying with her because . . . well, for a while." *Yippee!*

"Really?" Michael worked to keep the excitement out of his voice. "Are you having construction done on your house or something?"

"Well, sort of."

"*Sort of* construction?"

He won another smile. "Well, things at home are being, umm . . . refashioned."

"You are *refashioning* your house? What does that mean?"

"You don't know what refashioning your house is?" The *what are you, an idiot?* was implied.

Michael was too intent on getting her to tell him the truth to be offended. "No, I don't."

Kate exhaled an irritated burst of air. "Well, I don't know how to explain it to you."

"Because you don't know?"

"What?"

"Let's see . . . how do I make that clearer? Oh, I know— because you are talking out of your ass?"

Kate was able to maintain an offended expression for almost ten seconds before bursting into laughter. "Damn it! I was hoping if I sounded snotty and superior enough you wouldn't question me."

"Yeah, that's usually a good technique . . . if you are talking to a twelve-year-old girl."

"Are you implying that you are intellectually superior to your average twelve-year-old?"

"Only when it comes to seeing through your more basic distraction techniques. I'm pretty sure that even the bottom third of your average sixth-grade class has me beat in all things computer related."

"Oh my god, isn't that so true? They can work computers better than I can work a basic TV remote."

"Kate?"

"What?"

"Remember how I said I was good at seeing through basic distraction techniques?"

"Yeah . . ."

"Well, unless you were crying in the corner because of your lack of computer skills, my carefully honed antennae indicate that you're not telling me the whole story."

"I wasn't crying about my nonexistent computer skills."

"I am shocked," said Michael, clearly not shocked.

"Yes, I can see that. It's not really about my mother, either."

"That I *don't* believe. It's always about our mothers."

"Touché." Kate laughed. "But it's not *just* about my mother."

"I see," said Michael, beginning a terrible attempt at an Austrian accent. "And vould you like to tell me vhy you *think* that eet is not about your mother?"

"Are you doing Freud?"

"Are you avoiding the question?"

"Yes."

Michael let the silence linger, enjoying the small smile that had finally made it all the way to Kate's eyes. "You're not going to tell me what is really going on, are you?" he asked.

"Not yet," she acknowledged. "But I do feel better."

"Good," said Michael, thrilling at the future implied by her use of the word "yet." "I suppose that's something."

"Considering how I felt when I got here, it's a lot. Thank you."

"You're welcome." He decided to go for the golden ring. "Will I see you here tomorrow? I promise to pay for your coffee."

"Free coffee? Wow, that is tempting but, sadly, I have to work."

"Work? Oh my god, is tomorrow Monday already?"

"Yes, it is, my writer friend. I guess the days of the week mean less when you make your own hours. Do you write every day?"

"I have been lately, yes," said Michael, surprising himself with the realization.

"I've heard that's half the battle for writers—just getting the words down on paper."

"Yeah, that's what they say: writers write." *And I have been writing every day. Does that make me a writer?* wondered Michael, the very idea sending waves of excitement through his body.

"Well, I admire your discipline."

"Thank you. Actually, so do I." Would the sound of her laugh ever cease to please him? Michael thought not. "I'm sure your work takes discipline, too . . . whatever you do."

"Well, I'm an actress, so there *is* discipline involved in learning lines and getting to work on time, but once I get there, I am pretty much led through my day like a mentally challenged princess."

Deciding it was too early to say *I love you,* Michael said simply, "You are adorable."

Kate blushed, which made her even cuter. "Yeah, well, we'll see how adorable I am when my alarm goes off at four-thirty a.m."

"Is that an invitation?"

"No." She laughed. "It was a deflection. I don't take compliments well. I'm surprised you didn't pick that up with your deflection antennae."

"Touché, my adorable opponent. Now, why are you getting up at the ungodly hour of four-thirty a.m.?"

"I have to be at work at six."

"Ouch."

"Exactly," said Kate, thinking about the pain of dragging herself out of bed before dawn. Michael's "ouch," however, had nothing to do with Kate's early wake-up call. He was worried about his own. He, too, had to be at the *Generations* set tomorrow morning. How would "Michael the writer" explain his presence in Sapphire's trailer at six a.m.?

18

"Hello! I'm home!" Kate called into the empty foyer, hearing the familiar echo of her mother's empty house. Even her father, who had paid for every one of the dwellings her parents had called home, referred to each one as "your mother's house." Of course, in his case, it was really her mother's *life*.

Kate walked down the hall to the kitchen, idly viewing the photos that covered the walls along her route. She noticed something for the first time: her mother was in each and every photo. She was, of course, featured in the holiday photos her parents had done every October at the mall, her mom and dad posed in front of a foggy background of either brown or blue, depending on what they had chosen to wear (or, rather, what her mother had chosen for them to wear). But what Kate now noticed was that Marcia was also in all of her school photos, standing next to the teacher with the other class moms. Kate didn't have any memories of her mother working at the monthly bake sales or helping out her teachers on craft days, but she did remember watching her mother stride across the school yard in brightly colored dresses and high heels on photo days. She wondered if the other mothers had noticed that Marcia's version of being a class mom more closely resembled modeling than mothering.

Story of my life, thought Kate, wondering vaguely if her mother was playing the role of perfect mother at that very moment, regaling her Palm Springs friends with stories of her famous daughter—while her famous daughter sat at her house, depressed and alone. Sitting at the kitchen table, Kate waited for a fresh batch of self-pitying tears, but they never arrived. Instead, images of Michael kept floating through her mind. He had been so incredibly sweet this morning that she had come very close to spilling the whole story of her almost divorce and near homelessness, but the habit of protecting personal information was so ingrained in her that she had found herself dodging his direct questions. He probably thought she was a CIA spy protecting state secrets. If she was lucky enough to see him tomorrow, she determined, she would tell him the truth. She would change some names, of course, to protect the innocent . . . and the slutty. *Stop it,* she scolded. *You should not even be thinking about him.*

But he likes me.

It doesn't matter. You aren't looking.

Why not?

Because you are heartbroken and humiliated.

So?

So, you moron, that means you need to be miserable.

That's stupid.

You're stupid.

Real mature.

You're mature.

You're stupid and mature . . . infinity.

Touché.

"Oh, stop it!" she said aloud, hoping to break the (insane?) cycle of arguing with herself. She should be having this conversation with someone else. Granted, unless that someone else was a snotty nine-year-old, the banter would probably be at a slightly higher intellectual level, but the point was that she shouldn't be sitting in her mother's kitchen talking to herself.

She should be talking to her girlfriends. But the truth was, she didn't have any. She didn't have any college friends, mostly because she hadn't gone. She'd done some local commercials while still in high school, and when the subject of college had come up, her mother, never a big fan of education for education's sake, said, "Oh, Katie, why do you want to waste your time with college? We both know that your looks are your greatest asset. Why squander your prettiest years sitting in a dark classroom?" So she had forgone college altogether and started auditioning, cringing silently every time a well-meaning casting agent asked brightly, "So, where did you go to school?"

In the years on her own before she met Hamilton, she'd had a couple of friends, girls she met here and there on movie sets, but those relationships came and went with each new location shoot. She found it difficult to maintain friendships with women. She was never quite sure what was expected of her or what, if anything, of value she had to offer. Penelope's theory had been that Kate's insecurity with women came from the fact that she had never been able to hold her own mother's interest for long. Sitting alone in her mother's kitchen now, Kate was forced to admit that the theory had merit. Maybe she should call Penelope right now . . . or not. She was pretty sure that any contact with Penelope would be nothing more than a long, drawn-out *I told you so,* and that would feel the tiniest bit less than supportive.

She almost wished that she was working today so that she could see Paige. Paige would have something brilliant to say— brilliant and funny and wise. Actually, Kate had Paige's home phone number from the time she had done her makeup for an awards show. She could call her right now. Kate picked up her cell phone and looked at the time: eleven-thirty. It certainly wasn't too early to call. Was it too late? Paige was probably already out enjoying a busy day of bike riding, shopping, and brunching with friends. Or maybe she was settled in at home with the Sunday *New York Times,* feeling grateful to have a quiet day before the start of her grueling workweek. Either way, the last thing she needed was to get a call from Kate. It might even be ethically wrong to make a personal call using a number that had been given for work reasons. And poor Paige would probably feel like she *had* to take the call, since Kate was, for all intents and purposes, her boss. It was like sexual harassment without the sex: emotional harassment. How pathetic would it be if she got sued for using her position to force someone to be her *friend?* Maybe she could just hit on Sam instead. The lawsuit would be less humiliating and maybe he would talk to her afterward. Do you get postcoital cuddling and chatting with your sexual harassment?

It seems only fair.

Of course, if life were fair, Kate would be in Italy right now, eating pizza while Michael read her poetry that he had composed just for her. Well, maybe that would be if life were incredibly wonderful, but why bother fantasizing about a fair life? The truth was that Michael probably couldn't even afford to take her to Italy, certainly not the way she had gone with Hamilton.

With Hamilton, it was first class all the way, from the plane ride to the elegant hotel suites and chauffeur-driven BMW sedan. They ate in only the best restaurants and spent their days shopping in the best designer stores. In hindsight, it would have been easier— and cheaper—to just stay home and hire a limo to drive them around Beverly Hills. For Hamilton, though, the point of travel wasn't to experience another culture—it was to re-create all of the comforts of home in a place about which he could later brag at dinner parties. The actual place was much less important than how it sounded in the sentence "Yes, well, you know, Kate and I spent our holidays in [insert latest hot spot here]." Occasionally, when Kate had read about an interesting destination in a magazine and brought up the possibility of going there, Hamilton's first question had always been "Who has gone there?" His vacation-destination rating system was based on the number of celebrity visitors as much as the number of stars. The minimum amount required for each category was five.

★   ★   ★

When the phone rang, Kate was surprised to hear herself answering it in the strangely affected way she had been taught by her mother when she was six years old. "Keyes' residence, Kate speaking." Old habits . . .

"Hello, Kate. It's Hamilton." She wanted to tease him for matching her exaggerated formality, but she was pretty sure it wasn't appropriate to lovingly tease the man who had just left you for a tramp. She would have to check her mother's *Emily Post.*

"Hello, Hamilton."

"How are you?" Was he kidding?

"Are you *fucking kidding?*"

"I don't think that language is necessary, Kate."

"You know what, Hamilton? So many unnecessary things have happened to me in the past forty-eight hours that I really feel justified using whatever language I want."

"Well, I suppose I shouldn't be too surprised. Penelope warned us that you would probably exhibit some juvenile behavior."

"*Exhibit some juvenile behavior?* What does that even *mean?*"

"Which words are you having trouble with, Katie?"

"Hamilton, stop it."

"Well, I just don't know how far you have regressed. You sound like a thirteen-year-old, with your insolent tone and throwing the f-word around like it's going out of style. For all I know, your vocabulary has regressed as well."

"My vocabulary is fine," seethed Kate.

"That's good to hear. I know it's a sore spot for you because of your lack of education."

Ouch. "Hamilton, why are you calling?"

"Well, I was *hoping* to have a pleasant conversation."

"Well, then, perhaps you shouldn't have boinked another woman."

"Oh, Kate, grow up. I need to have an adult conversation with you. Can you do that?"

She stuck her tongue out at the phone and then said, "Yes."

"Good. I am actually calling on behalf of Sapphire. She is concerned that you might make things awkward for her at work."

"*I* might make things awkward for *her?*"

"Yes. I told her she had nothing to worry about, that you are first and foremost a team player. But now I am not so sure."

Kate wanted to tell Hamilton that he was right to feel unsure, that his darling Sapphire had *a lot* to worry about. She wanted to tell him that she was going to make life on the *Generations* set a living hell for his new girlfriend, that she would use her considerable goodwill with the crew to turn everyone against her—well, *more* against her than they already were.

But she didn't. Because she knew it wasn't true. "Tell her not to worry, Hamilton. I have no intention of causing problems at work."

"That's my good girl," he said, hanging up the phone.

19

10:30 p.m.
11:23 p.m.
12:54 a.m.
1:45 a.m.

At 2:15 a.m., Kate finally surrendered to her sleeplessness and got out of bed (well, cot). It was always difficult to get a full night's sleep when she had an early call at work. Her fear of over-sleeping was so intense and her anxiety about being late for work so overwhelming that she was never able to accomplish more than a light doze. Even that was peppered with panicky moments where she would jolt straight up in bed, sure that she had over-slept, often stumbling all the way into the kitchen before she calmed down enough to look at a clock. Her rule was that if it was before two a.m. she went back to bed, but anything after that meant she was allowed to doze on the couch with the television on, clutching an alarm clock like a security blanket. She was baf-fled by co-workers who strolled into work a half an hour late, who thought nothing of keeping the entire crew waiting while they treated the assistant director's panicked search for them as a wake-up call. She realized that sitting up watching the clock all night was probably not the healthiest counterpoint to such behavior, but until she could face being five minutes late without indulging in a self-flagellation fest, it was her best alternative.

This particular Monday morning, Kate had the extra, super-special sleep buster of knowing that she would be facing her husband's new girlfriend at work. Every time she closed her eyes she saw a different, hideous version of Hamilton and Sapphire together. She always envisioned them intertwined with their legs and arms wrapped around each other at improbable angles, and they were *always* laughing at her, but their location changed from scene to scene. Sometimes they were giggling away on their (Kate's) bed, whereas in other scenes they were standing in front of various romantic landmarks, such as the Eiffel Tower or the vineyards of Tuscany, miraculously holding their acrobatic embrace. None of the other tourists in Kate's nightmares seemed to notice the naked lovers. Maybe they were all enjoying a good night's sleep.

Kate padded into her mother's kitchen and set about trying to make a pot of coffee. Marcia couldn't stand clutter (outside of Kate's luxurious junk room, of course), so she immediately removed all foodstuffs from their original packaging and transferred the contents to her extensive collection of Tupperware. As a result, her pantry looked beautiful, but only she knew which blue-lidded opaque container held which food. Kate was forced to open each container one by one, breaking three fingernails before finally discovering the coffee grounds wedged between a pink powder that smelled like strawberry Jell-O and a white powder that she hoped was flour. She also hoped that the tiny *r* written on the underside of the lid stood for "regular." She was counting on caffeine to get her through today. If she had to face this day on a cup of decaf, she feared she would literally fall apart. Her parents would come home to find her reduced to nothing more than little bits of hair and teeth littering their floor.

Her mother would be furious about the mess. Then, of course, she would immediately pick up the pieces of her daughter and put them into the appropriate Tupperware container. Kate hoped her mother would take the time to label her. She would so hate to be mistaken for the Jell-O and made into a fruity mold for her parents' condo-association picnic.

Waiting for her coffee to percolate, Kate wondered idly if it might be a good idea to have some breakfast. She cringed as she remembered the humiliation of being covered up in what was supposed to be her sexy lingerie scene. She hated knowing that the group of people huddled around the camera pointing and staring at her had been discussing her body and that they decided it wasn't acceptable—that *she* wasn't acceptable. She could hear Paige saying, "You are not your body," but if Kate wasn't her body, then what was she? Or, more to the point, *who* was she? She stood in front of the open refrigerator, looking at the neatly displayed rows of nonfat, sugar-free packaged foods and tried to turn off the voice in her head that was repeating, "Less is more, less is more," on a continual loop. Her mind was like a computer that was programmed to locate the lowest-calorie food available in any given situation and choose only that.

But sugar-free Jell-O is not a healthy breakfast food.
It's only ten calories.
It is a cup of chemicals.
Yeah, but it's only ten calories worth.

She closed the refrigerator door and walked back to the counter, hoping that she could speed up the coffeemaker by staring at it. She would have her coffee here and then have breakfast at work. Paige could choose it for her. Maybe if Paige talked really loudly about the wonders of a healthy breakfast (as she was wont to do), she could drown out Kate's programming. It seemed especially cruel that the original programmer had used her mother's voice. She thought about another of Paige's sayings: "Of course your mother pushes all your buttons. She installed them."

Kate doctored her coffee the best she could using her mother's creamerlike diet powder and took her cup into the TV room. She glanced at her mother's exercise bike and pink three-pound hand weights and considered them carefully. She really should work out. Then a frightening thought occurred to her: *or not*. She could work out . . . *or not*. She looked around the room, half expecting her mother or Hamilton to jump out of a closet and scold her for such blasphemy.

But nothing happened.

She just continued to sit on the couch, a mere three feet away from a perfectly viable piece of exercise equipment, and sip away. No one yelled at her, and she was fairly certain that her clothes were not getting tighter by the minute. Of course, she was wearing flannel pajamas, so the true test wouldn't come until later, when she faced her day's costume, but she was feeling a new sense of mutinous glee. She was going to skip her workout and have breakfast. Granted, it didn't have the knife-wielding, rope-swinging drama of a real high-seas type of mutiny, but for a rule follower like Kate, it packed a very similar emotional wallop.

She pulled the chenille blanket down off the back of the couch and wrapped it around her shoulders, snuggling into the corner of the sofa with her warm mug and the TV remote. When she turned on the television and saw that there was a two-hour Bette Davis biography starting in exactly one minute, Kate felt that there was a loving power in charge of the universe. She knew that somehow she would be taken care of. For the next two hours, her caretaker would be the divine Bette Davis.

Kate's sense of goodwill carried her all the way through her shower and her drive to work. It wasn't until she pulled up to the gates of Starlight Studios that she felt the nauseating power of fear and dread begin to work their dark magic on her psyche. She really, really wanted to stay home from school today. Her childhood friend Cassie used to be allowed one mental-health day a year, when her mother would let her stay home from school for no reason other than that she wanted to. She and her mother would spend the whole day eating popcorn and watching soap operas and old movies on TV. *I need a mental-health day,* thought Kate, although she knew that she would be nurtured by the same empty house and plastic cup of sugar-free Jell-O that had embraced her as a child. *Oh, fuck it. If I am going to be lonely and miserable, I may as well get paid for it.* She managed to rally enough energy to offer the guard a smile and a halfhearted wave as she willed herself to drive through the gate and toward the soundstage where *Generations* was filmed.

She pulled into her assigned parking spot, noting with relief that Sapphire's spot was empty. Maybe there had been a change of schedule and she wouldn't be coming into work today. Wouldn't that be amazing? Kate relished the thought of just one day to work in peace, to pretend that her life hadn't fallen apart. She practically skipped from her car to the makeup trailer.

It wasn't until Paige opened the door of the trailer, a look of shocked disgust on her face, that Kate turned around to see Hamilton and Sapphire walking hand in hand across the parking lot.

20

Michael was watching them, too, from his less-than-macho vantage point of crouching inside Sapphire's trailer and peeking through the curtains like a busybody neighbor. He, too, had spent a sleepless night worrying about this day. He wasn't worried about seeing Sapphire, however. He had spent his anxious night plotting how he would get through his meeting with the Annoying Duo without being spotted by Kate. At four-thirty in the morning he had finally decided that his best course of action would be to arrive early and hide out in Sapphire's trailer, thus evading an awkward meeting with Kate. He knew that she would eventually discover that Michael the charming writer was actually Michael the moneygrubbing agent, but he wanted to make sure that she was good and in love with him when that day came . . . if not pregnant with their first (second?) child.

So at six a.m. he found himself stretching awkwardly over the couch/bed in Sapphire's trailer in order to see Kate through the tiny window. She looked devastated, and why wouldn't she be? She was watching her husband and her costar strolling into work like two teenagers in love. He had been hoping that a breakup was behind Kate's staying with her mother, but he wouldn't have wished the pain caused by this tactless display on anyone.

When Hamilton and Sapphire finally arrived at the door, Michael shifted his position so that they would find him sitting casually on the couch. Even so, he was forced to witness a mini make-out session in the doorway, complete with an ass grab and a couple of energetic pelvic thrusts. Wishing in vain for a hose to turn on the rutting twosome, he coughed loudly in the hopes of drawing their attention.

"Michael!" said Hamilton, casually disengaging himself from Sapphire. "Well, aren't you the early bird?"

Sapphire giggled as though he had said something very clever, and Michael wished he had thought to bring some ginger tea or saltines.

"So," said Michael, getting to his feet and straightening his jacket, "when did this, um, 'thing' between you two start?"

Hamilton smiled at Sapphire indulgently. "Well, Michael, that's difficult to say."

"And why is that?" asked Michael.

"Because we are *soul mates*," chimed in Sapphire, settling into the banquette and tearing the plastic wrap off a grossly oversize blueberry muffin.

"I'm not sure I follow," said Michael, turning his head to avoid witnessing the plunder.

"What's so hard to follow?" Sapphire asked, her eyes wide. "I called my psychic, Norman, last night, and he told me that he knows for a fact that Hamilton and I have been in love through several lifetimes."

Michael stared at Sapphire, hoping for any sign of irony. Finding none, he said, "Norman knows this for a fact, does he?"

"Yes," she continued. "He checked with his spirit guides and they told him that, in a way, we have always been together. You know, like Antony and Cleopatra."

Michael turned to Hamilton, who was gazing at Sapphire with

undisguised affection. "I'm not sure how much I really buy into all of this reincarnation stuff," he said to Michael, "but truth be told I have always felt a real connection to Mark Antony. Norman also mentioned that our past lives may have included King Solomon and the Queen of Sheba and, most important, Laurence Olivier and Vivien Leigh."

Sapphire loudly swallowed a chunk of muffin. "Isn't that incredible?"

"Right . . . incredible," said Michael. "Although in the case of Olivier and Leigh, I believe they were still alive when both of you were born."

Sapphire looked at him blankly. "So?"

"Well, my point is . . ." Michael began, but he soon realized that any attempt to interject logic or reason into this conversation would probably only prolong his misery. "My point is, we should get down to business. Is there something specific—and work related—you wanted to discuss this morning?"

"Yes, as a matter of fact, there is," said Hamilton, snapping to attention. "Sapphire mentioned that you have been working on a deal with Bob Steinman over at Cutting Edge Pictures for her to star in a Vivien Leigh biopic. We think this is very exciting news."

Oh no. "Oh . . . yes . . . very exciting," Michael hedged.

"Obviously, we feel that this is a part Sapphire was born to play."

"Well, *re*born to play," Michael said dryly.

"Exactly," said Hamilton, moving over to stand next to Sapphire, who had gobbled up the last of her muffin and was now meticulously sucking the remnants from the cellophane wrapper. "Can't you just see it? *Our* famous beauty playing *England's* famous beauty?" Sapphire looked up and smiled, revealing a blueberry stuck to one of her incisors.

"Oh, well, I hope that Sapphire told you that this project is still in the, uh, *beginning* stages," Michael said. "*Very* beginning."

"Yes, I understand that, which is why I think it's the perfect time for me to get involved. So here is my question for you: what do you see as our next step? I think we need to look at this as a hiatus project, which means we have got to get cracking. Should I just go ahead and give Bobby a call?"

Knowing that Bob Steinman's biggest pet peeve was being called "Bobby," Michael was tempted to say yes, just so that he could listen in on the other line while Hamilton got ripped to shreds by the famously short-tempered and hypersensitive studio head. The knowledge that *he* would be shredded next, however, reduced the humor value of that stunt quite a bit. "You know, Hamilton, I completely appreciate that you both want to get moving on this right away, but I really think it's best for me to handle this on my own for the moment. I don't know how much Sapphire told you, but the whole project is very hush-hush. I wasn't even supposed to tell her yet."

"Yes, she did tell me it was a secret, but you should know going forward, Michael, that she and I don't keep confidences from each other."

"Right, gotcha . . . However, we do still need to have secrets with studio executives. Agreed?"

"Agreed." Hamilton stood up and walked to the door, signaling the end of their meeting. "So, unless you have news sooner, we'll revisit this next Monday, six a.m.?"

"Yes, I look forward to it," said Michael, trying to catch a glimpse out the window as he headed to the door to make sure that Kate wasn't nearby to witness his exit. "Can I ask you one thing?" he asked Hamilton sotto voce, so Sapphire couldn't hear over the cellophane that crinkled as she unwrapped another muffin.

"Sure."

"How is your wife with . . . all of this?"

"You mean Kate?"

Michael held back the urge to slug him in the face on Kate's behalf. "Yes, Kate. Your *wife*."

"Well, Michael, Kate's a trouper. I really think, on some level, she can see that Sapphire and I are destined to be together. You know, everyone loves a great love story."

"Antgjrim anldk Cliohtllkfdd," added Sapphire from the muffin corner.

"That's right, honey, Antony and Cleopatra."

More like Judas and Benedict Arnold, thought Michael, glad to be leaving the happy couple—and any guilt he had about his feelings for Kate—behind.

21

Paige stood facing Kate with her arms crossed, a stern expression on her face.

"*What?*" Kate asked, hoping to deter Paige with a bitchy tone.

"Don't use that tone with me." *Damn it.* "You are going to tell me what is going on and you are going to tell me *right now.*"

"Why bother? I'm sure you'll read all about it in the tabloids tomorrow, complete with pictures of the happy couple."

Paige looked at Kate for a moment, then said quietly, "Is that what you want? You want me to read about it in the tabloids? Good to know that I rate right up there with all of the people who have never even *met* you." She turned away and began setting up her workstation, slowly laying out products and makeup brushes on the counter in front of the mirror.

"That's not what I meant," said Kate, surprised to see the impact on Paige.

"No?" Paige turned to face her. "What did you mean?"

"I don't know." Kate felt the last of her fight drain out of her and she began to cry. "I really don't know. I didn't mean to hurt you, of all people. I am so sorry."

"Oh, get over here, you poor thing." Paige held her arms out to Kate, who shuffled over and melted into her warm embrace. "I think I can forgive you some bratty behavior on the morning that your husband shows up holding hands with the Antichrist." Kate managed a small snort-laugh into Paige's shoulder. "I do want it clear, though: I am not asking you what is going on in order to have a titillating story to tell at my next cocktail party, okay? And that *isn't* just because I don't go to cocktail parties. I am asking because I care about *you* and I am worried about *you*. Get it?" Kate nodded without raising her head, and Paige shuffle-danced the two of them over to a chair and gently disentangled them, sitting Kate down and squatting in front of her so that they were eye to eye. "Now, do you think it would help you to talk things over with a friend?" Kate nodded again, keeping her eyes down. "You do realize that an important aspect of talking is the *talking*, right?"

"I know," said Kate into her own chest. "It just seems like if you were really my friend, you could read my mind."

"Oh, *really?*"

"Yes, *and* bring me Bon Bons and candy necklaces."

"So we have mind reading, ice cream, and candy. What are you, nine years old?"

"I *wish* I felt nine years old. That would be almost double digits. That would rock."

Paige was happy to see Kate smile, but she was determined to keep her on track. "Are you ready to talk now?"

"Are they going to call me to set any minute?"

"No, Sapphire has some sort of private meeting so they're pushing crew call. I guess no one called you, which is just par for the fucked-up course around here."

"No, they may have called me. I wasn't home. I'm staying at my mother's." Paige's gasp was so intense and sincere that both women burst out laughing.

"You're *what?*"

"I know, I know . . . but it was either that or spooning with Hamilton and Sapphire."

"Even so," said Paige, holding her palms up in an "all things being equal" gesture.

"Yeah, you're right. That spooning is looking better and better."

"Okay, as much as I love the image of you sandwiched in between those two lunatics, I still don't know what actually happened. I've just been watching you disappear before my eyes—literally and figuratively—and now you are living with your mother and your husband is walking the evil head cheerleader to school in the morning. What happened?"

Kate took a deep breath and began to tell her story. She found that once she started she didn't want to stop. Paige listened intently, nodding, gasping, and laughing in all the right places. She even cried with her a couple of times. Whenever Kate got to an especially shameful part of her story, Paige would chime in with an "Oh god, I have *so* been there" and Kate would find the courage to go on. By the end, Kate was searching her memory for the most humiliating moments, partly for the sheer pleasure of watching Paige shriek with laughter, but mostly for the profound relief she felt when Paige would offer up her own examples of the many times that she had abandoned herself for a man, for a drink, or simply because she didn't know any other way. When Kate confessed that she had allowed herself to be kicked out of her own house without a fight, Paige said, "Oh, honey, that's nothing. I once spent my last dime on a car for an old boyfriend, and the very next day he put my best friend in the front seat and my dog in the backseat and drove away. I was pretty drunk at the time, so I don't remember a lot of the details, but I am pretty sure I packed them a picnic lunch."

When her articulate, confident friend went on to admit that she had always felt as if she were stupid, Kate was floored. Paige was less surprised by Kate's admission that, in spite of her current low

weight, she still feared that she looked fat. Paige's own early struggles with body-image issues had taught her how difficult it can be
to see your own body realistically, but she approached this sensitive issue the way she did all others—with merciless, albeit loving,
teasing. "Fat compared to *whom?*" Paige asked. "An extraordinarily thin broomstick?" Kate couldn't believe that she was not
only telling her deepest, darkest secrets, but that she was laughing
about them. She had never known such freedom. When Sam came
in two hours after her scheduled call time, expecting to see a distraught Kate and an annoyed Paige, he walked in on two women
bent over double with tears of laughter running down their
cheeks.

"Ladies," he said, because he really had no idea what to say.

Kate and Paige both looked up at him at once, exposing red
eyes and even redder faces. "How long have you been standing
there?" Paige asked.

"I just got here," he answered. "Why?"

"No reason," managed Kate before collapsing again into a fit
of giggles.

"What's so funny?"

"Nothing," said Paige, although she was clearly having trouble
keeping a straight face. She gestured toward Kate. "She is just very
immature. I think it's the extra weight." Kate's tiny frame was
now helpless with laughter, sliding along the edge of the cupboard
on which she had been leaning until she was sitting on the floor
clutching her aching sides.

"Oh . . . shut . . . up . . . *stupid,*" she barely managed to choke
out, triggering a laughing fit for Paige that soon had her joining
Kate on the floor, leaving Sam feeling even more confused. And
more than a little envious of all of the fun they were having.

"Well," he began, not sure if they could even hear him through
their mirth, "I came in to tell you ladies that there has been a
change of schedule."

"Oh fuck," said Kate. The two women froze, their laughter

coming to an abrupt halt as they each took in the other's disheveled appearance. Paige turned to Sam.

"Please tell me they are not ready for her."

"Oh god, no. They're sending you both home. There's a problem with the permits for the location today and we can't do your scene. We have no idea what we are going to shoot, just that it won't involve you."

Kate felt as if she had won the lottery. "Are you serious?"

"Yes," said Sam. "I know it sucks that you had to come all the way out here just to be sent home, but—"

"Sam," interrupted Kate, "I don't want you to waste one minute of your life worrying about it. I have just had one of the best mornings of my life."

"And one of the worst," added Paige.

"Thank you so much for reminding me."

"That's what friends are for," trilled Paige happily.

"You are not a well woman," laughed Kate.

"That," said Paige earnestly, "is very true. However, I am extraordinarily attractive in an offbeat sort of way. Wouldn't you say so, Sam?"

Sam, surprised at being suddenly pulled into their strange banter, managed a clumsy "Yes, Paige, you are very attractive" before making a hasty exit.

"You scared him," giggled Kate.

"Yes," Paige said with a sigh. "I have that effect on most men. It's my stunning beauty. Or my shelf of dog-eared self-help books. I may never know."

"Hey," said Kate, taking in a deep, steadying breath in preparation for what felt like a huge emotional risk, "do you want to go grab breakfast or something?"

"That depends," said Paige thoughtfully.

"On what?" Kate asked, readied for rejection.

"On whether you are going to actually *eat* with me, or if you plan on sitting across from me daintily sipping lemon water and picking at a dry house salad while I tuck into a huge omelet."

Kate knew she'd just gotten nailed, and she had never felt more loved. "I promise to eat with you."

"Good," said Paige softly. "Then I would love to go to breakfast with you."

"Great," said Kate, relieved.

"Yes, you are," said Paige, and the two women gathered their things and headed out.

22

Michael tried to plot his next move as he drove. What he really wanted to do was head out to the Palisades and write on his computer while he hoped for a Kate sighting. But since he had just seen her on the *Generations* set and his cell phone was already ringing off the hook with business calls, he decided to bite the bullet and go straight into the office. He really had to figure out how to handle this Bob Steinman situation. It was possible that Bob was trying to reach him *at this very moment* to pitch him an idea about a Vivien Leigh movie for his client Sapphire Rose. Of course, it would be difficult to answer the phone, what with all of the pigs flying out of his ass.

In truth, it wasn't a terrible idea. Vivien Leigh had lived a fascinating life, full of drama, romance, and the pain of mental illness. It was a story that begged to be told, and Michael had a client who was begging to tell it. He knew that Sapphire saw this as her Academy Award picture, the role that would put her back on top . . . or at least back into the movie-star section at the Golden Globes. He also knew that she might be right and that was exactly what was making him feel so conflicted. He was so disgusted with her right now, so angry about what she and Hamilton were doing to Kate, that it was difficult to get excited about helping to make her self-centered dreams come true. Although you could also say that their astounding self-centeredness had actually created an opportunity for him to make *his* dream come true. Kate was devastated, true, but she was also available. Really, outside of being forced to witness her soon-to-be ex-husband canoodling with Sapphire at work, her life was probably better than it was before.

And soon, thought Michael, *she will be making out with her writer boyfriend at the corner table in Starbucks—coffee breath be damned!*

When he remembered how hurt she had looked this morning when she saw Hamilton and Sapphire holding hands, however, Michael realized he would need to take things slowly. He needed to get her away from them so that she could heal. He told himself that he wanted to help her because he was a generous man, but he knew that desire was playing at least as large a role as goodwill. Well, many good deeds had been done in the name of ego—why not testosterone? He and Kate could do all sorts of good deeds together, they could go to benefits together, donate money to worthy causes, even work in a soup kitchen or two . . . right after he got her naked. The point was that there would be plenty of time for changing the world *and* making out. But first, he had to deal with Sapphire.

If he could get her a deal with Cutting Edge Pictures to film a movie in, say, Prague for six months, that might really help Kate. If he could put Sapphire in a hotel with no phone or Internet access, it would make his life a lot easier, too. Maybe if she really liked it there, she would move there full-time and spend her days eating borscht and drinking vodka—or was that Russia? Either way, it was halfway around the world, and Michael was going for distance, not accuracy. What if he told her about all of the great writers who had come out of Eastern Europe? Sapphire fancied herself a writer now—maybe she would move there in the hopes of finding her muse. Of course, Michael remembered, Sapphire had already found her muse, and her name was Joan/Jane. Knowing Sapphire, she would probably just send her poor ghost-writer to freeze in a cheap pension while waiting for Sapphire to e-mail her an occasional inane comment that Joan/Jane was supposed to transform into a Pulitzer Prize–winning novel.

He suddenly hoped that his delusional client wouldn't decide that she wanted to "write" her own screenplay. So far, Emma Thompson was the only writer/actor that Sapphire was aware of, and because she hadn't approved of Emma's Academy Award dress, she thankfully had no interest in emulating her. Michael wasn't even sure if Sapphire had heard that Miss Thompson had won an Oscar for adapting *Sense and Sensibility*, since her limited attention span was usually reserved for the acting and directing honors. He knew for a fact she hadn't seen *Good Will Hunting*. Too much math.

So if he could keep her out of trouble and away from a typewriter—or BlackBerry—for the next few weeks, he just might have a shot at pulling this thing together. It was true that Sapphire would be a hard sell for the lead role in a movie, but if this thing with Hamilton hit the press as hard as Michael thought it would, maybe they could ride the wave of publicity all the way to a deal. The public loved to hate Sapphire, and he had faith that they would hate her even more when they found out that she had stolen "that sweet Kate Keyes-Morgan's husband right out from under her." Even if audiences just went to the movie to throw popcorn at her image on the screen, the studio would be virtually guaranteed a big opening weekend, and that was what Bob Steinman cared about most. And if the movie turned out, by some miracle, to be *good,* and if Sapphire was good *in* it, then the audience would get to watch something it enjoyed almost as much as witnessing a tragic fall from grace—a triumphant comeback. Then the people who had shaken their heads, saying to their friends,

"People get what they deserve—I knew that man-eater, Sapphire Rose, would get her just desserts," could turn to the same friends and say, "Wasn't she just *brilliant* in that Vivien Leigh movie? I am so glad that she found her soul mate in that handsome Hamilton Morgan."

Michael knew that even if he were able, through a series of divine interventions, to pull this project together, there wouldn't be a lot of up-front money in it for Sapphire, but his client was much more interested in the perks, anyway. He'd been through many frustrating negotiations with her during which he was fighting for more money, and all he could get her to focus on was the length of her trailer or how much of her wardrobe she would get to keep. God forbid she had just read an article about the contractual demands of an A-list diva, because he would then find himself giving back hard-won cash in exchange for such essentials as custom-colored M&M's or a youth-preserving brand of bottled water that had to be carted in from Uruguay on the backs of spiritually gifted donkeys.

He was getting ahead of himself, though. First he had to call Bob and convince him to back a movie about the life of a deceased movie star whom no one in his target demographic of twelve-year-old boys had ever even heard of, starring his difficult client, the ex–movie star and current campy man-eating television star.

It was going to be a long day.

★　★　★

Sapphire watched from her trailer window as Kate and Paige got into Paige's tiny car and drove away.

"Is that one of those cars like Cameron Diaz drives?" she asked Hamilton, who was sitting next to her on the couch, peeking out the other side of the window.

"Yes, darling, it's a Prius."

"It's tiny."

"Yes, it is. It is good for the environment, though, which makes for good press."

"Is that why Cameron drives it?" Sapphire had lost interest in looking out the window and turned to face the mirror, which never got boring.

"No, believe it or not, she really wants to conserve energy." Hamilton chuckled. "I mean, I am all for doing good deeds, but for god's sake, make sure that there is a camera nearby. Otherwise, you are just driving an uncomfortable car for no reason."

"I don't want to drive an uncomfortable car," said a worried Sapphire, torn between her desire for positive media attention and her obsession with being as comfortable as humanly possible for every single minute of the day.

"Don't worry, my little hothouse orchid," said Hamilton, pulling her into a comforting embrace. "I promise to wrap you in heated leather seats and surround you with polished wood finishes."

"But I want good press, too," she whined in the little-girl voice that Hamilton found so utterly irresistible.

"I know you do, baby, and daddy is going to get it for you. All we need to do is ride in a hybrid car when we go to awards shows. We don't even have to ride in it the whole way. We can take a limo to a block away from the event, and then we have to be uncomfortable only for a block or two."

"*One* block, okay?"

"*Less* than one block, if that's what will make you happy."

"It does," said Sapphire, jumping up off the couch and launching into a series of dramatic stretches as if she had just completed a long and arduous negotiation. She watched herself in the mirror as she reached her arms and legs out in different directions, checking to see which positions were most flattering. For her, "proper form" had less to do with avoiding injury than it did with showing off her body to its best advantage. She found an exceptionally flattering position and rotated her body so that Hamilton could enjoy how slim her waist looked when she held both of her arms over her head and extended her left leg while pointing her toe. "Do I have to work today?"

"Yes, you do, my princess," said Hamilton, clearly thinking that the combination of her tiny waist and submissive attitude made her almost unbearably attractive. "They changed the whole schedule for you, remember? Just so that you wouldn't have to see Kate."

"But I *did* see her," Sapphire protested.

"But only through your window, honey bear. Jerry has promised that you won't have to do any scenes with her."

"I don't want to see her at all. It upsets me." To illustrate just how much it upset her, she stopped posing and slumped into the banquette. Luckily, she was within arm's reach of the muffin basket.

"Well, you know that protecting you is everyone's first priority, but since you and Kate work on the same show, you will probably have to see her from time to time."

"Why?" Sapphire asked through a mouthful of chocolate croissant.

"Because you work together, darling."

"*Why?*"

Hamilton looked at the woman he now loved, her chocolate- and crumb-covered lower lip thrust out in a charming pout, and realized that he would do anything within his power to make her happy, even if it meant losing his hard-earned percentage of Kate's salary. "Would it be better for you if she wasn't here at all?"

Sapphire lowered her face before she raised her eyes to meet Hamilton's, ensuring that they would catch the light in the most flattering and effective way possible. She allowed a single tear to fall down her left cheek and nodded slowly to demonstrate that, although she would do everything she could to have Kate fired, she was in pain about it.

Hamilton came over to sit next to her, kissing the tear away. "I just can't stand to see you in distress like this, my sweet. I am going to go talk to Jerry right now and see if we can't figure something out." He pulled her close, planting another kiss on top of her head. "Would that make you feel better?"

Sapphire nodded into his chest. "A little."

"Well, that's a start at least," said Hamilton, heading for the door. Then he added, "Maybe my little girl needs a little trip to the jewelry store later to cheer her up. What do you think?"

Sapphire thought she was the luckiest little girl in the whole wide world.

23

"Palm Springs?" Paige couldn't believe her ears. "Your parents left you home alone the day after you broke up with your husband to go to *Palm Springs*?"

"Yeah," said Kate, taken aback by the intensity of her friend's response. "It's no big deal."

"Not a big deal? Are you *high*?"

"No," said Kate, knowing it was a rhetorical question but feeling a need to defend herself, nonetheless. "Why are you yelling at me?"

"Oh, honey, I'm sorry. I didn't mean to yell at you." Paige took a calming breath before she continued. "It is just that it is so fucked up and you don't seem to have any idea!"

"You're yelling again."

"No, I'm not!" yelled Paige. They looked at each other for a moment over their decimated veggie scrambles and burst out laughing.

"You do realize that everyone is staring at us," whispered Kate.

"No, *duh*," said Paige. "You're famous."

"No shit?"

"No shit."

"Wow. You'd think my mother would be nicer to me."

Exactly my point! bellowed Paige, causing almost all of the other diners to turn and stare at them again. Kate slumped down in her chair, giggling and trying to disappear. Some of the customers smiled, happy to be in on the game, but some people just looked annoyed at the interruption. The line was drawn directly between those who recognized Kate as a television star and those who didn't. For those to whom she was a celebrity, almost anything she did seemed charming and interesting, but for those to whom she was just a regular customer, she was one-half of an irritatingly loud twosome.

"This is *so* going to end up in the tabloids."

"As what? Kate Keyes-Morgan has a loud friend? I don't see that on the front page. Unless maybe you are about to change into an unflattering bikini. Cellulite always scores a headline."

"Oh my god," said Kate, terrified. "I would just die."

"I so wish you were exaggerating, but somehow I really don't think you are."

Kate shrugged. "Well, maybe I wouldn't literally *die*."

"But you're thinking that you just might kill yourself, right?"

Damn, she was good. "Let's just say that I hope I would recover . . . but I'm not so sure that I would."

"Well, let's just hope it doesn't come up until you are about three thousand times healthier."

"Agreed . . . as long as you are not using the word 'healthy' as a euphemism for *fat*."

Paige dropped her head into her hands. "Oh dear, we have so much work to do on you."

"Do you really think now is the time to bring up plastic surgery?" Kate asked with faux earnestness.

"If I thought that it would actually help your crippled self-esteem, I would drive you to the doctor myself."

"Don't even worry about it. For that, my mother would come back from Palm Springs."

Paige shook her head and said, "Please tell me you are kidding."

"Oh no, not at all. She's wanted me to get my boobs done since I lost the Miss Junior Orange County pageant in eighth grade. She probably thinks Hamilton left me because of my small boobs. Come to think of it, maybe he did."

"Don't be ridiculous," said Paige, then added, "He *probably* did."

"Oh god," said Kate. "It really is that pathetic, isn't it?"

"No, Kate, it isn't pathetic," said Paige, leaning forward in her desire to be understood. "It is infuriating . . . galling . . . maddening—not pathetic. Where is your anger for god's sake? Your husband left you for a brainless lunatic, and when you went to your mother for support, she took off to Palm Springs. You should be *furious!*"

Kate watched Paige getting more and more revved up. She didn't seem to care that people were staring at her or that they were probably thinking that she was crazy, irrational, or—god forbid—not nice. Paige seemed to get larger before her eyes, as if her anger were literally puffing her up. Yet Kate knew that when she felt angry, she got smaller, literally and figuratively. When she finally spoke, even her voice sounded small. "I do get mad when I talk to Hamilton. I'll have you know that I have thrown around the f-word more than once."

"Good for you. I am very happy to hear that," said Paige proudly, as though Kate had just brought home a straight-A report card. "Saying 'fuck' to, at, or near Hamilton is a very good start, but I think there has got to be some real butt-kicking rage in there somewhere that is looking for a way out. You are just too damn . . . *good* all the time."

"Well . . . I don't want to kick ass. I just want to take a nap."

Paige took a deep breath, readying herself for another motivational offensive, but instead of launching into an energetic tirade she exhaled slowly and sunk back in her chair. "You know what? I want to take a nap, too. Let's go get you moved out of your mother's house and onto my couch for an afternoon of Lifetime movies and catnaps."

Kate froze, confused. Was Paige inviting her to stay with her—which seemed *way* too good to be true—or just offering up an afternoon of trashy TV? "Okay, um, that sounds like fun. Let's go get . . . an afternoon's worth of stuff from my mom's."

Now it was Paige's turn to look confused. "Wait a minute. Are you saying that you want to move in with me only for the afternoon. And, if so, are you saying that because you really don't want to stay with me and are trying not to hurt my feelings or because you actually think I just invited you to move in *for an afternoon?*"

Kate blushed scarlet, wanting nothing more than to melt into her chair. "I don't know," she mumbled.

"Well, let me be clear: I am offering you a place to stay. It isn't glamorous, Lord knows, but you are welcome to stay with me until you remember that you are a rich television star and can actually afford to get your very own place."

Kate looked up, scared. "Do you think I should?"

"Should what?"

"Get my own place. Like you said."

"Oh dear," said Paige. "I can see that I am going to need to go *really slowly.* I was kidding about you getting your own place. You are definitely *not* ready to live on your own. I don't remotely trust you to feed yourself properly yet, and I have a feeling you are wearing your only cute outfit."

This was undeniably true. Kate didn't know what had possessed her to grab formal wear instead of sweats when she made her hasty retreat from her house, but when she unpacked her suitcase at her mother's house, it looked like an explosion at a designer-gown factory. "How did you know that?"

"I've been there, remember? When I left my second husband, I took only my slow cooker and my thigh-high boots. I was out of my mind."

"What were you going to do? Start a career as a slow-cooking dominatrix?"

"Hey, don't knock it 'til you've tried it," Paige said, checking the bill and throwing down enough cash to cover half. "Now, do you want to stay with me or not?"

"Nothing would make me happier," said Kate sincerely.

"Oh jeez. I'm offering you a place to sleep, not *proposing*, for god's sake."

"You say that now," said Kate, throwing in her half of the bill and following her friend out of the restaurant. "But stranger things have happened."

"I may need to rethink this," said Paige, laughing.

"Too late!" sang Kate happily.

"Oh dear," said Paige.

"See? You called me 'dear.' "

"*Help!*" called Paige out the window as she drove away, Kate giggling in the passenger seat beside her.

★　★　★

When the two women walked into Marcia's house twenty minutes later, it was buzzing with activity. Kate's mom was at the center of a group of young Hispanic men who were busily setting up tables and chairs in what had been a fully furnished living room six short hours ago.

"Mom, when did you get back?" asked Kate, pressing her

body against the entryway wall in order to allow a man struggling with the weight of a large box to get past.

"Your father and I drove home early this morning. We had planned to stay the week, but we had to rush back to set up for the party!" Marcia trilled, happy to be at the center of anything.

"What's the party for?"

"For the condo association. That's why we went to Palm Springs. We all went down for our big benefit dinner."

Paige squeezed through the crowded doorway to stand next to Kate. "Your condo association has a benefit dinner? What charity does it support?"

"The new pool, dear," said Marcia. "And who are you?"

"Oh, I'm sorry," said Kate, trying to forge a path through the sea of rented furniture to get Paige within handshaking distance of her mother. "This is my friend, Paige. Paige, this is my mother, Marcia."

Kate could almost see her mother's mental Rolodex spinning at full speed, searching for a famous identity to connect with her daughter's friend. "It's so nice to meet you, Paige. Do you work with my daughter on her show?"

"Yes, I do."

Marcia brightened. "Oh, isn't that lovely! And who do you play?"

"I just play with her makeup."

"I'm sorry?" asked Marcia, confused.

Kate stepped in before her mother could say anything too offensive or insensitive. Why should Paige have to experience Kate's reality? "Mom, she does my makeup. You know how you are always saying, 'Why can't you look as good as you do on your show?' Well, that's all Paige's doing."

Kate tried to ignore Paige's "Oh, that is so fucked up," even though it was cough-talked directly into her left ear.

"Well, isn't that *lovely*." Kate knew that in this case "lovely" was code for "*disappointing*." "Will you be doing Kate's makeup for the dinner tonight?"

"Uh, I wasn't planning on it." Paige raised her eyebrows at Kate in an oh-so-subtle "what the fuck is going on?" expression.

"Mom, you didn't tell me anything about a dinner tonight."

"Well, dear, I didn't know about it myself until last night— that's why we're all rushing around like crazy."

Kate assumed the "we" referenced the many workers running around the condo carrying tables, chairs, and boxes. Her mother never ran. Kate took a deep breath, trying to inhale some of Paige's self-confidence. "Well, Mom, I can't come to your party. We, uh, made other plans."

Marcia looked Kate directly in the eye. "You *can't* have other plans. This whole dinner is for you."

Kate's jaw dropped. "What?"

"Katherine, close your mouth. You look like a largemouth bass."

"Ouch," whispered Paige.

Kate snapped her mouth shut and said through clenched teeth, "Mom why are you having a party for me?"

"Well, sweetheart, it's because so many of your father's and my friends want to meet you."

"Really?" asked Kate, suspicious.

"*Really,*" replied Marcia, steely-eyed.

"Well, I gotta say, this seems like a lot of preparation for a friendly little get-together," Paige said, dodging two men carrying a portable bar.

"Well, we have a lot of friends," said Marcia proudly.

"That's *great.*"

"It really is."

"Yes, it is. Maybe the best part of having so many wonderful friends is that you'll hardly notice if one little person is missing. Kate, should we go ahead and get your stuff?"

"Huh?" Kate was staring at Paige in shock, watching her stand up to her mother.

Paige spoke painstakingly slowly, trying to break through Kate's paralysis. "Let's. Go. Get. Your. Things."

"Oh," said Kate, coming back into reality. "Right . . . my things."

"Yes, let's go get them, so that we can *go*."

Sensing freedom, Kate's survival instincts finally kicked in and she turned to lead the way down the hall to the junk room. Unfortunately, Marcia stepped in front of her. "I hope you girls are heading back there to start getting ready for the party. I saw that you brought some lovely gowns." Looking up and down Paige's well-fed body, she added, "I think I saw a forgiving dress with an empire waist in there that just might work on you, dear."

Hearing the thinly veiled insult directed at her friend endowed Kate with new strength. "Mom, we aren't going to the party. I told you, we have other plans."

"And I told you, Katherine, you *can't* have other plans. This party is for you."

"I don't *want* a party." Kate was overwhelmed with a sense of déjà vu. How many times had she had this same conversation with her mother? At least thirty, since every one of her birthdays had been marked by a luncheon "in her honor," during which she sat at a table in the middle of her mother's favorite restaurant, surrounded by her mother's friends. Chuck E. Cheese's gave her mother a headache, as did being surrounded by children, so Kate had learned very early that her birthday parties were really a celebration of her birth *mother*.

"Well, dear, you can't always get what you want."

"That is so true," said Paige, nodding sagely. "You *can't* always get what you want."

"Exactly," said Marcia, glad to have an ally. "I'm so happy that you understand. Now, if you could just explain it to my daughter, we can all get on with our day."

"Absolutely," said Paige to Marcia. To Kate, she said, "I am afraid that your mother is not going to get what she wants."

"*What?*" Marcia was aghast.

Kate, on the other hand, was giddy with the thought of her

impending emancipation. "We are going, Mom. It's like you just said: you can't always get what you want."

"No, Kate," said Marcia, getting more irritated by the minute. "*You* can't always get what you want. I *always* do."

"Well then, this will be a nice little life lesson for you, won't it?" Paige hooked her arm through Kate's and they began to weave their way through the piles of boxes and chairs.

"But, Kate, what am I going to tell everyone?"

"I don't know, Mom. Tell them I couldn't make it," Kate called over her shoulder.

"But . . . but . . . you are an auction item!"

The two women stopped and turned around. Kate spoke first. "I'm a *what?*"

Relieved that their exit had been stalled for a moment, Marcia plastered on her most charming smile. "You are an *auction item,* darling. Isn't that flattering?" When Kate didn't say anything, she went on. "It's actually quite an interesting story: Last night, your father and I were at that live-auction thingy they always have right after the benefit dinner. And, as always, we were watching everyone showing off, bidding outlandish sums of money for a weekend at so-and-so's beach house or an evening with some other muckety-muck's private chef, and we suddenly realized that we had something people would happily pay money for—right in our very own house!"

"Some-*thing?*" hissed Paige, pinching Kate's arm hard enough to leave a bruise.

"*I heard,*" Kate whispered back, yanking her arm away and rubbing the sore spot.

"So your father stood right up in the middle of the auction and said, 'We would like to donate a dinner party hosted by our daughter, television's Kate Keyes-Morgan!'"

"You call your daughter *television's* Kate Keyes-Morgan?"

"Not all the time," said Marcia, "but that is hardly the point. The point is that people started bidding like crazy, and the couple who bid the highest—ten thousand dollars, if you can believe that!—is leaving on a trip to Bhutan tomorrow morning, so we have to have the dinner tonight. I mean, planning a dinner for twenty people in less than twenty-four hours! I don't have to tell you, I am exhausted."

"Or at least your caterer is," mumbled Paige.

Kate's voice was preternaturally calm. "So, let me get this straight: while I was here, crying my eyes out over my marriage falling apart, you were whoring me out to pay for a swimming pool?"

"Oh, Kate, there you go with that language again."

"Mom!"

"Okay, okay, dear, calm down. Honestly, I am just so surprised to see that you are upset about this. Well, surprised and a little disappointed in you, to be quite frank. Your father and I have always tried to teach you that the best way to cheer yourself up is to help someone less fortunate. We just assumed that you'd be thrilled for the opportunity to step out of your little pity pot to help us with our fund-raiser."

"Mom, you didn't even *ask* me."

"I wasn't aware that I needed to ask my daughter—who is staying in my home *free of charge*—if she wanted to have dinner with her father and me."

For the first time ever, Marcia's pouting had no effect on her daughter. "Well, you do," said Kate simply.

Marcia's gasp was interrupted by Paige exclaiming, "You go, girl!"

Dropping all pretense of being hurt, Marcia moved right into bully mode. "Can't you girls throw this ridiculous tantrum tomorrow?"

"No, we really can't," said Paige, checking an imaginary date book on her open left palm. "Tomorrow we are getting our nails done, Wednesday we have yodeling class . . . Yup, just like I thought—today is the only day this week that we can fit in a tantrum."

"Well, it's obvious that you both see this as nothing more than a joke. Maybe you see *me* as nothing more than a joke."

"Don't bite, don't bite," Paige muttered under her breath.

Kate breathed in her friend's strength. "I don't see you as a joke, Mom. I just don't want to go to your party."

"Well, first of all, it isn't *my* party, it is *your* party, but I can see that your father's new pool means nothing to you."

Rallying more internal resolve than she ever imagined she possessed, Kate said, "No, Mom, it really doesn't."

"Well, then, Katherine," said her mother, narrowing her eyes in preparation for her final attack, "I don't see how it will be possible for you to stay in our home anymore. I'm afraid it would be too uncomfortable for your father."

"But where will she stay?" asked Paige, wide-eyed.

"I really don't know," said Marcia smugly, sensing victory.

"That's the thing, Mom," said Kate, linking her arm through Paige's. "I do."

With that, they headed down the hallway to collect the gowns.

24

"Hamilton Morgan on two," squawked the box on Michael's desk.

Crap.

Picking up the phone, Michael forced out a hearty "Hello, Hamilton!" Overkill? Perhaps.

"Well, hello to *you*, Michael! It's nice to hear you sounding so chipper."

Chipper? Okay, definitely overkill. "How can I help you this morning, Hamilton?"

"It's not me who needs your help, my friend. It is our favorite client, the beautiful Sapphire Rose."

Michael sat back in his chair, instantly exhausted. He didn't want to be talking to Hamilton Morgan, nor did he want to be talking about Sapphire. When had his life become so full of things he didn't want to do? "Yes, Hamilton, I'm all ears."

"Well, it seems that our little girl is feeling increasingly uncomfortable at work. I'm afraid that it is my fault, in a sense, in that my ex-wife is the cause of her discomfort."

"*Ex*-wife? That was fast." *That rocks.*

"I just think it's easier for all concerned if we start using our new titles as soon as possible." Did that mean that Hamilton and Sapphire would expect to be called Antony and Cleopatra? Or, even worse, Emperor and Mrs. Emperor?

"Does that mean that you are definitely going forward with a divorce?"

"As soon as humanly possible. You know, I feel so deeply connected to Sapphire that still being married to Kate almost feels like unintentional bigamy."

"Unintentional bigamy? Is that considered legal grounds for divorce?"

"No, I think we will probably go with 'irreconcilable differences.' I don't see a problem. The truth is, it was always more of a business deal than a love match." Michael wondered if Kate had been let in on this little tidbit or if she had been under the mistaken assumption that she had married for love.

"Well, good for you, Hamilton." *And good for me . . . if Kate is ever able to trust a man again.* "I'm still not clear what you need from me this morning. I haven't had time to call Bob Steinman yet, so I don't have any news on that front."

"No, no, I wouldn't expect any . . . yet. I'm calling about *Generations.* More specifically, how we can work together to make our client more comfortable there."

"Correct me if I'm wrong, Hamilton, but isn't Sapphire's comfort the reason behind both the recent scheduling changes *and* the weekly six a.m. meetings?"

"Absolutely," said Hamilton. "And they have certainly helped, but our princess is having difficulty with being forced to see Kate on a regular basis. It upsets her."

"I see," said Michael, wondering how he had ended up on the wrong side of this miniature battle between good and evil. "And what are you proposing?"

"I think it would be better for everyone if Kate was replaced."

Michael held the phone out in front of him and stared at it, aghast, like an actor on a campy soap opera. Regaining his composure somewhat, he said, "I just can't imagine how that would be better for Kate, Hamilton."

"Well, you don't know Kate like I do." *Not for lack of trying,* thought Michael. "She has trouble letting go and moving on. When I met her, she still had jackets in her closet with shoulder pads, for god's sake!" Michael did not join in on Hamilton's laughter.

"What does that have to do with her job?"

"I just don't think she is capable of seeing it for the unhealthy situation it is. I mean, think about it: she's working with her exhusband's new love. On some level, that has got to hurt."

"On many levels."

"Exactly. So I think what we are talking about is doing for Kate what she can't do for herself."

"And making your 'new love' more comfortable in the process."

"Precisely. It's a win-win."

"You know, Hamilton, I am still having trouble seeing how losing her job is a win for Kate, much less a win for the show."

"The show?"

"Yes. I know that you view Sapphire as the star—"

"She is the star."

"—but Kate has a solid fan base, too, and it is very dangerous to mess with the chemistry of a cast that works as well as *Generations*'s does."

"I admit that you make a good point, Michael. However, Kate is an ingenue, and pretty girls are a dime a dozen in this town. We could even keep the character as is and just change the actress."

Michael's heart ached for Kate. Had this asshole shared his cruel, inaccurate opinions with her? "How about this, Hamilton: how about we let things settle for a few days, see if things quiet down on the set, and revisit this idea on Monday morning."

"I don't know, Michael—Sapphire really wants us to act on this thing. She has to pass Kate's trailer every day and it upsets her."

Oh lord. "Well, maybe the set decorating department can create some sort of a shield to protect her delicate eyes," said Michael sarcastically.

"That's a great idea," answered Hamilton sincerely. "And maybe I can get Jerry to make up some special call sheets so that Sapphire doesn't have to see Kate's name. That bothers her, too."

"Of course it does."

"Yes, she is very sensitive. Her femininity is one of the main things I—and her public—love about her."

Michael wondered what was so feminine about being narcissistic and hyperemotional, but his drive to get off the phone was much stronger than his curiosity. "Listen, Hamilton, I've got to run."

"Me, too. Busy day!"

"Yes, I imagine that Sapphire keeps you hopping."

"Like a bunny, my friend, like a bunny!"

Picturing Hamilton in a Playboy bunny costume, hopping around behind Sapphire, gave Michael his first sincere chuckle of the day.

25

Kate woke up and stretched as long and languidly as Paige's pull-out couch would allow. In spite of the metal bar that insisted on making itself known through the middle of the thin mattress, she had slept like a log, for the first time in weeks. She was filled with a sense of optimism, as if she had finally hit rock bottom and her fall was softened by this lumpy hide-a-bed.

"Well, the good news is that there's nowhere to go but up," she said aloud.

"What?" she heard from the general direction of Paige's kitchen. "Did you just ask if I was up?"

"No," she called back. "But are you?"

Paige walked into the room. "No."

Kate laughed. "Shut up. It's too early to confuse me. What time is it, anyway?"

"Six-thirty. I have to be in at ten to do some guest actors for that party scene. Do you have to go in today?"

Kate searched her body for the familiar feeling of panic that usually arose when she wasn't sure of her schedule but found only a sense of mild curiosity. "You know, I really don't know. I assume they would have called me if they needed me, right?"

"Yes, assuming they know where to find you. Do I need to go over the whole 'assuming makes an *ass* out of *you* and *me*' thing again?"

Panic struggled to force its way to the surface, but Kate's hopeful mood won out. "They have my cell number. But I'll give Sam a call anyway, just to be sure. I've barely even looked at this week's script. Am I in it?"

"Yeah," Paige said over her shoulder, heading back into the kitchen. "Don't you remember? This is the episode where you do that stunt where you swing naked on a trapeze over the garden party. Don't worry, though—I have pasties to cover all of your private parts."

"Great," Kate answered, not fooled for a minute. "I don't think I want to use the pasties, though. I fear they might stanch the flow of my creativity."

"It is way too early in the morning to use the word 'stanch.' Do you want coffee?"

"I do. Do you want to go out for it?"

"Sure," said Paige. "There is a little coffee shop right up the street."

"Or . . ." said Kate with a mischievous smile. "We could go out to the Palisades."

"For *coffee*? Why don't we just go to the moon? There would be less traffic."

"Maybe," agreed Kate. "But there would also be fewer supercute writer guys to talk to."

Paige took in Kate's raised eyebrows. "What are you talking about? Have you been reading *LA Weekly* again? Trust me, I have been to every one of their 'hot spots to find hot guys' for the past ten years, and all I have ever found are crowds of disappointed women."

"What if I were to tell you that there was a *specific* cute writer guy there?"

"*What?*" Paige covered the five steps to the bed in 0.03 seconds, roughly the speed of light. "Have you been holding out on me? Here I have been coddling you like some wounded little bird, when all along you have had some hot romance going with a sexy writer? Scoot over—you should be taking care of me."

"No, I don't have a hot romance. There is just a very nice guy I have seen a couple of times at Starbucks, whom I would very much like to see again."

"*And . . .*"

"And . . . marry him and have his kids and live happily ever after in a Cape Cod house on Martha's Vineyard, where he will write all day and I will make jam with the strawberries we grow in our very own garden."

"I see. And how much time have you spent with this guy?"

"Let's see . . ." Kate raised her right hand and began writing imaginary numbers on an imaginary chalkboard. "Carry the five . . . Multiply that by three . . . Subtract seventeen . . ."

"Kate!"

Kate dropped her hand. "About an hour and a half."

"Oh, great," said Paige. "It's good to know that you aren't rushing into anything."

"I'm not." Kate laughed.

"Ha!" said Paige with a flip of her hair.

"*Ha?* Did you really just say 'Ha!' and flip your hair? What are you, a 1940s detective?"

Paige pointed a finger at Kate and tried not to laugh. "Don't you try to distract me, young lady. If you are going to get married and move to an island with this boy, I demand more details. Does he have a job? Is he married? Does he have any single friends?"

"I don't know. I hope not. And if it will make you drive me out to the Palisades, then yes, he has lots of single friends."

"You wouldn't lie to me, would you?"

"For a ride across town? Absolutely."

Paige stood. "Good enough for me. Let's go."

"Wait a minute. I need to pretty up."

"I have to be at work by ten. There isn't time for prettying up." Paige reached across the bed and dragged Kate to her feet. "Besides, I hate to give you a big head, but you are pretty damn pretty just like you are."

Kate was touched. "That is so sweet."

"You may want to brush your teeth, though."

"That was less sweet."

"I could say the same about your breath. Go!"

Kate literally ran into the bathroom.

26

Michael stared at his laptop. He had opened and closed the latest draft of the short story he was writing about his father no fewer than three times. Every time he settled in to work on his story about a man and his son who escaped the pain of a mentally ill wife and mother by watching the news, he was distracted by thoughts of Vivien Leigh. He'd been awake most of the night, completely engrossed in a biography of the beautiful actress. He was preparing for his pitch meeting with Bob Steinman, which was scheduled for late Thursday morning. He had two days to learn enough about Ms. Leigh to convince the president of Cutting Edge Pictures to put money behind a movie about her life . . . starring Sapphire Rose. He had no doubt that Sapphire was perfect for the role, but he also knew that he would have to walk a delicate line between convincing Bob that she was crazy enough to be brilliant in the role, but not so crazy that she wouldn't behave in a professional manner. He'd have to use a lot of words like *sensitive* and *creative* and avoid phrases like *off her rocker*.

He was under time pressure, too. Kate was in serious danger of being fired. He needed something to distract Sapphire from the incredibly narcissistic pain of working with the woman whose husband she had stolen. If he didn't feel such an affinity for animals, he would consider getting her a tiny dog. That might distract her, but he would have to surrender his membership to the ASPCA immediately. However, if he could remember the name of that little animal—was it a ferret?—that had taken a chunk out of Paris Hilton, he would overlook his reservations and buy one for Sapphire right now. Was it too much to hope for a rabid one?

What Sapphire really wanted, of course, was a role in a movie. Michael was convinced that it wasn't working with Kate that really bothered her—it was working on a television show. She was just projecting her displeasure and misery on everyone around her. If she was going to be dissatisfied, so was everyone else. So, it followed that if he wanted to make everyone else (Kate) happy, he would have to bite the bullet and make Sapphire happy, which meant getting her what she wanted.

He needed to go into this meeting with all of his ducks in a row. Unfortunately, he didn't have any ducks. He didn't even have a screenplay. He racked his brain for a talented writer he could wrangle at the last minute to accompany him to his meeting with Bob. He needed someone he could trust to keep his or her mouth shut, both during the meeting and afterward. Michael really thought he was on to something with this idea and he didn't want anyone stealing in and running with it. The last thing he wanted was the competition of another Vivien Leigh movie in production at the same time, god forbid with an actual movie star. He didn't need Sapphire Rose going up against Charlize Theron at the Golden Globes. His fame-obsessed client would be sent back to the TV seats so fast, her head would be spinning. No doubt green vomit would also be shooting out of her mouth, which would make a win for best actress a long shot.

So, he needed to move fast and he needed a writer. His fingers tapped lightly on his computer keyboard as he thought. A writer . . . a writer . . . a writer—his fingers froze over the keys. A *writer*.

No, that was crazy. He couldn't write a screenplay. He was an agent, for god's sake, who dabbled in thinly veiled autobiographical short stories. Who was he to write the story of a manic-depressive woman?

Only the son of a manic-depressive woman.

His heart beat faster in his chest. He tried to step back from his own intense fantasies to look at his idea objectively. Objectively, he liked it.

He felt the agent in him come to life. Wouldn't the pitch to Bob Steinman have more impact if he showed up with a script in hand, or at least an outline? He couldn't come right out and tell him that he wanted to write it himself. Between that and pitching Sapphire as the lead, it would start to sound too much like the vanity project it actually was. He would need to create a nom de plume and pitch the hell out of his alter ego. Why couldn't, say, *Mark Green* write a treatment for a feature about the great Vivien Leigh? For that matter, why couldn't he write it with Sapphire Rose in mind for the lead? He could. Not only that, he would.

Michael checked his watch: 8:15. He had a good hour before he had to head into his office. He had only about fifty hours before his meeting with Bob, though, and a treatment for a movie to write. He would call his secretary and tell her he was sick. He would spend two days doing nothing but immersing himself in the life of Vivien Leigh. He would read biographies and watch her movies and hope to be struck by a lightning bolt of inspiration—or at least hammer out an outline. He started packing up his laptop and gathering his things when he heard a familiar voice say, "Hello."

He looked up to see Kate smiling shyly down at him. *Adorable.* "Hello," he said back.

She gestured to the gear he had been gathering together for his exit. "Are you leaving?"

"What?" he asked, stalling for time. "Oh, no, I wasn't leaving." He quickly dropped his briefcase and made a show of positioning his computer on the table in front of him. "I just got here."

Kate looked around at the empty coffee cups and crumpled napkins that littered his workstation. "I see. Wow, whoever sat here before you was a real slob."

"True," said Michael, pulling out a chair for her. "But he is working on it."

"Good to know," she said with a heart-melting grin.

Remembering his manners, Michael offered to get her a drink.

"My friend is getting it for me." She gestured to the long line and Michael recognized the woman he had seen holding open the makeup trailer door for Kate at the *Generations* set. "Oh good," he said, but he thought, *Oh great—another person I need to hide from during my weekly six a.m. torture sessions.* "You girls don't have to work today?"

"I don't. She does."

"Oh, that's nice." Michael racked his brain for something—anything—to say. There was so much he really did need to talk to her about: her job, her breakup, his client who had caused her breakup. But since he wasn't supposed to know about any of it, he couldn't. How could he make "How are you?" sound sincere when he really wanted to say, "I'm so sorry about what is happening to you, and I need to warn you about danger ahead"? So he settled on the very clever "Would you and your friend like to join me?"

"Oh," said Kate, "I don't know. I'll have to check with her—"

"Hi, Michael," said Paige, appearing with three cups balanced precariously in her hands. "I brought you a latte. I figured it's still too early for a mocha caramel candy frappuccino."

Michael looked at Kate, who immediately dropped her eyes, embarrassed. *Her friend knows my name. Kate told her my name.* Was it just him or was the world suddenly glowing with brilliant white light?

He took two of the cups from Paige before all three came tumbling down. "I couldn't agree with you more," he said. "My hard and fast rule is no milk shakes before nine a.m."

"Good to know you are a man of principle," she said, sitting in the chair he offered.

"That's my only one, but I feel it is more than enough to hang my hat on."

"In Hollywood, I believe even one solid principle qualifies you for the priesthood."

Michael laughed. "I will remember that if I'm ever looking for a career change that entails converting to Catholicism and embracing celibacy."

Kate finally pulled herself together enough to speak. "If you two are done, I would love to introduce you. Michael, this is Paige. Paige, meet Michael."

"Oh dear," said Paige, realizing her faux pas. "I already said your name, didn't I?"

"*Yes, you did,*" hissed Kate.

"It's all right," said Michael. "I just assumed it was a lucky guess. It's a pretty common name."

Kate smiled at him, grateful for his attempt to alleviate her embarrassment. "So . . . fancy meeting you here."

"Yeah," he said shyly, holding her gaze. "What are the odds?"

"Pretty good when you drive all the way across town," said Paige. Kate looked at her with a horrified expression. "What?"

Kate slid down low in her chair, her freckles disappearing in the bright red of her cheeks.

"So, Paige," said Michael, turning his attention toward her in order to allow Kate some time to regain her composure. "You work with Kate?"

"I do. And you're a writer?"

"*Oh god,*" whimpered Kate, sinking lower.

"Oh, sorry," said Paige, grimacing at her second faux pas. "What I meant to say was, 'What do you do . . . guy I've never heard of?'"

Michael laughed again. Even Kate managed a small chuckle in spite of her mortification. "Well, I guess you could say I'm a writer, but mostly I just sit here with my computer hoping that your friend comes in."

Still not quite ready to raise her eyes, Kate smiled into her chest.

"Is there a lot of money in that?"

"The writing or the waiting?"

Paige laughed. "Either."

"So far, no," said Michael, wondering at how much easier it was to talk to Paige than to Kate. Why did attraction turn his verbal skills to mush? "The problem with both career options is that they are very dependent on other people."

"Well, speaking of dependent, I have to go to work and Kate here is depending on me for a ride home. Unless . . ." She looked pointedly at Michael.

"*Paige,*" groaned Kate, now little more than a puddle on the floor.

"Well, I can't just leave you here," she said innocently.

"No, you can't," agreed Michael. "I would be honored to drive Kate home . . . after breakfast."

"Is that breakfast today or tomorrow?"

Now it was Michael's turn to say, "*Paige.*"

Paige raised her hands in a gesture of surrender. "Just making sure."

Finally, Kate looked up. "You know, I am a little hungry."

★　　★　　★

As Michael feared, all of his conversational skills left with Paige. He and Kate sat staring at their individual cups, pretending to be fascinated with the list of coffee possibilities written on the side.

"So," Michael finally managed, "do you like Café Vita?"

"I do," said Kate.

"Do you want to go there?"

"I do."

"Do you think that once we get there you will say more than 'I do'?"

Kate grinned. "I really, really hope so."

Michael laughed and started gathering his computer, phone, and BlackBerry, each item reminding him of how much he had to get done today. He should be on his way into his office to start getting ready to pitch Bob Steinman on a script that he should have written already, but somehow he just didn't care. He remembered reading somewhere that if you had what you needed, suddenly you needed a lot less of what you wanted. Right now, he needed to get to know Kate.

They walked the half a block to the restaurant in silence, jolts of electricity shooting through Michael's body every time Kate's shoulder accidentally bumped his. They settled into a corner table and looked at each other shyly.

"So . . . are you still staying at your mother's?"

"No!" said Kate with so much enthusiasm that Michael actually flinched. "Sorry," laughed Kate. "Obviously, I am quite excited about moving out."

"Obviously. What happened?"

"I'm staying with Paige."

"That's good," he said, cursing himself for not offering up his own place when he'd had the chance.

"It really is," Kate said. Then . . . nothing.

They busied themselves with pretending to read their menus, but soon the waiter came over to take their orders and, to both of their great dismay, took the menus with him when he left.

"She made me an auction item," blurted Kate.

"She what?" asked Michael, completely lost.

"My mother. She made me an auction item. For her condo association." Michael still looked confused. "That's why I left."

"I'm sorry, I still have no idea what you are talking about," said Michael with a kind, albeit baffled, smile.

"No," sighed Kate. "*I'm* sorry. I tend to blurt things out when I'm nervous."

"You what?"

"I blurt. Usually it's inappropriate, deeply personal things."

"Like your mother trying to sell you into slavery?"

"*Oh no,*" laughed Kate. "Is that what you got from what I said?"

"Pretty much."

"Oh, man, now you see why I don't like to do interviews."

"Why?"

"Because when I get nervous there is no telling what will come out of my mouth, and once it's out, it's out. I mean, what if you were a reporter—you're not, are you?"

Michael laughed. "No, I'm not."

"Good. Anyway, if you were a reporter and I tried to tell you about how my mother donated a dinner with me to an auction—"

"Oh, a *dinner* with you."

"—but it came out all wrong and you thought I had said that she had tried to sell me into slavery—well, you can see how that might be an issue."

"Well, if I were that reporter, I would be quite excited."

"Sure." Kate laughed again. "It would be a very good story."

"In fact," said Michael earnestly, "you might want to leak that story. It has everything: human interest, danger, intrigue—"

"Crazy mother."

"Exactly. Everyone thinks their mother is crazy. Of course, in my case it is actually true."

Kate stopped laughing. "Are you serious?"

Michael realized he may have just done his own blurting of

inappropriately personal information. "Actually, I am. She was institutionalized for much of my childhood."

"Wow," said Kate quietly. "That must be tough."

"It was. She's gone now. She died three years ago."

"I'm sorry."

"Thank you."

Kate looked around the restaurant—at the other diners, out the front door, anywhere but at Michael.

He asked, "Did that freak you out?"

"What?"

"What I told you about my mother?"

"Oh no," said Kate definitively. "I . . . I'm just embarrassed that I was complaining about my mother when, well, you obviously had real problems."

"Look, I did have a hard time with my mother, but I lucked out in the dad department, so it all balances out. Besides, it's all relative, you know? Just because my situation with my mother was so serious doesn't mean that it doesn't hurt when *your* mother tries to use you in order to look important in front of her friends."

Kate flinched. "Ouch."

"Exactly. It would have been very difficult for my mother to organize a dinner from inside an institution, so really, I won out."

"I promise you, my mother would have found a way."

Michael laughed. "Did she have to cancel the party when you left?"

"Oh, I sincerely doubt it." Kate moved her water glass to make room for the waiter to place her basil and feta omelet in front of her. "I'm sure she just told everyone I was in the bathroom with intestinal distress and then proceeded to charm everyone to distraction. I would bet anything that after three minutes no one even noticed that the guest of honor was missing and that the evening turned out to be a great success. She had always been the true star of every party anyway."

"It sounds like she should have been the actress."

"Yeah, I have thought that many times," said Kate, taking a big bite of her breakfast.

"Do you like what you do?"

"Sometimes. Do you?"

Michael took a long time to spoon strawberry jam onto his toast and spread it carefully across the bread, stalling. *This is the time to come clean*, he thought. "Sometimes." *Tell her*.

"Why sometimes?"

"Well, the truth is . . ." *Tell her*.

"What?" asked Kate, with genuine interest. It had been so long since an attractive woman had looked at Michael with genuine *anything* that he was momentarily taken aback.

Now. Tell her now. "The thing is, um . . . well, I'm not really a writer."

"Damn it," said Kate, dropping her fork onto the table and shaking her head.

Oh shit. "Listen, I'm sorry I—"

"No, no, I'm not upset with *you*. I just get so mad at the attitude of this town," she said passionately. "I mean, of course you are a writer. You are a writer because you *write*."

"But—"

"No buts. You know, before I was on a successful TV show, people would ask me what I did, and when I told them that I was an actress, they would say, 'Oh, yeah? What restaurant do you work at?' As if I couldn't claim to be an actor unless I was being paid to do something they could see me in. I think it's so admirable that you write every day. In fact, I think it is all the more admirable that you do it without being paid." She paused her zealous diatribe and then asked, "Do you get paid for your writing?"

Michael was thrilled to have a question he could answer honestly. "No, no one pays me to write."

"I think that's great," Kate declared.

"Well, I don't know if it's *great* that no one wants to pay me."

Kate laughed. "No, I know that. Of course it is better to earn your living doing what you love, but there is something so pure, so admirable, about the fact that you are doing your art for its own sake."

Pure? Admirable? Those are words an agent rarely hears. "Well, I can honestly say that writing is something I do for myself."

"And I think that is so much better than if you were selling your soul for some stupid paycheck, you know? You see that so often, especially in Los Angeles. Too many people give up their dreams for a fancy car and a condo in Malibu. It is just sad."

"That is sad," Michael said, wondering how soon he could sell his condo.

"But look at you," Kate said brightly. "You are living the *true* dream."

"Yeah, that's me." Michael managed a weak smile. His desire to tell her the truth was no match for her admiration. He just wasn't ready to risk losing it quite yet. "Living the dream."

Well, living the illusion, at least.

27

When Paige tried to open her front door at six o'clock that night, she felt it hit something soft.

"Ow!" Kate yelped, scooting out of the way.

Paige carefully pushed the door a little more, peeking around it nervously, afraid of what she might find. She was pretty sure it would be either naked bodies or dead bodies. Neither option was very appealing. "Kate? Are you okay?"

"Yes, I'm fine," Kate said, yanking the door open while rubbing her right butt cheek. "Except for the bruise on my ass."

"Oh my god!" exclaimed Paige, berating herself for leaving Kate with an ass-bruising stranger. "What did he do to you?"

"*He* didn't do anything. *You* rammed the door into me!"

"I did what?"

"You *bashed* me with the door," said Kate. "I was just standing here minding my own business, and you came in willy-nilly and hurt me."

"Okay, slow down. Why were you in front of the door?"

"That is a very good question," said Kate, all but skipping

into the kitchen. She called over her shoulder, "I was very busy swooning."

"*Swooning?*" asked Paige, accepting the bottle of water Kate took out of the fridge for her.

"Yes, swooning. I got home a few minutes ago, closed the door behind me, and leaned up against it to enjoy a little bit of reminiscing about my fabulous breakfast date with Michael, when—*bam!*—the door crashes into my backside, injuring me terribly. I just hope there isn't any permanent damage."

"I wouldn't worry about it," said Paige. "I think most of your permanent damage happened a long time ago."

"That's where you're wrong," said Kate, dropping into a chair in the breakfast nook and opening her own bottle of water. "I am one of the lucky few who made it through her childhood virtually unscathed."

"Okay, now I know you are not in your right mind," said Paige, laughing. "What has gotten into you?"

"I'm happy," sang Kate, doing a jerky, seated dance.

"This is you happy? Uh-oh—I think I liked you better depressed."

"I'm no expert," said Kate, "but I am pretty sure that 'liking you better depressed' is not high on the list of qualities to look for in a friend."

"It would be if the author of the list had seen your little chair dance."

Kate dropped her jaw in an expression of shocked outrage. "I'll have you know that I won best dancer at Middletown High."

"Well then," said Paige, "I stand corrected." Kate nodded nobly, a dancing queen forgiving an errant subject. Paige continued, "I assume that Middletown High was a school for the blind?"

"That is a very cruel thing to say," said Kate with an offended scoff, "and I would be *very insulted* if I didn't know for a fact that I am a truly terrible dancer."

Paige laughed. "Just out of curiosity, how did you win best dancer?"

"I didn't. That was my dream, but the only thing I actually won was Girl Most Likely to Help a Stranger."

"That's the saddest award I have ever heard of."

"Yeah, I didn't have a lot of girls campaigning against me."

"You campaigned for that?"

Kate mumbled unintelligibly.

"What?"

"I said, 'Just a few buttons.'"

"Oh dear."

"And maybe a poster or two."

Paige plopped down into a chair next to her. "That is the saddest thing I have ever heard."

"I didn't say it was my proudest moment. What did you win in high school, Madam Superior?"

"Oh, lord only knows. I'm sure I cut the assembly where they gave those things out."

"You cut the assembly?" asked Kate, her sincere shock making her look like the innocent fourteen-year-old she once was.

"Oh yeah, I cut everything. I'm still not sure how I graduated. In fact, I'm still not sure *that* I graduated. I cut graduation, too."

"Oh my god! Didn't the school call your parents?"

"Probably, but my mom wasn't exactly a disciplinarian. She's sober now, but she was well into her box o' wine most nights when I was growing up."

"Wow," said Kate, unable to picture a world where calls from the school were ignored by tipsy mothers.

"Yeah, it actually sounds more dramatic than it was. God bless her, my mom always managed to defrost a hearty meal, and every night she sat with me and my brothers while we ate it. Granted, she was drinking her wine and smoking the whole time, but that was way before anyone knew anything about secondhand smoke. I think I smelled like an ashtray my entire childhood. Wait a minute—I just thought of something. Do you think that's why I didn't make cheerleading?"

"Did you try out?"

"You know, you ask a very good question. I don't think I actually made it to the tryout. I believe it was scheduled at a bad time for me."

"A bad time?" asked Kate.

"Yes. I seem to remember that it was scheduled for three o'clock in the afternoon, which was generally the time I had set aside for getting stoned behind the bleachers."

"In other words, you had a scheduling conflict."

"Precisely!" said Paige in her best proud-teacher voice. "Were you a cheerleader? You certainly look like you could have been."

Kate looked at her suspiciously. "I don't quite know how to take that. Are you insulting me?"

"Not consciously, but who knows? My high school self was secretly jealous of the cheerleaders, which manifested in a quiet rage that I treated with marijuana. I no longer smoke pot, so if you were a cheerleader, I may have to hit you."

"Well, this may be the very first time I can sincerely say that I am happy I did not make the cheerleading squad."

"But you tried out?"

"Oh god, yes. All four years. My mother was devastated."

"Your *mother* was devastated?"

"Yeah, she couldn't figure out what she was doing wrong. She even hired a 'cheer coach' and put me on a diet of Slim-Fast bars and carrot sticks. I was skinny, but I was so weak I could barely raise my arms, much less do a cartwheel. She cried for hours when I was cut at the tryouts my last eligible year."

"Did you cry?"

"Yeah, but I think I was crying more for my mother than for myself. It was really her dream."

"Wow, that's a lot of pressure."

Kate was quiet for a moment. "Yeah, I guess it was."

"*Is,*" said Paige quietly.

"What do you mean?" asked Kate.

"I just wonder how much you are still living your mother's dream, instead of your own life."

"Well, part of my mother's dream, the handsome husband part, just left me, so . . ."

"How is she going to feel about the struggling writer?"

"She'll probably cry again and say something sensitive like 'You know, Katie, if you had been a cheerleader, Hamilton probably wouldn't have left you and you wouldn't have to date a man with no future.' "

Paige laughed. "Nice."

"Yeah. Well, for all we know, she may be right. Who knows where you and I could be right now if we had made our respective cheerleading squads."

"Probably president and vice president."

"No doubt."

"You know, I always thought I could work wonders with the White House," mused Paige. "Just give me free reign and a few throw pillows and I could warm that place right up."

Kate sipped her water and looked around the charming little fifties-era kitchen. It was so perfectly Paige: warm, low-key, and welcoming. The painted wood chairs looked ancient, perfectly mismatched in their chipped and peeling shades of blue, green, yellow, and red. The windowsill was lined with old salt and pepper shakers, and the open shelves were stacked with an appealing assortment of dishes and bowls, each beautiful and unique. Kate knew she would never have had the confidence to choose the kitschy furniture that fit so perfectly in this room, unless, of course, it had been re-created for the Pottery Barn catalog and sold as a set.

"I like this room a lot," she said. "I really would like to see what you could do with the White House."

"Thank you, but I don't think the president and I would see eye to eye about serving state dinners on mismatched china."

"You could decorate other houses, though. Do you ever think about that?" asked Kate. "I would hire you in a heartbeat."

"Oh, that's very sweet. I do have a fantasy of opening an antiques shop in a sophisticated little tourist town one day. I have such an affinity for things that have seen better days but are still beautiful in their own way, you know?" Paige got up to put on a pot of tea. "Everything in here comes with a story. I don't know that all of it actually goes together in the real world, but the story it tells of my personal history of boyfriends and swap meets is perfect."

Kate said, "I think when I get my own place I am going to decorate it with stuff from swap meets."

"Hey, when you get your own place, you can do it up in all custom-designed furniture with perfectly finished wood and fabulous fabrics. Trust me, if I had an actress's salary instead of a makeup artist's salary, this kitchen would be a lot less kitschy and a lot more elegant."

Kate was a little taken aback, embarrassed. "I didn't mean I wanted to steal your ideas."

"Oh, honey, you can steal the *furniture* if you want to. I'm just saying that you can afford to do whatever you want with your own place. It may look like this, or it may be something completely different. The only important thing is that it is a reflection of you."

"I don't even know what that would be," Kate said, suddenly a little sad.

"Don't beat yourself up about it. It's not easy to figure out what you really like, especially right after a relationship where who you are got so lost in who he wanted you to be," said Paige gently. "I mean, after my last big breakup, I spent an entire weekend clearing out roughly three hundred Laura Ashley dresses from my closet."

"Laura Ashley dresses?" Kate couldn't picture Paige in anything other than her requisite True Religion jeans and low-heeled boots.

"Oh, yeah. Right after I got sober, I met this very handsome, very successful guy who completely swept me off my feet. Within two months, he put a gargantuan ring on my finger and set me up in a gorgeous house in Orange County."

"Wow."

"Yeah, *big* wow. I was so tired and raw at the time, and I was so grateful that this guy was going to rescue me from my life of toil and strife."

"Toil and strife?"

"Well, working to support myself, which back then felt like a life sentence of drudgery. Anyway, he appeared like a knight in shining armor and promised to take care of me and buy me a Mercedes station wagon. All he asked for in return was that I morph into the perfect housewife and spend my days making casseroles and learning how to play bridge."

"What happened?"

"Well, at first I made a lot of casseroles and played a lot of cards, but then three things happened: I remembered it wasn't 1953, they added Lycra to denim, and I realized that acting like the perfect wife twenty-four hours a day was a lot harder than working at a regular job for eight."

"So you left?"

"I did. I left the six-thousand-square-foot house with panoramic ocean views and moved into the nine-hundred-square-foot palace you now enjoy." Paige swept her arm across the room. "Seriously, though, it was the best move I've made. Be it ever so tiny, it is all mine."

"What about the guy? Was he heartbroken?"

"Oh, lord no. He immediately replaced me with a newer, more obedient model. He was never quite happy with me anyway. Even in my pretty dresses, methodically crumbling potato chips over tuna fish and noodles, I couldn't quite pull it off."

It was so hard to picture Paige turned out in long dresses and lugging Jell-O molds to church picnics. "I just can't see it," said Kate.

"I'm happy to show you pictures, but they aren't pretty—literally or figuratively."

"But . . . you're so strong."

"Oh, and you are so sweet," Paige said, smiling. "But I am just as vulnerable to all the fucked-up fantasies we're fed from the time we are two years old. Who doesn't want a handsome prince to come in and save the day? It's hard to stand up to an entire culture built on the idea that a woman's greatest value is in being taken care of by a man. It doesn't matter how happy and fulfilled a single woman is—our society still looks at her as if she is somehow sad and incomplete."

"That's depressing."

"Yes, and trust me, it is much, *much* more depressing to be in the wrong relationship than it is to be single. I am actually very happy in my life right now. Honestly? I don't know where a man would fit into it."

Kate, baffled by the concept of a life without a man, said, "Do you really think you might spend the rest of your life single?"

"I don't know what is going to happen. What I do know is that I don't want another relationship like the ones I have had. It scares me when I look back and see how easily I've given myself up, adapted myself to fit someone else's image of who or what I should be."

Kate was floored. "I'm so surprised to hear you say that. You just seem so, I don't know, on your own side or something."

"Do I? Maybe I'm working on the wrong side of the camera. Seriously, though, I may look strong and independent now, but god forbid I fall in love with a horse-riding chef tomorrow—I will be showing up at work in jodhpurs and a big white hat."

Kate laughed, but as she did she felt her earlier excitement about Michael draining out of her. Maybe it was a bad idea to get into another relationship. Maybe she was just trading one crutch for another. She couldn't even remember if she actually liked omelets or if she had eaten one just to please Michael. Paige noticed the change in her mood and said, "Hey, what's wrong? I almost miss the chair dance."

Kate worked up a small smile. "I was dancing because I was excited about Michael."

"And that's great."

"I thought so," said Kate, uncertain. "But now I feel like I am just jumping from one mess into another. I mean, if *you* can't hold your own in relationships, what chance do I have?"

"Oh dear," said Paige, turning her head to the side and raising her eyebrows. "Look what I've done—I've spilled my issues all over you." Kate managed another small smile and Paige continued. "Look, Michael seems like a very sweet guy and it sounds like he is as taken with you as you are with him. You deserve to have some fun, and—"

"But I don't want to lose myself in another relationship—"

"—and I *promise* you, on my supersecret but still disgusting tuna casserole recipe, that I will watch you like a hawk for signs that you are morphing into a different person, okay?"

Kate sighed. "I really would like to see him again."

"Good. I think you should."

"Do you have any more of those dresses lying around?"

"I do, but unfortunately for you they have all been turned into dishrags," said Paige, as the teakettle began to whistle.

28

Michael sat at his kitchen table, watching the sun rise over the ocean. It was a view that never failed to amaze him. *If there is a God*, thought Michael, *He is definitely an artist.*

He wondered if God also did some writing in His spare time—you know, in between miracles and stuff—and if He did, if He would be willing to give Michael some tips on working through writer's block. Michael had been staring at a blank computer screen for almost twenty hours straight. Well, it wasn't totally blank; he had taken the very important step of writing "The Untitled Vivien Leigh Project" in boldface letters across the top of what he hoped would be his title page. Could it be called a title page if no story actually followed it? There were those who thought a great title was the true selling point. Of course, those people had probably squeezed out an additional sentence or two.

What he really wanted to write was *Michael and Kate: A Love Story.* He would definitely start with the characters' first kiss, because it was *high fucking time*. He had almost kissed her when he had dropped her off at Paige's house yesterday, but he had been too damn scared to pull the trigger. He was desperate to call her, to try to move the relationship forward, but he was afraid that every step forward would be another nail in his coffin when she found out that he wasn't being completely honest with her. In fact, if he really did the math, the lies probably outweighed the truth, and that was a great way to win the heart of a woman whose husband had just deceived her and left her for her costar and rival.

Not.

His only hope, outside of Superman appearing and rotating the earth backward on its axis to turn back time so that he could tell her the truth from the beginning, was an equally miraculous *Pride and Prejudice* moment, in which his Darcylike machinations to save her job were so successful and romantic that she not only forgave him for lying to her, but she immediately threw herself into his arms and (please, please, please) kissed him. Of course, this being modern times, she could also throw him to the ground and make mad, passionate love to him, which, along with high-speed Internet access, was a benefit of living in the twenty-first century.

But first, he had to *focus*.

Become a screenplay. Become a screenplay. Michael focused all of his concentration on the blank screen and tried to will it to life. He so desperately wanted it to work, he half expected words to begin scrolling across the page, coming together to create a brilliant first draft of a screenplay. *Brilliant first draft*, he thought, shaking his head to break the hypnotic pull of the unbelievably blank screen. *Now I know I've lost it.*

He looked at the clock and, after a quick calculation that cost him twenty precious seconds, realized he had less than forty-eight hours until his meeting with Bob Steinman. He needed inspiration and he needed it now. Looking at his phone, he wondered if help was just a call away. Dial-an-Inspiration? Dial-a-Screenplay? He knew neither one existed, but when he was through this crisis, he was definitely going to look into creating 1-900-Break-a-Block. Considering what he would be willing to pay right now to cure his own writer's block, he would be rich beyond his wildest dreams.

Of course, writers weren't known for having a lot of disposable income, which could definitely impact the venture's profitability. However . . . if he were able to accept credit cards, he could—

Focus.

Focus, focus, focus, la-la-la-la-la. How was it that any word, when repeated repeatedly, could become a song? Why was it fun to say "repeated repeatedly"? That could be a song. Maybe not a rap song, per se, because it lacked a certain edge. That *is my problem*, thought Michael. *I lack edge. I need edge.*

I need focus.

I need a snack.

Clinging to the theory that low blood sugar was behind his complete inability to put words on paper (or his computer screen), Michael headed into the kitchen, hoping against all logic to find something other than olives and champagne in his refrigerator. Maybe he could call Kate and see if she wanted to meet up for a quick breakfast. Or, even better, he could bring her back here for breakfast, and as the eggs were cooking, he could ravage her right there on the kitchen table . . .

Focus.

Turning on his heels, he forced himself back into the chair in front of his computer. *Just write,* he scolded himself.

Write what?

Write anything.

Anything?

Anything.

So he did. He wrote his grocery list (olives, coffee). He wrote a long list of all of the things he *wouldn't* miss about Sapphire if she were to suffer a tragic hair-product accident and a much longer list of "Kate's adorable traits," which almost became a poem but was too nauseatingly cutesy to ever show to anyone. Then he started writing about how terrified he was to start writing and how afraid he was of the humiliation of failure, and how his deepest fear was that by allowing himself to actively pursue such a pro-

found and personal dream he would somehow chase it away forever. He wrote pages and pages about the many ways he could fail
and have his heart broken by his creative ambitions, but how he
felt a drive to move forward anyway, even if it meant risking his
comfort and security.

And then he found himself writing about Vivien Leigh.

The research that had kept him up all night flowed together with
his imagination and his personal experience, and his fingers were
suddenly flying across the keyboard. He found that he understood
his subject not just through the eyes of a young boy who had lived
with mental illness in his home, but also as an artist with frustrated
ambitions striving to communicate his creativity in the face of society's expectations. He struggled to get his ideas down before his mind
raced ahead to the next scene, the next action. He felt as though a
dam had broken and his rapid-fire typing was the only thing saving
him from drowning in the rushing waters of his imagination.

Michael didn't take a break or even look up from his computer
until his ringing phone broke his concentration. Reaching for it,
he was surprised to see that it was completely dark outside. What
time was it? How long had he been writing?

"Hello?" he croaked.

"Hello, Michael, Hamilton here. Did I wake you?"

"No," said Michael, although he did feel as if he were coming
out of a deep sleep. "I was just, um, watching TV. What time is it?"

"It's a few minutes after eleven. Sapphire and I just got back
from the Save the Diamonds benefit."

"Save the Diamonds?" Michael knew he was tired, but was he
losing his hearing, too?

"Yes. Apparently there are some misguided people who have
taken issue with the working conditions or some other blah-de-
blah happening in the diamond mines. If those of us who love
diamonds don't act fast, these nasty gem-haters and their demon-
strations may even impact supply."

"Wow, Sapphire must be beside herself," said Michael, masking his disgust with sarcasm. "I remember how devastated she was when they cut down on the baby-seal clubbing and she couldn't buy the fur coat she had set her heart on."

"Yes, she is quite upset. She has had far too much loss in her life, as you know."

Only if you count her mind, thought Michael. "What can I do for you tonight, Hamilton?"

"Well, as I said, Sapphire is quite upset. This issue with the diamonds has made her feel very vulnerable. She has always felt that jewelry was the one thing she could really count on to keep her warm at night when the chips are down."

"What about you, Hamilton?"

"Oh, I buy her *lots* of jewelry."

"No, I mean, don't you keep her warm at—oh, never mind. What were you saying?"

"Just that Sapphire is feeling very vulnerable right now, and when we were at the dinner tonight, several people asked me about Kate. It was very awkward. I mean, don't they read *People*?"

"Did you two do a story for *People*?" asked Michael, his heart breaking for Kate.

"Yes, *and* we had brunch at the Ivy, went shopping at Kitson, and had dinner at Mr. Chow. We even sat on the swings at the Malibu Country Mart. Anyone who can't figure out that we are together is just not paying attention."

"Maybe you need to do a story in the *New York Times*."

"Well, we did send out a press release. It's not our fault if the *Times* can't recognize a good story."

"Well, they are probably just distracted by the war."

"Maybe, but I'll be honest with you, Michael. People are bored with all of this war talk. That's why newspaper sales are down. If those snobby *New York Times* editors want to boost distribution, they need to take a page from the book of *Star* magazine. Those full-color photos sell newspapers like crazy."

Michael decided against pointing out that *Star* magazine

wasn't actually a newspaper, preferring to let Hamilton's stupidity speak for itself. "I don't know how to help you with the press, Hamilton. It sounds like you are doing everything you can to announce your new couplehood."

"I think we are, too, Michael, and that is why we're so frustrated."

"Frustrated?"

"Yes. Despite all of our efforts, people just can't seem to forget about Kate."

"Well, you did break up a week ago, Hamilton."

"Isn't that *amazing?*" asked Hamilton, stunned by the realization. "I mean, my relationship with Kate feels like a tiny blip on the radar screen compared to the meeting of the souls that I share with Sapphire."

"Tell me you didn't say that to *People* magazine, Hamilton."

"Of course I did. I believe it's the title of the piece."

" 'A Tiny Blip on the Radar'?"

"No, no—'A Meeting of Two Souls.' I don't believe Kate's name even came up."

"How could her name not come up, Hamilton? She is your soon-to-be ex-wife and a television star."

"Exactly why I called you, Michael."

Finally. "Yes, Hamilton."

"Well, I don't have to tell you how short the public's attention span is. The way I see it, if Kate wasn't on television every week, people would stop thinking about her, and if people stop thinking about her, then they will stop asking Sapphire about her, which, as I mentioned before, upsets her."

"I thought she was upset about the possible diamond and fur shortage."

"That, too. She feels like her world is falling down on her, Michael."

"And how do you think Kate is going to feel losing her job right after her husband left her for another woman?"

"Have you read *Codependent No More,* Michael?"

"What?" asked Michael, trying to adjust to the conversational U-turn.

"I just notice that you keep bringing up Kate's feelings. But her feelings are her own responsibility, Michael, not mine. And certainly not yours."

Oh dear. "Thank you for the psychological checkup, Hamilton."

"You're welcome."

"But I wonder if firing Kate is really in Sapphire's best interest. It could be a real image-killer if word gets out that Sapphire ordered the execution."

"I don't think we need to kill her, Michael."

"I was speaking metaphorically, Hamilton."

"Good, because nothing turns the tide of public opinion like untimely death. Kate could be turned into some kind of saint."

"Too bad for her she wouldn't be alive to enjoy it."

"True, although I could never get her to understand the importance of a good public image."

"Yes, nothing kills a marriage faster than public image incompatibility."

"Amen."

Michael allowed the silence to hang between them, using the few moments of peace to strategize about how to keep Kate employed. Although the more he talked to Hamilton, the more he began to think that getting fired and getting as far away from this creep as possible could be the best thing for her. He was at a loss as to how to communicate with Hamilton anymore. What he really wanted was to be left alone to write and pursue a relationship with Kate. Maybe he should just sit back and let Hamilton and Sapphire fire her. They could fire him, too, while they were at it. Worse things could happen to both of them than to be rid of the Annoying Duo. It might be a hard sell, though: "Great news, Kate! I got you fired so you will have more time to date me! I realize you just got divorced and could probably use the money you earned in the good old days when you were employed, but I can support both of us with the money I don't earn as a writer!"

Maybe not.

"Listen, Hamilton, you make a lot of good points." *I couldn't name any if pressed to do so . . .* "But I really feel that we need to put some more thought into this before moving forward. Let's keep our focus on Sapphire's film career. She is in a completely different league than Kate." *Let's call that league "outer space."* "I think the next meeting we should have with the suits over at *Generations* is one that focuses on clearing her schedule for the Vivien Leigh project."

Hamilton perked up. "Is that imminent?"

"Well, let me put it this way, Hamilton: the script is in the works."

"Well, that is great news, Michael. Maybe that will take poor Sapphire's mind off her troubles."

"God willing," said Michael, thinking he couldn't live through another conversation about his rich, spoiled client's difficult life of privilege and wealth.

"When is your meeting with Bob Steinman?" asked Hamilton.

"In a couple of days," said Michael casually, doing an internal calculation that put the exact time frame at thirty-five hours and thirteen minutes.

"Great. We can't wait to hear all about it. When can we get a look at the script?"

Never, if you don't let me off the fucking phone. "Soon, Hamilton. As I said, it's in the works."

"Great. Super. I'm off to comfort our sensitive little flower. It wouldn't hurt for you to give her a call, too, Michael. She needs her friends right now."

Then she should really go make some. "Right-o, Hamilton. I'll get right on that."

Just as soon as the sun starts rotating around the earth . . .

29

Sapphire was inconsolable.

"Why does no one care about *me?* When is it going to be *my* turn to shine?" She threw herself onto the floor of her trailer. Luckily, her fall was cushioned by the huge pile of discarded designer clothes that covered the ground.

"Sapphire, darling, we are all here for you. We all want to help you shine." Hamilton took it upon himself to speak for the group gathered by the door. Jerry eagerly nodded his agreement. Claire tried to maintain an outward expression of concern while inwardly rolling her eyes.

"It's true, Sapphire. And nothing means more to me than doing my part to help," she said dryly.

"Absolutely!" piped in Jerry excitedly. Claire watched him, searching for any sign of sarcasm or irony. She found none. Amazing. "Just tell me what more I can do to make your life easier and I will run and do it right now," he said, turning to face the door and placing a hand on the doorknob to illustrate his sincerity.

Claire's eye roll snuck to the surface. "Thank you for that, Jerry, but before you charge out into the world in search of dragons to slay in honor of our shiny star, we really need to focus on getting her dressed for this scene. Everyone else is ready and waiting on set." The fact that this point should have been made by the producer, not the costume designer, was just one more reality that seemed to float right over Jerry's head.

"Everyone else can just wait, then. Sapphire *is Generations.*" Jerry delivered his serenade directly to Sapphire, not even bothering to glance at Claire as he spoke.

"Honey-bunny, we really do need to get dressed soon," said Hamilton gently. "Claire has been kind enough to bring out everything in your size from the trailer, as well as sending her assistant to buy everything in your size from Saks and Neiman Marcus. There must be something here that will work for you."

"No, there's not!" wailed Sapphire. "I want the blue jersey Calvin Klein dress I saw in *Vogue.*" She sat up just far enough to create the momentum necessary to throw herself back onto the clothing pile with a dramatic "Nobody ever cares what *I* want!"

"I do!" said Jerry, rushing forward to help as if Sapphire had accidentally fallen instead of hurled her body in a tantrum.

Claire thought about her mortgage and car payment and realized that, sadly, she really did need this job. "I do care what you want, Sapphire, but that dress is not available."

Hamilton knelt down next to his sobbing girlfriend, displacing Jerry, who offered Sapphire a tiny bow before scurrying back to his position by the door. "Did you hear Claire, honey? That dress is not available. We need to find you something else to wear today."

"But that's the one I want," said Sapphire in a little-girl voice, looking up at Hamilton with sad eyes.

Hamilton turned to Claire and Jerry with an indulgent "isn't she precious?" expression. Jerry smiled back, but Claire was on the verge of drawing blood in her palms from the pressure of her clenched fists. "Sadly, my beauty, we don't always get what we want."

"But *I* should," said Sapphire, pouting. "*I'm* the star."

"Yes, Sapphire, I believe that has been made clear." *Painfully clear*, Claire thought. She continued, "I understand that you are a special case, but the dress you want is simply not available, for you or anyone."

"I bet Gwyneth Paltrow could get one."

"But you're not Gwyneth Paltrow." The words were out of Claire's mouth before she could stop them. There was a collective gasp from the floor at her blasphemy.

Not surprisingly, Jerry jumped to his star's defense. "Of course you're not Gwyneth Paltrow . . . because you are so much *better* than Gwyneth Paltrow. She only *wishes* that she could hold a candle to—"

"Thank you, Jerry," interrupted Hamilton. "I think we are all in agreement about who deserves our loyalty and admiration." He stared pointedly at Claire. "And those of us who are confused about that should really be working for Ms. Paltrow."

Claire allowed herself a brief moment's fantasy of dressing that elegant, yoga-toned body before saying, with just the subtlest hint of sarcasm, "What could be confusing about working on a hit show with the biggest star in the business?" She had to literally bite her tongue to keep from expounding on the many applications of the term "biggest."

"Amen to that," Jerry said.

Sapphire seemed comforted by the comparisons between her and the stunningly beautiful Gwyneth, unrealistic association being the cornerstone of her inflated self-image. She began the slow process of pulling herself together, sniffling and wiping her nose on the nearest piece of cloth, which, to Claire's dismay, was a four-hundred-dollar silk blouse that she had hoped to return to Fred Segal. Maybe she could sell it on ebay. If Britney Spears's half-eaten corn dog could sell for two hundred dollars, who knew what fortunes could be made from a snot-stained designer blouse?

Sensing a possible end to the standoff, Hamilton shifted into manager mode. "So, short of finding you that blue dress, is there *anything* we can do to help you get ready for your scene today?"

"Well . . ." Sapphire sniffled again, her face the picture of wide-eyed innocence. "There is *one* thing."

★　★　★

"That's weird," said Kate, closing her cell phone.

"What?" Paige was just finishing loading their breakfast dishes into the dishwasher. They had taken advantage of Kate's day off and Paige's late call time to enjoy a midmorning breakfast of mammoth proportions. It gave Paige great pleasure to see her friend tuck into a big bowl of oatmeal with nuts and berries. They'd be sharing clothes in no time. Too bad it wouldn't be Kate's tiny designer wardrobe. Maybe they could sew a few things together to make one normal-size outfit.

Kate got up to pour herself another cup of coffee. "That was Sam. They want me to come in."

"Oh shit," said Paige, reaching up to feel her messy topknot. "I am a good hour away from being anywhere near presentable. When do they need us?"

"That's what's so weird. They don't need *us,* just me."

"That doesn't make any sense." Paige's face paled. "Unless they are replacing me. Do you think they are upset that you are staying here? Maybe they think it's inappropriate."

"Well," said Kate, concerned, "Sam did say something about hearing through the grapevine that you are trying to fatten me up."

"Really?"

"No." Kate grabbed a dish towel and threw it at Paige. "And the proper response to that statement isn't 'Really?' The proper response would be 'That's crazy! I could never fatten you up. You are lithe and beautiful like a panther.' "

"Okay, panther-head, if I tell you that you are still skinny, will you tell me whether or not I still have a job?"

Kate sat down at the kitchen table, suddenly serious. "Honestly, he didn't say anything about you—and I asked. He said I wouldn't need makeup because I was just coming in for some sort of meeting."

"No scenes?"

"Not of the acting variety, but lord only knows what Sapphire has up her sleeve."

"Probably a leg of lamb," quipped Paige, lightening the mood.

"I just hope she doesn't hit me with it," said Kate.

"Or if she does, that she at least has the good grace to share it with you afterward. Remember how greedy she was with those lamb kebabs? You would have thought that somewhere on those industrial-size trays there was an extra kebab or two."

"Oh, don't remind me," said Kate, wrinkling her nose. "I can still smell lamb sometimes when I close my eyes at night. I think it is seared into my nasal passages. Why can't she ever go on a diet that smells good?"

"Beats me. Remember her Kombuchi tea phase, when the whole set was covered with Tupperware containers of big, slimy mushrooms that procreated like Trebles? It was like living in a giant petri dish."

Kate tried unsuccessfully to stifle her laugh in a failed attempt to keep coffee from shooting out of her nose. "Oh great," she said, grabbing a napkin to wipe her face. "Now I am going to be smelling coffee all day."

"Better than lamb."

"True," said Kate. "But not as good as chocolate."

"When have you ever had chocolate come out of your nose?"

"You don't want to know," said Kate, shaking her head earnestly. "I was young and he was Belgian. The details are too painful."

"Speaking of painful," said Paige, bringing them back to reality, "what do you really think is going on at work?"

Kate felt her stomach do a rather athletic gymnastics routine. "I don't know. It's probably another scheduling change. Maybe Sapphire has decided she wants to work only on alternate Thursdays during the year of the cow."

"It wouldn't surprise me. Do you want me to go with you for moral support?"

Kate was so touched by the offer that she got flustered. "Oh, I don't know. I mean, wouldn't it be boring for you?"

"Yes, it would be boring and painful and I would resent you forever," said Paige with a dramatic sigh. "That's why I offered. I am going for full-on martyrdom."

Kate smiled, her eyes filling with grateful tears. "Well, I wouldn't want to get in the way of your martyrdom."

"Thank you," said Paige, heading to the bathroom to get ready to go. She continued to talk while she walked down the hall. "Wait a minute—why am *I* thanking *you*? *You* should be thanking *me*. In fact, we should probably stop at a Barneys on the way so you can pick up a thank-you gift for me. I would like a pair of Manolo Blahniks, please."

"Never mind," called Kate through her laughter. "Your generosity is going to be too expensive for me!"

"Too late!" yelled Paige, just before she shut the bathroom door. "You are stuck with me!"

"Well, that sucks!" Kate yelled back.

But she was really thinking, *How did I get so lucky?*

30

Michael pushed back from his computer and stood up for the first time in six hours. His shoulders were tight, his neck was stiff, and his lower back ached . . . and he felt like a million—no, a bazillion—dollars. He felt like a writer.

With the exception of a brief sleep between midnight and three a.m., he had worked straight through the night, and he now had his first-ever completed outline for his first-ever script. He wanted to call someone to share his joy, but the only person in his life who knew him as a writer was Kate.

Oh, fuck it, he just plain wanted to call Kate.

He wanted to *see* Kate, to pick her up in a bear hug and twirl her around in a victorious dance that would, of course, culminate in a tender but sexy kiss. Or just a plain sexy kiss. At this point, it would take a mammoth amount of self-control to manage the tender part, but he had seen enough chick flicks to know that it was an important stop on the road to sexy town. Of course, he could go right for the *Officer and a Gentleman* version by picking her up and smashing her face in with a dramatic snog, but that always looked a little bit painful. Speaking of painful, all of this thinking about making out with Kate was giving him a very painful hard-on. So, the old saying was true: love hurts.

He laughed at his own play on words, wondering if Kate would be flattered or offended if he shared his sophomoric erection humor with her. *He* knew that his hard-on was the highest compliment, but women could be touchy about those things. It was probably not the best way to begin their first phone call. Sadly, his other opener was something along the lines of "So, I've been lying to you about pretty much everything. Want to grab a bite?"

Maybe it would be best to wait to call until he had some obviously good news, such as getting Sapphire off her back. If his meeting this morning went well, he just might be able to make that call this afternoon. He glanced at the clock to see how much time he had until his meeting—*oh shit!* He had forty-five minutes to shower, get dressed, and drive to Bob Steinman's Beverly Hills office. The drive alone could take forty minutes. Oh well, his grooming and wardrobe would have to suffer. Hopefully, Bob didn't use "cutest outfit" as the primary basis for his business decisions. Michael hit the print button on his computer and raced to take a shower while his outline printed out.

His outline.

He allowed himself the briefest moment to enjoy the sound of that wonderful phrase, then charged ahead into the frantic rush of trying to make it to his meeting as close to on time as the traffic on the Pacific Coast Highway would allow.

While in the shower, he heard both his cell phone and landline ringing insistently. He glanced at the caller IDs while he zoomed around his bedroom, shoving arms and legs into whatever clothing was easiest to grab, his only concession to fashion being that legs went into pants and arms into shirts. Hamilton Morgan's number came up on both phones. No doubt he wanted to put in his two cents before today's meeting. Well, he would just have to wait. This was Michael's meeting, and Hamilton and Sapphire would wait patiently until he rode in on his white steed to save the day for Kate.

And if that didn't work, Michael just prayed that this meeting wouldn't be a total career-ending, dream-killing disaster.

Either way, he decided that he wasn't going to call Hamilton until the meeting was over. Struggling writers had to take moments of feeling powerful wherever they could find them.

Two hours later Michael was leaving Bob Steinman's office, stunned. He ran the meeting through his mind, trying to piece together what had happened. An hour and ten minutes earlier he had literally run into the company's sleek outer lobby, doing his best to make up the time he'd lost in traffic. For a brief, terrifying moment he thought he might have missed the meeting altogether—a secretary saying "Let me see if I can find him" is never a great sign—but when Bob walked into the waiting room three minutes later, he was holding two take-out cups of coffee. He offered one of them to Michael and said, "Sorry I'm late. I thought I could feed my latte addiction and be back in time to meet you. Clearly, I was wrong." He smiled and pointed to the cup in Michael's hand. "That's a peace offering. I hope you like cappuccino."

"Love it," said Michael, trying to hide both his relief at escaping reproof for his own tardiness and his shock at witnessing a studio executive who made his own Starbucks runs.

"Great, then I will consider myself forgiven," Bob said, opening the nearly invisible door that led to the inner sanctum of executive offices. "Should we get started?"

"We should," said Michael, taking a deep breath and silently repeating his newly invented mantra to himself: *why the fuck not?*

Why the fuck not, indeed.

The rest of the meeting was a blur of laughing, nodding, and hand shaking. Bob loved the idea. He loved Sapphire (. . . in theory. Thankfully, they'd never met in person. That could happen *after* the contracts were signed . . .). He *especially* loved the outline. His only question was "How soon can I see a full script?"

I don't know, thought Michael. *How long does it take to write a script?* Luckily, the agent in him kicked in. "How soon do you want it?"

"As soon as you can get it to me. Is the writer available to start right away?"

"Yes, he is," said Michael, thrilled to be asked a question he actually knew the answer to. "I happen to know for a fact that he would love to get started on this as soon as possible."

"Great." Bob shuffled the pages of the outline, looking for something. "I didn't see a name here. Is this writer someone I should know?"

"That is a very good question," said Michael, stalling. "And one for which I have a very good answer . . ."

"Which is?" asked Bob, leading.

"Which is . . . that, yes, you should know him, but not because you've seen his work before. You should know him because I believe he has a very bright future." Knowing how much producers loved to claim discovery rights, he added, "You hold that future in your hands."

"He's never sold anything?"

"He hasn't sold anything *yet*. He is someone I've just discovered, but for whom I have very, very high hopes." Going in for the kill, Michael said, "Of course, we understand that his lack of experience affects his fee."

"Well," said Bob, smiling, "of course we want the best script, but saving money on a first draft never hurt anyone. I'll have business affairs contact you about the details, but I think we should count on moving ahead as fast as possible."

"Great," said Michael, physically gripping the edges of his chair to hold himself back from jumping up and down and letting loose an earsplitting victory cry. "I'll tell him to get started immediately."

"Good, because time is of the essence. It's a perfect twist of fate that you would bring this idea to me today. All of our research is telling us that this is the right time to do projects with female leads. Apparently, women make up half of the ticket-buying population." Bob chuckled at his witty observation, and Michael joined in with a hearty guffaw (a little brownnosing never hurt). "And the beauty of casting Sapphire Rose is that she not only brings with her a built-in audience of *Generations* fans, but she also helps ameliorate the highbrow factor that a biopic can sometimes project. You know what I mean?"

"Absolutely. There is very little worry of highbrow where Sapphire is concerned."

"Which is just perfect. We want megaplex, not art house. Am I right?"

"Right as rain, Bob."

"That's what I like to hear! Now, why don't you go out and light a fire under the ass of that writer of yours and I'll get my people started on the paperwork."

"Consider it lit," said Michael.

★　★　★

Michael now stood in front of the building that housed Cutting Edge Pictures, the company that, unbeknownst to them, had just hired him as a writer. Even as an unproven, fledgling writer, he could make one hundred thousand dollars for a completed first draft. Man, that number felt big now that he was on the other side of the artist/agent split. Ninety percent really was a lot better than ten. This explained all the big houses on the star our maps.

He was walk-skipping to his car, almost bursting from joy and the overriding feeling that all was right in the world, when he felt the vibration of his phone in his jacket pocket: Hamilton Morgan. Michael flipped open his phone, excited to have someone—anyone—with whom to share his great news.

"Hello, Hamilton!" he crowed.

"Hello, Michael," said Hamilton, sounding somber.

"Is something wrong?" asked Michael, hoping that Sapphire hadn't ruined both of their lives by deciding to enter a nunnery. Not very likely, granted, but if someone had recommended the Nunnery Diet, it was all too possible.

"No, I wouldn't say anything is *wrong,* per se, but these things are never easy. Tears always upset Sapphire."

"Why is she crying this time?" asked Michael, annoyed that her emotionality was ruining his victory buzz.

"Sapphire isn't crying, thank goodness."

Oh shit. "Who is crying, Hamilton?"

"Well, I'm afraid it's going to be my Sapphire pretty soon, because she's worried that she looks like the bad guy, but I keep telling her that—"

"Hamilton, stop!" He stopped. "I need you to slow down and tell me why someone might think that. What did she do?"

"She didn't do anything, Michael, except try to do her best to protect the future of *Generations,* which, as you know, is her whole life—outside of the profound love that she and I share, of course. Didn't you get my messages?"

Oh double shit. "What messages?"

"I left you several messages on your home and cell phones," said Hamilton. "To be honest, we're both a little peeved at you. This has been quite traumatic for Sapphire, and she really could have used your support, as could I, to be perfectly frank."

Wow, honest *and* frank. It was Michael's lucky day. "Hamilton, I apologize for missing your messages. I have been in meetings all morning with Bob Steinman."

"Oh!" said Hamilton, brightening. "With everything that has been going on around here, I completely forgot about our big meeting. Tell us the good news, buddy!"

Michael was so annoyed by Hamilton saying "our" meeting that he almost wished he *didn't* have good news . . . *almost.* "Actually, Hamilton, I do have good news. Very good news indeed. Bob is very excited about our project and very, very interested in Sapphire Rose for the lead. He wants to get started as soon as possible."

"Well, isn't that terrific!"

"I think so," said Michael modestly.

"Although the timing is a little awkward."

"What? How could the timing be awkward?" Michael asked, annoyed to have his news greeted by anything less than a victory parade in honor of the miracle he had just performed.

"Not awkward for *us,* Michael. For us, the timing is *brilliant.* The whole thing is brilliant!"

"That's what I thought," said Michael, trying "brilliant" on for size and finding he liked the fit.

"I just think it's going to be difficult for the group here at *Generations.* It's going to be quite a blow to lose Sapphire, too."

Oh no. "Sapphire, *too?*"

"Yes, so soon after Kate leaving. It's going to be tough for them to recover from that. Oh well," said Hamilton, changing gears, "I guess that's not our problem anymore, is it? I mean, now that we have a movie star client, right?"

"Right. Movie star client. But could we back up for just a minute here, Hamilton? Did you say Kate is leaving the show? Did she quit?" Michael held his breath.

"Yes. She's leaving the show to pursue other interests." *Oh, thank god.* "Or at least that's what the press release will say," Hamilton added.

Michael's heart sank. He knew that "leaving the show to pursue other interests" was code for fired/canned/kicked out on your proverbial ass. Poor Kate. "How did she take it?"

"She was sad, I think. There were some tears. I like to think that it helped to have me there, a friendly face and all."

"I'm sure having you there to share in her humiliation was like a warm blanket, Hamilton."

"I like to think so," said Hamilton. "Although she seemed resistant when I went to give her a hug."

"That's surprising," Michael said sarcastically.

"Not really," said Hamilton. "She never could accept my support. That is one of the things that drove us apart. She just couldn't accept affection."

"Yes, Hamilton, I can see how that would be difficult for you. Now, can we get back to the problem at hand?"

"What problem?" asked Hamilton, oblivious.

The problem of you being an insensitive fuck-head. "The problem of getting Kate her job back."

"Why would we want to do that?"

"Because with Sapphire leaving to pursue other interests, it's the right thing to do." Michael could tell from the silence on the other end of the phone line that Hamilton had no context for such high-minded ideals. He tried another tact: "Also, Sapphire has ownership in the show and you get a percentage of Kate's salary, so keeping the show on the air makes good financial sense."

"Ah, I see your point," said Hamilton finally. "She's already been fired, though. And I don't mind telling you that it was hard enough to convince the powers that be that it was in their best interests to get rid of her. It would be uncomfortable to go back in and ask them to change their minds."

"I think the last thing any of us wants is to make you uncomfortable, Hamilton." *Except maybe Kate, who just lost her job.* "But maybe this is worth the risk of being the tiniest bit ill at ease."

"Again, you make some very good points, Michael," conceded Hamilton. "And if this were just about me, I would agree with you. But we have to answer to a higher power."

"I'm pretty sure God would be all for Kate getting her job back."

"What does God have to do with this? I am talking about *Sapphire*," said Hamilton, as though Sapphire as deity was the most obvious concept in the world. "Actually, I should really go check on her. You know, she has not had an easy day, although your news about the movie will go a long way toward cheering her up. In fact, I am going to go tell her right now how well all of our hard work has paid off."

Michael didn't have time to be offended by the dial tone that took the place of good-bye or by Hamilton's rather liberal use of the word "our." He ran to his car and peeled out of his parking space, racing to get to the *Generations* set in time to try to reverse some of the damage caused by Hurricane Sapphire.

31

Kate sat on her little dressing-room couch, a half-full cardboard box of belongings on her lap. She was supposed to be packing up her personal items, but she felt incapable of standing up, much less moving objects from one place to another. She felt Paige's hand on her arm. "Are you okay?"

"Yes," she said vaguely. "I mean, I think so. Does this box weigh four thousand pounds? It feels like it does."

"I can imagine." Paige lifted the box off Kate's lap and put it next to them on the couch. "I think you are probably in shock or something. I am."

Kate felt tears gathering behind her eyes. "Did I just get fired?"

"That's what you said. I wasn't actually in the room."

"I wish you had been. Did I tell you that Hamilton tried to hug me?"

Paige couldn't help it—she laughed. "Yes, you did."

"Did I tell you that he was offended that I didn't want to hug him back?"

Paige laughed again. "Yes, you did."

"Is it just me, or is that fucking *whacked?*" Kate looked up with an expression of genuine curiosity.

"Yes, honey, it is fucking whacked." Paige reached up to brush Kate's hair out of her eyes. "This whole thing is fucking whacked."

"That's what I thought." Kate's voice sounded flat. "Was my mom in the room?"

"What? Why would your mom have been in the room?"

"Oh, I don't know. It just seems like she would have wanted to be there."

Paige leaned in close to Kate's face, looking for signs of a breakdown. "Kate, that doesn't make any sense."

"It makes as much sense as the rest of it." Paige sat back. Kate had her there. "I just think she would have wanted to be there to get her 'I told you so' in right away," Kate went on, offering a wan smile. "On the bright side, I guess that gives me something to look forward to."

"True," said Paige. "On the even brighter side, your cachet as an auction item has just fallen through the floor . . ."

". . . so that'll save some time," finished Kate, her smile widening.

"Exactly." Paige stood up and offered a hand. "Should we collect your oral-hygiene products and get out of here?"

Kate allowed herself to be pulled off the couch. "Shouldn't the fact that my life as I know it has just come crashing to a halt warrant a 'get out of flossing free' card?"

Paige took hold of both of Kate's arms and looked intensely into her face. "You can cry your eyes out. You can lie in bed for three weeks eating Krispy Kreme doughnuts and watching *True Hollywood Story.* You can even get your very own Home Shopping Network membership number, but I cannot allow you to ignore your dental health."

"How about my mental health?"

"Mental health is for sissies." Paige turned Kate so that she was facing the bathroom and handed her the box. "Now, get packing. We want to get to Krispy Kreme before all of the really disgustingly creamy, candy-coated doughnuts are gone."

Kate walked the three steps to the tiny bathroom. "Don't you have to work today?"

"No."

"I thought you had to come in to do extras for that restaurant scene."

"I did . . . until I quit."

Kate dropped the box into the miniature sink and turned to face Paige. "You *what?*"

"I quit."

"Oh no," said Kate desperately. "No, no, no—don't quit just because I got fired. It's not worth it. *I'm* not worth it."

"First of all," Paige said definitively, "you *are* worth it. Second, don't flatter yourself. I didn't quit because you got fired. This is not some misguided show of support. I just don't want to miss the doughnut extravaganza."

"Paige, be serious. Please." Kate felt too vulnerable to be teased anymore.

"Okay. In all seriousness, I quit because you were the only thing that made working here bearable. Besides, how long do you think it's going to take Sapphire to decide that having *me* here upsets her delicate constitution? It's just not worth the anxiety of waiting for the ax to fall."

Kate squinted at Paige, trying to figure out if she was telling the truth. Paige squinted back, mirroring her. Kate said, "I'm not going to share my doughnuts with you."

"I'm still quitting," said Paige, squinting harder.

"Okay, then." Kate broke the stare-down and turned back to the bathroom. "You have officially passed the comfort-food with-holding test. I am happy to inform you that you can now join the unemployed depressives."

"I'm so excited," said Paige, grinning. Kate glared at her. Paige immediately slouched and turned her mouth into a frown. "I mean, I am *so depressed.*"

"Much better," said Kate, laughing and continuing to pack. She picked up the few pens and notepads that were scattered around her trailer and tossed them into the box, along with the framed photographs of her parents (her mother's yearly start-of-production gift), and her toothbrush. Standing by the door with Paige at her side, she did a scan of the room that had been her home for two years. Why didn't she have more personal items to pack up? In the past week, she had moved out of her home and her dressing room, with just a few boxes and a couple of suitcases to show for it. Where was the evidence of her life? She felt Paige's gentle touch on her arm.

"Are you ready to go?"

"I guess so," she said, grateful for the feel of Paige's hand guiding her out the door. Without that proof of her physical being, she may have doubted that she existed at all.

32

Kate stepped out of her trailer into the brightness of the sunny afternoon, the light momentarily blinding her. When her eyes adjusted enough to take in the parking lot, she saw what she at first thought was a mirage.

"Michael?" she asked dubiously, half expecting the handsome man in the suit to tell her that she was mistaken, that he didn't know anyone named Michael. Instead, he stopped dead in his tracks, looking like a frightened child caught with a hand in the cookie jar.

"Kate," he managed, his eyes darting around rapidly. "I thought you'd left."

"You thought I'd *left?*" asked Kate, completely confused but thrilled to see him. "Why are you here? Did Paige call you and tell you to come?"

"No," said Paige from behind her. "I don't know why he's here. I don't even have his number."

"Then how did you know to come?" Kate looked at Michael with a look of such openhearted wonder that he was struck dumb. Where was a white horse when you needed one?

"Um, well, it's sort of a long story," he stammered, searching desperately for a way to confess to being a gutless liar that wouldn't immediately snuff out the admiration in Kate's eyes.

"Well, time is one thing I have a lot of," said Kate with a brave smile. "It's a job I lack." Saying the words out loud brought reality crashing back down on her, and her eyes filled with tears. Between the pain of her morning and the unexpected joy of seeing Michael, her emotions were a whirlwind.

"Oh, Kate," Michael said, wrapping her in a hug. He couldn't stand seeing her in pain, but he couldn't think of anything he could say that wouldn't cause her even more. He looked over Kate's shoulder and locked eyes with Paige. She, too, looked at him with a mixture of curiosity and hero worship. He offered her a weak smile, knowing that she wouldn't view him as a hero for long. He held Kate while she cried, allowing himself the indulgence of breathing in the scent of her hair and trying to commit to memory the feeling of her body close against his. Try as he might, he couldn't figure out a way to avoid this being the last time he would hold her, the last time she would turn to him with anything but anger and disappointment.

"*There* you are, Michael!" called a shrill voice from behind him, the accompanying clicking of stiletto heels removing any doubt as to whom the voice belonged to. He inhaled one more deep, heavenly breath of Kate's scent before turning from the entrance to face his fate.

Sapphire had apparently spotted Michael through her trailer window while she was somewhere in the middle of her beautifying process. Her hair was half in rollers, half teased almost straight up. She had one eye done in bright shades of lavender and one completely free of makeup. She looked like a half-man–half-woman character from a carnival. The female half looked a lot like Cruella de Vil.

"Where have you been? I have been waiting for you all day!" Sapphire fell into Michael's arms. Well, it would be more accurate to say that she fell into *Michael,* since his arms remained straight at his sides.

He turned his head away from the teased and perfumed mass that hung from his neck to look at Kate. Her eyes were still wet with tears and she looked completely lost. Behind her, Paige had clearly passed through the denial stage and was already closing in on anger. "I see you know Sapphire, Michael," she said. "That's interesting."

Michael turned his eyes back to Kate, desperately searching for his voice. His mind was racing, rifling through his few precious memories of Kate, of all the times he could have told her the truth but chose not to out of fear. Now all of those times came back to prosecute him, and he could see in Kate's face the jury waiting for him to take the stand in his own defense. He opened his mouth to speak, deciding that any half-assed defense was better than walking silently to the firing squad. "Kate, I—"

"Kate?" screeched Sapphire, finally finding the strength to disentangle her arms from around Michael's neck and stand on her own two feet. "Why are you talking to *Kate? I'm* the one you came here to see."

Kate looked from Michael to Sapphire and back again, bewildered. She searched his face, her beseeching vulnerability breaking Michael's heart. "I don't understand what's going on here, Michael."

Before he could answer, Sapphire broke in. "Why does it matter what *you* understand? You don't even work here anymore. *Hamilton!*" she called over her shoulder toward her trailer. "She's still *here!*" Hamilton's head appeared around the door, cell phone at his ear. He took in the scene, held up his free hand in a "just a second" gesture, and disappeared back into the safety of Sapphire's dressing room. Michael watched him slam the door, wondering if there was room in the trailer for him, too. When he turned back around, he faced three females in various stages of confusion and anger.

"Michael, why *are* you here?" asked Kate.

Paige stepped forward to stand next to her friend in a show of moral support. "Yes, Michael, I think we'd *all* like to know what's going on."

Sapphire looked at both of them with disgust. "What I would like to know is why you two are *still here*." She moved so that she was standing next to Michael and slid her arm through his. "And why you are talking to *my agent*."

If the world didn't literally stop on its axis, it did a very good impression. Kate gasped and took a step backward, almost losing her footing. Michael moved forward to help her but was stopped by Paige, who held out a warning hand toward him as she steadied her friend with her other arm. He finally found his voice, but all he managed was "Kate, I can explain . . ." before he realized that, in fact, he couldn't explain, not here in front of all of these people.

Sapphire snorted her disgust. "There is nothing to explain, Michael. She doesn't work here anymore, *I* do, and I need you to come take care of me." She tightened her grip on Michael's arm and turned him back toward her trailer, saying over her shoulder, "Let those two lesbians take care of each other."

"*Sapphire!*" scolded Michael, allowing himself to be pulled away from Kate in order to protect her from whatever other vitriol might pour out of Sapphire.

"What?" Sapphire asked innocently as they walked away. "It's true. I just feel bad for my Hamilton, wasting so much time trying to make a marriage work with that muff diver."

Michael turned back for one last look at Kate. Her shock made her look six years old. *I can explain,* he tried to say with his eyes. *I can fix this. Just give me some time . . .* Sapphire yanked his arm, pulling his gaze back to her and his body into her trailer.

★　　★　　★

Kate didn't move. "What just happened?"

"I really don't know," said Paige, moving forward to wrap a stabilizing arm around her. "Maybe God is starting up with the plagues again. Do you see any locusts or frogs?"

"It isn't funny," whispered Kate, and Paige felt Kate's shoulders begin to tremble as she surrendered to the tidal wave of emotions that had been building for the past week. Paige turned her toward the parking lot and half carried her to the car so she could have her well-deserved breakdown in peace.

"I'm sorry, honey," she said gently, holding Kate tighter. "I know it's not funny. It's not funny at all."

33

Michael slumped on the couch in Sapphire's trailer, numb to the manic chatter that surrounded him. Sapphire and Hamilton were quite proud of themselves—getting Kate fired and landing a possible movie deal were making this a banner day for them both. Michael could hear them prattling away near and at him, but he couldn't be bothered to make sense of anything they were saying. For once, he was grateful to both of them for their incredible narcissism: being heard didn't seem to be the point of their exercise. It was enough for each of them to be talking continuously and at full volume.

How had his day turned to such complete shit so quickly?

A few hours ago he had been reveling in his newfound status as an almost writer/white knight, preparing his brave stallion so he could gallop in and save the day for his lady love. Now he felt more like an incredibly depressed court fool, trapped for all eternity in the trailer/castle of King Bombast and Queen Narcissia.

A knock on the door brought the ego party to a standstill. Sam stuck his head in and started to remind Sapphire that she was needed on set. One look at her half hairdo and lopsided makeup application told him that that need would go unmet for the foreseeable future. Sam just sighed and closed the door, too upset about the news of Kate's firing to pretend to care.

"Don't you think you should get ready?" Michael asked, vaguely curious about how long her vanity would allow her to stay half done.

"What did you say, Michael?" asked Sapphire, momentarily halting her self-aggrandizing diatribe. "Did you say Bob Steinman is ready for me?"

Once again awed by her selective hearing, Michael said, "No, I asked when you were going to finish getting ready for work." She looked at him blankly. "Work. Here. Today. They are ready for you." He exaggerated his enunciation and slowed his speech dramatically in an attempt to be understood.

Instead of answering him, Sapphire looked to Hamilton and asked, "Do I have to?"

Unable to contain his annoyance, Michael snapped, "What do you mean 'Do I have to?' Of course you have to—it's your *job*."

Hamilton looked at Michael as though he had just struck an innocent child. "Now, Michael, I don't think there is any reason for such a tone." Sensing her advantage, Sapphire thrust out her lower lip and sniffled dramatically. "Oh, my poor, sweet baby," said Hamilton, crossing the room to take her in his arms. "He didn't mean it." He looked pointedly at Michael over her shoulder. "*Did you*, Michael?"

Looking at the grotesque tableau in front of him, Michael wondered how he had ended up there. Having spent his entire adult life trying to distance himself from his childhood, he was once again in the position of being asked to support the insane delusions of an unstable woman who had way too much power over his future. Without Sapphire, he had no production deal. And without a production deal, he had no way to help Kate.

"Of course he wants you to be happy, my darling," said Hamilton, in an attempt to cover Michael's silence. "That's all any of us wants."

Sapphire wasn't fooled. "I want to hear it from *him,*" she said, pointing at Michael, her annoyance at his reticence turning her voice cold and hard.

He just stared at them, unmoved.

"I'm sure he is just looking for the perfect words to describe how much he—"

"*Shut up, Hamilton!*" Sapphire moved away from her anxious boyfriend in order to stand directly in front of Michael, all pretense of little-girl vulnerability replaced by straight-backed imperiousness. "Michael, I need to know that you are on my side . . . *no matter what.*"

She said the last part with such intensity that Michael almost laughed. Instead, he sighed and said, "Sapphire, haven't I always taken care of you?"

She smiled and batted her eyelashes, reverting to her default personality of flirtatious, spoiled toddler. Behind her, Hamilton almost swooned with relief. "You see, darling, we are all your friends here. Michael was just teasing you."

"You silly-willy," she said, shaking her finger at Michael before turning away and heading to her mini refrigerator. She opened it and took out a giant chocolate bar, a large square of which she immediately popped into her mouth. "You shouldn't tease a woman on a diet. We can get cranky, you know."

Michael had to ask: "What diet allows you to have a chocolate bar the size of a child's torso?"

"The Chocolate Diet," said Sapphire and Hamilton at exactly the same time, both looking at him as if he were the stupidest person in the world. Then Sapphire added her life's motto: "Everyone who is anyone is doing it."

"Apparently, it's how Angie Jolie lost all of her baby weight so quickly," said Hamilton, reaching for a hunk of the gargantuan candy bar.

"Really?" Michael said, using their interest in the snack to cover his move to the door. "I was under the impression that it was her humanitarian work and parenting three children that helped *Angie* slim down."

"No," Sapphire said through cocoa-coated teeth. "Chocolate."

"Interesting," said Michael, feeling like he was sneaking out of a crack den. "Well, I'll be going now. I'll call you about, um, everything . . . soon."

He stood outside of her trailer, looking across the parking lot to where he had been embracing Kate just a few short minutes ago. It seemed like a dream—a very good, very beautiful dream, but a dream nonetheless. He knew he would probably never experience that joy again, that he didn't deserve to, but that didn't mean he couldn't do his best to play the role of the knight in shining armor behind the scenes. He squared his shoulders and took a deep breath before heading over to Jerry's office to do what he had done so many times before: plead Sapphire's case.

34

Paige and Kate rode home in silence, Kate staring out of the passenger-side window, her head resting on the cold glass. She felt as though all of the life had been drained out of her body, leaving a rag doll without the stuffing. When they pulled up in front of Paige's apartment, the short walk from the car to the front door looked insurmountable, like a trek up Everest. Paige placed a gentle hand on her shoulder.

"Come on, honey. Let's go in and get you settled on the couch. There is no reason you can't be depressed *and* comfortable."

"You go ahead," said Kate, cuddling up to her new best friend, the car door. "I'm good here."

Paige got out of the car and walked around to open the passenger door. Kate spilled out. "Fuck."

"Well, said," said Paige, dragging her friend to her feet and starting the slow walk to the front door. "I can see this is going to be a day of scintillating conversation."

"Who the fuck cares?" Kate looked and sounded like an old drunk, shuffling slowly up the path.

"Scintillating," repeated Paige, as they stepped up onto the porch. "Can you stand here on your own while I open the door?"

"Of course," Kate answered, but when Paige stepped away, she immediately sat on the ground. "What?" she snapped when Paige turned around a moment later. "You were gone *forever*."

"I turned around for roughly two-thirds of a second—" Paige started to argue but stopped herself. It was no fun to kick a wounded kitten. Instead, she opened the door and offered Kate a hand up. Kate reluctantly accepted her help and continued her Thorazine shuffle into the living room, where she promptly fell onto the couch, wrapping herself in a throw blanket. Paige perched on the edge of the cushion at Kate's feet. "Can I get you a cup of cocoa? Maybe a sandwich?"

Kate stared at her. "A sandwich? I'm not devastated enough for you? Now you want to fatten me up?"

"Oh dear," sighed Paige, standing up and walking to the kitchen. "Now I know what it's like to have a brokenhearted teenager with PMS and body dysmorphic disorder."

"You forgot unemployed!" yelled Kate.

"I also left out annoying!" Paige yelled back. "I was being kind!"

"Kind of *mean*, maybe!" called Kate, turning her body around until she was lying on her stomach facing the kitchen, the top of her head and eyes visible over the arm of the couch. She looked unbearably young and vulnerable.

"Oh, sweetie, you look like you are about five years old."

"I wish I were. Then none of this would have happened."

"That's true," said Paige, turning on the heat under the kettle and walking back into the living room, where she squeezed onto the couch next to Kate. "Of course, if you were five, I would be your real mother."

"Yeah, and if you were my real mother, you would be out shopping or golfing, so I would finally get some peace."

"Do you want some time alone?" asked Paige sincerely.

"Why?" asked Kate, resigned. "Do you have somewhere you need to go?"

"No," said Paige, settling deeper into her tiny corner of the couch. "I am exactly where I want to be." Kate smiled gratefully, relaxing back into the cushions. As if on cue, the kettle began to scream its earsplitting whistle. "Will you be okay while I go throw that horrible thing out the window?" asked Paige.

"I can't hear you over the hideous whistling," Kate said, laughing. "Go throw it out the window and then come back and talk to me."

Paige went to the kitchen and poured two cups of strawberry vanilla tea, thinking that the closer she could get to the taste of Kool-Aid, the more comforting it would be. She also filled a plate with crackers, cheese, and grapes on the off chance that Kate would be willing to eat something. Feeling her own stomach growl at the sight of sliced cheddar, she knew it wouldn't go to waste.

She put the plate down on the coffee table in front of Kate and was surprised to see her pick up a slice of cheese and pop it into her mouth. Her shock must have shown on her face, because Kate said, "What?"

"Nothing," Paige lied, and then amended it with "I don't think I have ever seen you eat cheese."

"Well, get used to it," said Kate, grabbing another slice and following it up with a handful of grapes. "I am done dieting. Dieting doesn't fucking work."

Paige looked at her friend's ultrathin figure and raised her eyebrows. "I would say it worked a little *too* well for you."

"No, you don't get it," said Kate, the energy of her epiphany pulling her into a sitting position. "I am thin, as thin as I ever wanted to be. I am also unemployed, heartbroken, and smack-dab in the middle of a nasty, humiliating divorce."

"Come on, Kate, don't beat yourself up."

"I don't want to anymore, that's my point. It doesn't do any good to beat myself up—or rather, starve myself down. *It doesn't fucking work!*" she shouted.

"*Why are you yelling?*" Paige shouted back.

Kate stood up from the couch. "*Because I am done being quiet and small and . . . and . . . inoffensive!*"

Paige jumped up to face her and screamed at the top of her lungs, "*I think that is just great!*"

"*Great!*" screamed Kate.

"*Really great!*" screamed Paige.

"*Can we stop yelling now?*" yelled Kate.

"Oh, please," said Paige, falling back onto the couch. "I am exhausted."

"*You're* exhausted? I just had a life-altering revelation."

"Really? How did I miss that?"

"Oh, shut up," said Kate, plopping down next to Paige. "You never miss anything."

"So true," said Paige sagely. "But just so I can be sure that *you* understand . . . what did you learn?"

"I learned that I can be the thinnest, nicest, most obedient girl in the world and I can still lose everything."

"So?"

"So . . . I may as well just go ahead and live my own fucking life."

"Exactly," said Paige, smiling. "But I have to ask—is the swearing going to be a big part of your new personality?"

"Fuckin' A."

"Charming."

"*Fucking* charming."

Paige leaned over and moved the cheese tray closer to Kate. "If I offer you cheese, will you stop swearing for a minute?"

"Maybe while I am fucking chewing," said Kate, popping a slice of cheddar into her mouth. "Mmmmm, cheese is good."

"Isn't it? I remember the day I decided to stop dieting and how shocking it was when the world didn't stop spinning and I didn't balloon to three thousand pounds."

"Oh god," said Kate, halting her next chunk of cheese halfway between the plate and her mouth. "Did you have to say 'three thousand pounds'?"

"I said I *didn't* balloon to thousands of pounds, you loony. You need to hear complete sentences."

Kate reluctantly took a bite and chewed thoughtfully. "What I need is a job."

"Honey, maybe what you need is a rest," said Paige kindly. "I'm sure you have enough money saved to buy yourself a little bit of time to process everything that has happened."

"I don't know."

"*I* know," said Paige definitively. "You need time."

"I'm not arguing that," said Kate. "But I don't know if I have any money."

"How could you not know if you have any money? Of course you have money. You've been a star on a hit TV series for almost three years."

Kate shrugged. "Hamilton handled all the money. I haven't signed a check since the show started."

Paige sat back, stunned. "What about the house? You must own half of the house."

"I think it's leased."

"You *think* it's leased? You don't know?" asked Paige, aghast.

"Don't be mad at me," Kate said in a small voice. "I already feel like an idiot."

"I'm sorry." Paige reached out and put her hand on Kate's knee. "I've been on my own and on a budget for so long; it's just hard to imagine not knowing where every penny goes."

"I know. It's embarrassing. It's like I was Hamilton's toy instead of his wife. Like he controlled my money, food, and career, and in exchange I sat on his shelf waiting for him to play with me." Kate covered her face with her hands and her head fell back against the pillows. "Ugh," she groaned. "That makes me sick. I went straight from being my mom's doll to being Hamilton's doll.

That's pathetic." She dropped her hands and looked at Paige. "I almost went right into being Michael's doll."

"Give yourself a break, Kate. You don't know that that's what would have happened with Michael. He seemed really different."

Tears filled Kate's eyes. "Yeah, he did. Until he turned out to be a total lying bastard."

"I'm not saying he was *perfect*," said Paige, happy to see a tiny smile emerge on her friend's sad face. "Just that you guys seemed to have a sweet connection."

"Yeah, we did. I was really falling for Michael the unemployed writer," said Kate wistfully. "It's Michael the backstabbing agent of the horrible woman who stole my husband and got me fired whom I have issues with."

"Your problem is that your standards are too high."

"So true," said Kate. "Unless he is a philanderer or a liar, I don't even give a guy the time of day."

Paige laughed. "Maybe it is time to rethink your dating criteria."

"You think?"

"I do," said Paige earnestly. "First we are going to find out if you have any money, then we are going to spend all of it on intense, cultlike therapy for you."

"Or clothes?"

"You're right. Clothes are a better investment." Paige thought for a moment, her right index finger held against her pursed lips. Then she nodded somberly and added, "Clothes and infomercial skin-care products."

"We are going to be rich in no time," said Kate, laughing.

"Just follow my lead, little lady," said Paige, waving her arm around her funky little apartment. "And all of this could be yours."

Kate wondered if Paige had any idea how desperately she wanted exactly that.

35

Michael sat in his car in the parking lot next to the *Generations* soundstage, too exhausted to start the engine. He stared at the set of keys dangling from the ignition but couldn't gather the strength necessary to raise his arm and turn the key the quarter turn it required to properly do its job. Its job . . .

His job.

He was just doing his job. It was his job to work for his client, to make sure that she was taken care of, coddled, honored in a way that made it possible for her to bestow the gift of her great talent on the world.

Michael opened his car door and leaned out, feeling as though he was going to throw up one of the fourteen cups of coffee that had been his sole sustenance on this glorious day. He dropped his head onto the shelf made by his arm braced against the open car door and stared at the dirty concrete of the parking lot. The nausea passed and he found that he missed it—at least it had been a feeling. Now he just felt numb. Numb with a touch of sadness and a smidgen of self-loathing.

36

"Your purse is vibrating," said Paige, pointing to Kate's loudly buzzing brown suede handbag.

"I know," said Kate, ignoring her insistent cell phone and picking up a typical lobby magazine. After their talk the day before, Paige had offered to accompany Kate to her lawyer's office so that she could find out if she had enough money to relax for a while or if she would have to start doing street theater. Or porn. Her purse buzzed again.

"It's making me batty."

Kate put down her magazine and looked at Paige earnestly. "First of all, no one—or no thing—can make you batty unless you let it." Paige rolled her eyes and snorted with disgust at her friend's cheesy psychoanalysis. "Second," continued Kate, ignoring the miniature tantrum, "I am not going to answer the phone, because it is either my mother, who actually *does* have the ability to make me batty, or Jerry, who is no doubt calling so that I can make him feel better about firing me. Either way, the buzzing is much less annoying than answering."

"Maybe it's Michael," offered Paige hopefully.

"How could it be Michael? He doesn't even have my cell phone number."

"He could have gotten it from Hamilton."

Kate stared at Paige, stunned. "There is so much wrong with that statement."

"I'm sorry," Paige said. "You're right. I shouldn't have brought up Hamilton."

"Or Michael."

"Okay."

"I mean, why would I want to talk to him, anyway?" asked Kate, getting wound up. "Why would he even be calling? So that I can comfort him through his realization that he is a lying scum?"

"Maybe he has a good explanation for what happened."

"A good explanation? Are you high?"

"Nope. Eight years clean and sober."

"Cute," said Kate dryly.

"Aren't I?" asked Paige, batting her eyelashes.

"No!" snapped Kate. "You are so *not* cute. And you are so not helping. Here I am, trying to be tough and cool, and you are telling me to talk to the guy whom I am trying to be tough at!"

"Tough *at?*"

"You know what I mean!"

"I do," said Paige gently, reaching a hand out to touch Kate's arm. "I didn't mean to mess with your head. It's just that he seemed so sweet and you were so excited about him."

"Well, judging from my track record with men, maybe the fact that I was excited about him was a bad sign."

"Maybe," agreed Paige. Under her breath, she said, "But I don't think so."

"What?" asked Kate, but before Paige could fumble through an answer, the receptionist called them into Frank Gilman's office.

"Hello, Kate," Frank said, holding open the door to his office. He shook her hand warmly, avoiding the standard Hollywood air kiss and half hug, then turned to Paige. "I'm Frank Gilman."

"Paige Carter. Good to meet you."

"Okay," he said, gesturing to a small couch and settling into the chair across from it. "First of all, I'd like to say that it's nice to see you, Kate. It's been a long time since you've been here in the office."

"Yes, I'm sorry about that. Hamilton sort of took over a lot of stuff."

"There's no need to apologize. I'm just saying it's good to see you, although from our phone conversation I gather this is not just a social call."

"Well, I guess you could say that." Kate paused to collect herself. "My husband left me and I lost my job."

"I'm sorry to hear that," Frank said, admirably calm. "Now, what questions do you have for me?"

"She wants to know if she will be living on my couch for the rest of her life," said Paige.

"I see," said Frank, reaching for a file folder on his desk. "I don't think you need to worry about that."

"What do I need to worry about?" asked Kate, her fear making it difficult to breathe.

"Well, first of all, you need to worry about how you are going to spend the money that NBC owes you."

"For the last episode?"

"No, for the next—how many episodes do you have left for the season?"

"I don't have any episodes left to do. They fired me for annoying Sapphire Rose."

Frank started to laugh, but when Kate and Paige did not, he asked, "Are you serious?"

"She is," said Paige. "It is as true as it is stupid. And they have eight episodes left to do this season." She answered his unspoken question with "I do her makeup on *Generations*. Well, I did do her makeup, but I quit in a show of respect. And because I forgot that I am not independently wealthy." She turned to Kate. "Can I sleep on your couch?"

Kate smiled. "If I can afford a couch, you can sleep on it."

"Unless there are gambling debts I don't know about, you can afford a couch for each of you," interjected Frank. "Your contract is pay or play, meaning that you get paid whether they use you or not."

"Really?" asked Paige. When Frank nodded, she added, "That rocks."

"It *super* rocks," said Kate, breathing in air and relief.

"So, you are making, I believe, fifty thousand dollars per episode this season?"

"Yes," said Kate.

"Holy shit," said Paige. "I'm going to have to be a lot nicer to you."

"So," continued Frank, "eight episodes times fifty thousand is four hundred thousand dollars."

Paige turned to Kate. "I am so charging you couch rental."

"Now, obviously, that's pretax, precommissions, but your net should be about two hundred thousand dollars."

"Wow," said Kate. "That is . . . that's just great."

"What about her divorce?" asked Paige. "Will she get anything from that?"

"Not immediately," said Frank, rifling through the open file folder. "After you called, I had Richard send over all of your financials and—"

"Who's Richard?" asked Paige.

"My business manager," answered Kate.

"I thought Hamilton managed all of your money."

"Him and Richard," Kate said.

Paige fell back into her corner of the couch, overwhelmed. "*Jeez*, you have a lot of people."

"Anyway," Frank said, getting the meeting back on track, "the simple truth is that you and Hamilton do not have much in the way of savings. Your house is leased, so there is no equity there, and most of your salary went right into his business. Also, as your manager at the time of the contract, he is entitled to receive ten percent of your payout from NBC."

"Well, that sucks," said Paige.

"Perhaps, but that is the law," said Frank.

"Then the law sucks."

"Well, I can see why you would think that, but let me explain the other side of the coin: just as Hamilton 'owns' a part of Kate's contract, Kate has a real case for part ownership of Hamilton's business."

"What does that mean?" asked Kate.

"It means that you may very well be entitled to a percentage of his earnings as well."

"So, she gets ten percent of *his* ten percent of *her* income?" asked Paige, confused.

"No," said Frank with a chuckle. "Although that would be interesting, wouldn't it?"

Kate was too nervous to join in the laughter. "Frank, what does it *mean?*"

"Well, it means that if the court agrees that you have basically bankrolled his business, which should be fairly easy to prove, since yours is the only traceable income, you may be entitled to a percentage of his income in perpetuity—and certainly to a piece of any business deals that were agreed to during the course of your marriage."

"Wow, that's great," said Paige.

"Yeah," snorted Kate, "until you realize that I'm his only client."

"No, you aren't," said Paige, grinning. "You are forgetting Sapphire Rose."

"Oh my god," gasped Kate, the pieces falling into place. "Does that mean that I could get a percentage of Sapphire's earnings?"

"If he was in business with her before your divorce, you have a very good chance, yes," said Frank.

"Well, then I wish her all of the success in the world," said Kate. "And today, I actually mean it."

"Ditto," said Paige. "Although I also wish for her to lose all of her toes in a freak lawn-mowing accident."

"I didn't hear that," said Frank.

"Do you need me to say it louder?"

"No." He laughed. "I just need you to stay away from Home Depot."

"That, sir, may be the easiest promise I have ever made."

"So, are we done here?" asked Kate.

"For now," said Frank, standing up and offering his hand. "My secretary will set up another appointment so that we can go over everything in greater detail, but I think we have covered the important points. Do you feel better?"

"Much," Kate said, gathering her things. "Thank you, Frank."

"My pleasure," he said warmly.

Kate turned to Paige and said, "Ready to go?"

Paige stood but made no move to leave. "Actually, I have a question for Frank, if that's okay."

"Sure," said Frank and Kate simultaneously.

Paige hesitated and then turned to Kate. "Um . . . is it okay if I meet you in the car?"

★   ★   ★

Kate was on page forty-three of her car's owner's manual when Paige knocked on her window.

"Finally!" snapped Kate, trying not to sound as pathetically hurt and left out as she felt. "Where have you been?"

"Having sex on your lawyer's desk," said Paige, sliding gracefully into the passenger seat and buckling her seat belt.

Kate gasped. "You liar!"

"A: I am offended," said Paige, looking offended, "and B: of course I am lying. What do you think I am? A slut?"

Kate raised her eyebrows. "Do you really want me to answer that?"

"No, I suppose I don't. I never should have told you about that Christmas party. I still believe that I would have held on to my honor had it not been for those musical panties."

"They are the devil's workshop."

"So true," said Paige, nodding wisely.

Kate waited patiently for roughly three seconds before blurting, "So, are you going to tell me what happened in there or not?"

"Man, you are like a dog with a bone!"

"Ruff, ruff," said Kate dryly. "Now *spill*."

"Fine. Mr. Gilman and I are going to have lunch to discuss a business idea I have."

"Uh-huh," said Kate dubiously. "Business or *bid*-ness?"

"Business," said Paige. "What's with you and the smut talk?"

"Oh, I don't know. Honestly, I have no idea what I'm saying half the time right now. I feel like I'm still in shock or something."

"You probably are," said Paige. "I mean, how could you *not* be in shock after everything you have been through this past week? My God, it's a miracle you aren't curled up in the fetal position, rocking back and forth and humming incoherently."

"That's a nice image."

"Isn't it?" Paige laughed. "Sorry about that. Believe it or not, my intention was to compliment you on how well you are holding up in the face of an extraordinary amount of stress."

"Oh, well, in that case, thank you."

"You're welcome."

After a few minutes Kate said, "I really don't feel that strong."

"That's okay," said Paige, reaching over and placing a comforting hand on Kate's shoulder.

"And I really am sad about Michael."

"Of course you are," said Paige gently.

"It's so stupid. I mean, I only knew him for about a minute and a half, but I felt like he really *got* me." Kate sighed. "Of course, it was probably all lies. He probably only talked to me to get information for Sapphire." She dropped her head onto the steering wheel. "I am such an idiot."

"Oh, honey, you are *not* an idiot. And I don't think you were the victim of a spy plot, either. Did you see the expression on his face yesterday? He was devastated. He looked like an animal with his paw caught in a trap—"

"Sapphire's trap," interrupted Kate.

"Yes, Sapphire's trap. But for all we know he is chewing off his arm as we speak."

"Doubtful," said Kate. "He needs both of his arms to carry all the money he makes off her."

"All I'm saying is that we don't know the whole story."

"Maybe," allowed Kate. "Can we change the subject now? This is too depressing."

"As a matter of fact, my newly wealthy friend, there is something I wanted to discuss with you."

"Paige, I am *way* ahead of you," said Kate, reaching into the backseat for her purse. "I need to pay you rent and back rent and give you money for food and—"

"Would you stop it?" Paige grabbed Kate's hand before she could get out her checkbook. "I don't want rent money. I have a business proposition for you."

"Really?" asked Kate, surprised and flattered.

"Really," said Paige, and then proceeded to share her idea with an increasingly excited Kate, both of them ignoring the insistent buzzing coming from Kate's brown suede bag.

37

When Paige and Kate pulled up in front of Paige's house, they couldn't even see the front door—it was completely blocked by a gargantuan bouquet of roses.

"Wow," said Kate as they got out of the car. "Who are those from?"

"I don't know," said Paige, reaching for the card. "They're so beautiful, it hardly even matters. I think you may be sleeping on the couch tonight."

"I already sleep on the couch."

"Really?" asked Paige, opening the envelope. "That seems wrong, somehow. I think I may need to move you to the porch."

"You spoil me," said Kate.

"I'm not the one who is spoiling you," said Paige, handing over the card.

Kate's breath caught in her throat when she saw the name at the bottom: Michael. She looked at Paige, who smiled at her before opening the door and going inside, leaving Kate alone on the porch. She sat down on the step to read.

Dear Kate,
I don't have words to express how sorry I am. I am not
sorry for the time I had with you, but for the price I
must pay for my deception. I suppose I was trying to
present a version of myself that felt worthy of you. I
don't know how I missed the fact that liar was probably
not high on your list of positive attributes. I know that
saying I'm sorry doesn't fix the pain that I caused you
during an already painful time, but nonetheless I am
sorry. I do want you to know that the version of myself
that I presented to you wasn't a thoughtless affectation
but the man I have always wanted to be. Your
authenticity and honesty are inspiring. I hope one day to
be deserving of those titles. And of you. I think of you all
day, every day.
Michael

Kate stared at the card. *Now what?*

The door opened as Paige stuck her head out. "You okay?"

Kate looked up. "I really don't know."

"Are you hungry?"

"I am," said Kate, surprised. "That's weird."

"That's healthy," said Paige, pulling Kate up onto her feet and heading back into the apartment.

"I think I have weird and healthy all mixed-up," said Kate, stopping to pick up the flowers.

"So does everybody," said Paige. "Only the truly disturbed think they are not weird."

"That's ridiculous."

"It is not. Everyone in the world thinks that they are a big, dark, embarrassing secret, but the simple truth is that most of us just hate our bodies or secretly believe that nobody loves us."

Kate knew there was some truth in what Paige said, but she

also feared it was too good to be true. "What if you are the one person who is really, truly unlovable?"

"Are you Ted Bundy?"

"No," laughed Kate.

"Then don't worry about it."

"Come on, don't you think there is a gray area between serial killer and worthy of love?"

"Honey, sit down." Paige pulled out a chair at the little breakfast table and leaned into Kate. "I read Michael's note."

"I wasn't talking about Michael," protested Kate.

"Of course you weren't," said Paige, her voice dripping with mock sincerity, "but bear with me for a minute. I'm not excusing the fact that he lied to you or that he lied to you at a very bad time, but I do understand why he did it: he is just as afraid as the rest of us that he isn't enough, that the ways he has traded himself for money or security make him unlovable. One of your favorite things about him was that you thought he didn't recognize you from your show. Why? Because you wanted to be seen for *you*, not for what you do for a living and all of the baggage that comes along with that. He wanted the same thing. I'm not telling you to forgive him. It's up to you to decide if you can learn to trust him again. I'm just telling you that most of us are afraid that we are not as lovable as we really are."

"I find that a little hard to believe. *Most* of us?"

"Absolutely," said Paige, getting up and going back to the counter to work on the tuna salad she was fixing. "There may be three or *possibly* four people who got everything they needed as children and have grown up to believe that they are perfect and worthy of love all the time, but I like to believe that those people are boring and that they secretly wish that their lives could be spiced up with some angst and self-doubt."

"Personally, I'd like a little less spice with my angst."

"Me, too. Truthfully, if I am ever lucky enough to have children, I hope that they are completely boring and well adjusted, even if they *are* less fun at the dinner table."

Kate sat quietly for a few minutes, deep in thought. "I just don't know if I can trust him."

Paige brought the two plates of salad over and sat down. "I don't know if you can either, or if you should. First you need to learn to trust yourself, and then it matters a lot less what anyone else does."

"Okay . . . and how do I learn to trust myself? Is there a pill I can take or something?"

"No—unfortunately, pills don't work. Trust someone who has tried every conceivable combination."

"I'm guessing you are going to burst my bubble about alcohol being the road to high self-esteem, too."

"Well, my experience is that alcohol did work . . . for a minute. But somehow I always ended up with my head in the toilet, which was not a real confidence builder."

"Thanks for the nice visual," said Kate, laughing. "Do you have any *real* advice?"

"My first advice is to eat this yummy lunch I have prepared," said Paige, handing her a fork. "Then I think you and I should start writing out a business plan, and pretty soon we will be so busy doing important things that we won't have time to beat ourselves up."

"Oh, I don't know. I think one must always find time for that which is really important."

"Do you want to know what I think?" asked Paige.

"Probably not," said Kate, laughing.

"I think one must shut up and eat."

So they did.

★　　★　　★

Three hours later, Paige and Kate were downright giddy with excitement. The more they talked about Paige's idea of opening a small furniture and design shop, the more enthusiastic they became. Kate was thrilled at the prospect of some time away from the camera, and the idea of spending that time driving around to small-town swap meets collecting inventory with Paige sounded almost too good to be true.

"Oh my god," said Kate, stretching her arms above her head and sighing contentedly. "If this works, I will never have to be photographed wearing lingerie again."

"At least not until we shoot our ad campaign," chided Paige.

"Would you really do that to me?" asked Kate.

Paige nodded. "If I thought it would bring in a wealthy clientele, I would post pictures of you naked with farm animals."

"So, basically, your plan for bringing in upscale customers for our new design business involves photographing me naked, sitting on a donkey?"

"Yes. I see a large mural."

"Wow. I am so blessed to be working with such an astute businesswoman."

"Stick with me, kid, you'll go places—" Paige's very bad Jimmy Cagney impression was cut short by Kate's buzzing handbag. "Okay," said Paige, turning serious, "if you don't answer that, I am going to flush it down the toilet. That buzzing is making me mental."

"Okay," said Kate calmly. "Flush it."

"Answer it!" yelled Paige.

"No!" Kate yelled back.

"Why not?"

"It might be Michael," admitted Kate, "and I don't think I can face talking to him."

Paige reached into the purse and yanked out the vibrating phone. *"Caller ID!"* she shouted, holding the display up in front of Kate's face.

"Oh, right," said Kate meekly, taking the phone. "You know, Hamilton always complained about how technologically challenged—"

Paige threw up her hands in disgust. *"Answer it!"*

"Fine," said Kate, looking at the display before flipping open her phone. It was the number for the *Generations* production office. *Great,* she thought, *more bad news.* She answered with a resigned "Hello?"

"Kate! Hi there! It's Jerry!"

"Hello, Jerry." She shot Paige a scathing look for forcing her to take the call. Paige smiled guiltily and skulked into the kitchen.

"Well, aren't you a difficult lady to get on the phone. I'm not afraid to tell you that you had us all a little worried over here on your old stomping grounds!"

"I'm not suicidal, Jerry," said Kate, annoyed beyond politeness. "So now that I've allayed your fears, I guess we can both go on with our lives. Good-b—"

"Wait! Don't hang up, Kate! It took me too darn long to track you down!"

"Jerry, you just fired me two days ago. That's hardly enough time to send out a search party."

"Oh, I know, I know." He chuckled nervously. "It's just been a crazy couple of days here and I really expected to hear back from you sooner. Did you get any of my messages?"

Kate was in no mood to apologize for not checking her voice mail. "Why don't you just tell me why you are calling, Jerry?"

"Well, Kate, as I said in my messages, Sapphire has decided to leave the show."

"What?" Kate blurted out loudly, enough to bring Paige running in from the kitchen. For her benefit, Kate repeated, "Sapphire is *leaving the show?"*

"Holy shit!" whispered Paige, dropping into the chair next to Kate and leaning in close to listen in on the call.

"Yes," continued Jerry. "Apparently, she has her heart set on doing some movie about Vivien Leigh. She decided she has to leave immediately to 'begin her process,' whatever the hell *that* means. I'm sorry to use that kind of language, Kate, but this has come as quite a shock to us all, especially after everything we did to make her happy."

"Like *firing* me?" asked Kate, earning her a thumbs-up from Paige.

"Well, yes, that may have been our biggest mistake."

"Uh, *yeah,*" blurted Paige.

"What was that, Kate?" asked Jerry.

Kate smacked Paige before answering. "I said, *yeah*, that certainly seems to have been a mistake, Jerry, but I still don't really know why you are calling me."

"Well, that's the good news!"

"What's the good news, Jerry?" asked Kate, fearing that she knew what he was going to ask.

"We want you back!"

"*Do* you, now?" asked Paige dryly.

"We do!" said Jerry energetically.

Kate's heart sank. She felt as though she were being welcomed back into the brawny arms of an abusive ex-boyfriend. She thought about how happy she had been just a few short minutes ago when she was planning her new venture with Paige. How joyful she felt thinking about spending her days running her own business, shopping and creating designs with her friend, away from the critical public eye. Then she thought about early call times at *Generations* and the endless hours wasted waiting for so many things that were out of her control. She didn't want to go back to feeling that powerless. She didn't want to go back, period.

"Kate? Are you there?" asked Jerry, his enthusiasm giving way to the intense insecurity that was always lurking right beneath the surface.

"Yes, I'm here."

"Well, what do you think of my great news?" He sounded like a cheerleader rooting for the losing team—forced and desperate.

Paige gestured for Kate to cover the mouthpiece. "It's okay if you want to go back," she said. "Don't worry about the shop. We can still go to flea markets on weekends, and we can use all of the cool stuff we find to decorate the wonderful place you buy with all your new loot."

Deeply touched by Paige's generosity, Kate covered her vulnerability by saying, "Are you kicking me out?"

"Never," said Paige. "I'm just hoping that you will buy a place on the beach and let *me* sleep on *your* couch instead."

"Hello? *Hello?* Kate? Are you there?" Kate rolled her eyes at Jerry's growing panic.

"Yes, Jerry, I'm here. I'm just thinking."

"Thinking about how fast you are going to say yes, I hope. Ha ha."

"Actually, no," said Kate.

"No?" squeaked Jerry, his voice almost shaking. "You don't mean that, Katie-Kate. I mean, what choice do you have?"

That did it. "You know something, Jerry? I actually have a lot of choices. And right now I am choosing to *not* go back into a situation where I ended up feeling powerless, used, and betrayed most of the time."

"*Wow,*" whispered Paige.

"Wow," said Jerry a beat later, as always a little bit behind the crowd. Then, under his breath, he said, "I guess he was right."

"What?" asked Kate, both she and Paige straining to make out what he had said.

"Nothing." Jerry sighed deeply, then continued. "We really need you, Kate."

"Maybe you should have thought about that sooner, Jerry." Blown away by Kate's newfound assertiveness, Paige was thrusting her fist into the air and doing a spastic, silent victory dance.

"What if we were to offer you more money?"

Paige leaned into the phone and said, "We're listening."

Kate jabbed her with an elbow. "It's not about the money," she said, ignoring Paige's wide-eyed, openmouthed attempts at communication.

"I know," said Jerry, resigned. "I know that you were not treated as well as you should have been."

"You *think?*" blurted Paige, earning another elbow jab.

"I do," he said. "And I am truly sorry for that."

"Sure, now you are," Paige murmured.

"What was that, Kate?"

"Nothing, Jerry." Kate covered the mouthpiece and hissed, "Could you please be quiet?" at Paige, who just shrugged and smiled. Kate shook her head and said, "Anyway, Jerry, I appreciate your apology and your offer, but I just can't see putting myself back in that position."

"Well . . . what if I could offer you *more* than money?"

"What do you mean?" asked Kate, trying not to laugh at Paige's raised eyebrows and thrusting pelvis.

"Well, what if you came back as an actor . . . *and* a producer?"

Kate couldn't believe her ears. "A producer?"

"Yes. I am offering you a producer position, with all that that entails."

Kate covered the mouthpiece and whispered to Paige, "What does that entail?"

"Being in charge of things and people and stuff," whispered Paige quickly. "You'll be brilliant. Find out how much it pays."

"Kate, are you there?"

"Yes, Jerry, I'm right here. I know I said it's not about the money, but just so I have all of the facts, is there a pay raise with the new position?"

"Yes, of course. There is a twenty-five thousand dollar fee per episode."

Kate and Paige silently screamed at each other: *OH MY GOD!*

"I see," said Kate calmly.

"Here's the thing, Kate," said Jerry, sounding more desperate by the minute. "I really shouldn't tell you this, but we need you. You and Sapphire were the show, and with both of you gone, the truth is, we've got nothing. I know you probably have a lot of offers already, but I'm hoping none of them have offered you the chance to have a real say in how a show is run."

Holy shit, mouthed Paige. *I know*, mouthed Kate. She said into the phone, "I'm going to need to give this some thought, Jerry. Can I call you back?"

"Of course . . . but could you make it as soon as possible? I'm really on pins and needles here."

"Understood. I'll call you back within the hour," said Kate, somehow succeeding in keeping her voice level. "I just need to discuss my options with my people." Paige pointed to herself and mouthed, *Your people?* Kate grinned broadly and nodded, then said, "I do have one question, Jerry."

"Of course," he said.

"As a producer, would I have a say in the budget for the hair and makeup department?"

"Among other things, yes, of course."

Paige thrust her fist into the air again, this time in a victory salute, and Kate did her best to keep her voice neutral as she said, "That is good to know, Jerry. I'll call you back within the hour with my answer."

Kate closed the phone and placed it carefully on the table. She and Paige sat quietly for a moment staring at it, then looked at each other, grinned, and let out an eardrum-bursting victory roar.

38

Three short days later, Kate stood outside of the conference room at the *Generations* offices, scared to go in. As the most recent addition to the *Generations* producing team, she was required to attend the weekly production meeting, during which scheduling, budgets, and any special details of the episodes were discussed. She clutched her script tightly in her damp hand and snuck a peek into the window, hoping to see a friendly face among those gathered around the long conference table. She had been standing in the same spot for ten full minutes. If she couldn't force her feet to move in the next five, she would be late for her first day at her new job. She willed her body to move through the door, but she was frozen with anxiety.

What if her fear that she didn't belong there was echoed back to her by the twenty people already established around the table? What if they thought she was just a stupid actress, overstepping her bounds and stealing power that wasn't hers? What if—

"Good morning, Kate! It is so great to have you here!" Claire, the head of the wardrobe department, interrupted Kate's self-punishment fest with a warm hug. "We are all so excited to have you back and to have you here at this meeting!" She leaned in conspiratorially and said, "For a minute there, when Jerry said they were bringing one of the actors on as a producer, we all thought he meant Sapphire. Can you *imagine?* Oh lord, we'd all be scrambling to find palm fronds and jewel-encrusted thrones! Anyway, we need to get in there or we are going to be late. I know a little bit about what the past week or two have been like for you, and I am totally available if you need someone to vent to. Or, for that matter, if you just need some help managing the ins and outs of your new responsibilities, my door is always open."

"Thank you," said Kate, a bit overwhelmed. "You may regret the offer when I am camped outside of your trailer with a list of questions."

"Never," said Claire, opening the door of the conference room and standing aside to let Kate in. "I will enjoy every minute. You, my dear, are a gem."

Kate wanted another hug right then and there, but with the door open and twenty faces staring up at her, she was afraid that clinging to Claire for dear life might look a little unprofessional. She forced her feet to carry her into the room, expecting to see eye rolls and snide whispers, but instead of the anticipated "Who do you think you are?" she was greeted with a hearty round of "Kate! It is so good to see you—have you here—have you back! We missed you!"

Overwhelmed, Kate could barely manage to spit out, "I was really only gone a few days, guys."

"But they were *long* days," shouted Bill, the set decorator, to peals of laughter.

"And they were about to get longer," added the stunt supervisor, Mike.

"Oh my god," said Kate, settling into a chair after a brief round of hugs. "What happened while I was gone?"

"Well," said Claire, sitting next to her, "first we heard that they fired you—"

"Which *sucked*," interjected Mike. Kate thanked him with a wide smile.

"Well said, Mike," continued Claire. "And then word came down that Sapphire was demanding that both she and Hamilton be hired as producers—"

"*Oh no!*" Kate covered her mouth with her hand, seemingly unable to stop her mouth from hanging open in shock.

"Oh *yes!*" said Bill. "She felt she needed him in a position of power to oversee the new direction of the show."

"What new direction?" asked Kate.

Claire took over the thread once more. "The new direction that had Sapphire playing *twins*. Apparently, she realized that letting you go would leave a hole in the show—"

"And you know how she loves to fill her hole," said Bill under his breath.

"Bill!" scolded Claire. "That was inappropriate . . . albeit funny and true." When the laughter died down she went on. "Anyway, she felt that the best person to play opposite her was . . . her."

Kate looked around the room suspiciously. "Are you pulling my leg?"

"Oh, would that we were," said Bill, "but as God is my witness, this is all totally true. So, basically, we all thought that we would be sitting here this week with Hamilton at the head of the table, telling us to find a believable way to introduce Destiny's somehow younger—and no doubt thinner—twin sister into our story line."

"I didn't sleep for three days," said Claire. "I can't get *one* Sapphire dressed—can you imagine what it would have been like with two?"

Mike leaned across Claire to pat Kate on the shoulder. "So, needless to say, we are all quite happy to have you back."

"Don't you mean to have *both* of us back?" asked Kate.

"What do you mean 'both' of you?" asked Claire.

"Well, me and my twin sister, Dramatica, of course. She is a foot and a half taller than I am, and she is an African-American trapeze artist. But I don't see that posing a problem for production, do any of you?"

The room broke into an exaggeratedly earnest chorus of "Oh no—not a bit—shouldn't be a problem at all—we'll get right on that!" before breaking into a loud and genuine refrain of laughter.

☆   ☆   ☆

Two hours later, Paige threw a Chanel lip liner down on the make-up counter in mock disgust. "I am very happy that you had a good morning, but if you don't stop talking long enough for me to do your lips, we are all going to have a very long afternoon."

"Sorry," said Kate, clamping her mouth shut and holding perfectly still. Paige picked up the liner again and was just beginning to trace Kate's lower lip when Kate blurted out, "But it was just so cool Paige. I mean, I felt like I really belonged, like I really had a lot to contribute—"

"What you have," interrupted Paige, "is a long red line on your chin because you can't seem to stop moving! Man, this is like trying to work on a toddler!"

"Sorry," said Kate again, but it was clear from her silly grin and her joyfully swinging legs that she was far more excited than sorry.

Paige smiled indulgently. "Okay. I am not going to ruin your fun for a pretty lip line. If you decide you want to have a visible mouth for this scene, you can slap on some lipstick before they roll." She plopped into the chair next to Kate's. "Why don't you just go ahead and finish telling me about your morning, and if anyone yells at us, I'll just tell them that the producer said it was okay."

"I'm pretty much done, though, right?" asked Kate, checking herself out in the mirror. "I don't want to hold anyone up."

"Oh, *now* you're worried?" teased Paige.

"I know, I know . . . I'm not quite myself today, am I?"

"You are, actually," said Paige. "You are just a very happy, confident version of yourself . . . with very pale lips."

"I do feel good. I really do. I didn't realize how much support I had here. I mean, I always knew you were on my side, but . . ." Kate stopped midsentence and looked at Paige intently.

"What?" asked Paige.

"Are you sure this is okay for you? You were so excited about our design business and now here we are, back at *Generations*."

"Oh god, yes."

"Really?"

"Yes, *really*. Kate, I meant what I said to you. It is so much better for me to work a little bit longer and save some more money. I had always planned on opening the shop when I was a little bit closer to retirement, but when the shit hit the fan here, I guess I sort of saw it as a sign."

"It *was* a sign—a sign that the inmates were running the asylum."

"Yeah, and the craziest part is that they didn't get fired—they got promoted to a better asylum."

"Well, that's Hollywood for you," said Kate.

"You should talk," said Paige. "Your life has pretty much turned into a Hollywood screenplay, Madam Producer."

Kate sighed. "No—if this were a screenplay, Michael would come through the door right now with a brilliant explanation and a bouquet of flowers and pull me into a deep, hard-to-watch tongue kiss."

"Ugh." Paige wrinkled her nose in disgust. "You had me right up until the end."

Kate batted her eyes. "And you had me at 'hello.' "

Paige grabbed a towel off the counter and threw it, narrowly missing Kate's face. "Hey!" said Kate. "Watch the face. The face is the fortune!"

Paige shook her head. "No, the *girl* is the *crazy*."

A knock at the door froze both women in their tracks. *Michael?*

"Come in," called Paige.

The door opened abnormally and painfully slowly to reveal . . . Sam.

"Hello, ladies!" he said cheerfully.

"Hey," they said together, with very little enthusiasm.

"Uh-oh," he said. "Have things gone south already? We haven't even started yet."

"Love troubles," said Paige.

Kate shot her a look. "More like *friends who can't keep their mouths shut* troubles."

"Oopsie," said Paige.

Sam cut in. "I didn't hear a thing. I just came in to say welcome back."

"Thank you."

"You are welcome. Also, we are twenty minutes away from your scene, and when you are done with your actress duties, Claire has some wardrobe questions for the producer part of you."

"Thank you from both of my parts."

"You are welcome to both of your parts," said Sam, heading out. He paused briefly before closing the door to say, "It really is great to have you back. You were missed."

"Thank you, Sam. That means a lot to me," said Kate right before the door clicked shut. "It's not a tongue kiss, but I guess it will have to do."

"A: gross, and B: I bet if you asked really nicely, Sam would give you a tongue kiss."

"Okay, I can see I need to explain something to you." Kate tried for a professorial expression.

"Are you constipated?" asked Paige.

"No, I'm being serious."

"Huh. You look constipated."

"Can I please get to my point?"

"Okay . . . if you're sure you don't need to use the bathroom first."

"Stop it!" shouted Kate, silencing Paige. After a few moments of silence she said, "Of course, now I can't remember what I was going to say." Paige giggled. "Oh, now I remember! I was going to explain to you that even though you, as a recovering slut—"

"Hey! Hold on a minute!"

"What?"

Paige shrugged. "Nothing. Carry on."

"Thank you. My point is, regardless of what you learned at slut school, it is important to be selective about whom you tongue kiss."

"Well, nobody is going to kiss you if you keep saying 'whom.' "

"Good grammar is very sexy."

"Oh yeah, I think I read that in *Hustler*."

"See? Slut," Kate said, pointing at Paige.

Paige pointed back. "See? Crazy."

Kate laughed. "Hey, if the producer in me eats an omelet, will the actress in me still fit into her costumes?"

"Well," said Paige, getting up and heading to the door, "if she doesn't, the producer can just order new costumes."

"You're right," said Kate. "That kicks ass."

"Yes, it does. You know, the producer can also approve a raise for the star's makeup artist."

"Really? Even the slutty ones?"

"Especially the slutty ones."

Paige and Kate continued their slutty debate all the way to the catering truck, where they each had a huge piece of cheesy frittata and a cinnamon roll on the side. Constipation be damned.

★   ★   ★

Kate's scene was filmed without a hitch. She was so intent on learning more about what each person on set was doing that her acting was completely relaxed and natural. She felt as if her eyes had been opened or at least turned outward for the first time in years. Suddenly, she was aware of how constricted she used to feel by all of the eyes trained on her. Now, thanks to her new producer point of view, she could see that the time spent watching her do her work was no more or less than the time spent looking at the flags placed by the grips or the lights placed by the electricians. It was a team and she was one member. Well, one member who now wore two hats.

Donning her producer hat, she headed over to the wardrobe trailer to meet with Claire about the next episode's costumes. She was pretty sure that her character, Melania, wouldn't be wearing lingerie anytime soon.

Jerry met her outside the trailer and held the door open for her. "After you, Madam Producer."

"Thank you, Jerry."

"You're welcome," said Jerry, without his usual simpering obsequiousness.

"You know, Jerry, you seem calmer. Are you taking copious amounts of Valium?"

Laughing, he said, "No, no Valium. I guess I just feel more relaxed around you now that you are a fellow member of the production team. I tend to get a little bit nervous around actresses."

"No! *You?*" teased Kate.

"Yes, *me*," said Jerry, nodding earnestly and proving that even though he was less nervous, he still had no ability to discern sarcasm. "Sapphire always sent me into a total tailspin."

"Well, in your defense, she had that effect on a lot of people."

"Oh, right, your husband," he stammered. "I am so sorry about all of that. I didn't mean to bring up a sore subject. I just—"

Kate stopped him with a raised hand. "Enough, Jerry. There is nothing to be sorry about. There is no sore subject. I mean, look how well this has all turned out, right?"

"Wow, you really are handling this incredibly well. Michael was right."

"What?" Kate managed, even though time had seemed to stop and she was having trouble taking a full breath.

"I said Michael was right about you. It was his idea to bring you back on as a producer. To be completely honest with you, I thought he was crazy. No offense."

"None taken," said Kate, offended but not wanting to stop the flow of what Jerry was saying. "Go on . . ."

"Oh, okay. Well, when Sapphire quit, she obviously left us in a bit of a jam, and Michael called me just as I was trying to figure out how I could possibly lure you back. He suggested that you might be tempted with a position that wielded a little more power and control."

"Really?"

"Yeah. He also said that you were smarter than you had been given credit for around here and that you were being sorely under-utilized."

"Wow," said Kate, stunned.

"That's exactly what I said. I mean, I didn't even know you guys knew each other, and here he is pitching his ass off for you. I gotta say, though, so far he has been right on. Obviously, it's only your first day, but everyone was very impressed with you in the production meeting. I have a very good feeling about this."

"Thank you, Jerry," said Kate, spontaneously pulling him into a hug. "I have a very good feeling, too."

"Oh, well, okay," sputtered Jerry, the public display of affection bringing him back to his old flustered self. "Well, uh, I think we should get on with this meeting, don't you?"

After one more torturous squeeze Kate released him and said, "Yes, let's get on with our meeting. And let's make it quick, okay? I have to get home and make a phone call."

39

Kate and Paige sat across from each other at the kitchen table, the phone between them.

"Call him," said Paige.

"I'm scared," whimpered Kate.

"Well, snap out of it!" said Paige, pretending to wind up for a slap.

"Are you doing an impression of Cher from *Moonstruck*? Is that how you're going to help me?"

"No, I am going to slap you into action. The Cher bit was just to distract you while I wind up for the big finish."

"You're crazy."

"No, you're crazy if you don't call Michael right now."

"You're right," said Kate, getting as far as placing her hand on the phone. She paused. "I can't pick it up. What is wrong with me?"

"You're just scared. Do you need a Snickers bar?"

"Why would I need a Snickers bar?"

"Well, I don't have any alcohol in the house, and sugar always calms my nerves."

"No. You think sugar calms you, but in reality it turns you into a speed-talking lunatic."

"Okay, I can't really argue with that," admitted Paige. "Do you want one?"

"No. I don't want to sound like Minnie Mouse on crack when I call Michael, thank you very much. I want to sound like a Zen master."

"How about you just try to sound like *you?*"

Kate rolled her eyes. "How about *you* try to stop sounding like a bad self-help infomercial?"

"How about *you* try to stop yelling at me and call Michael?"

"Touché," said Kate, beaten. She took three deep breaths and picked up the phone. She got through calling information and getting the number for the BAM agency without passing out, which she and Paige took as a good sign. She let out a brief, tension-relieving scream, then dialed the number and asked the receptionist to connect her to Michael Frankel.

"I'm sorry. He no longer works here."

"What?" asked Kate.

"What *what?*" whispered Paige.

Kate held up a finger and mouthed, *Hold on.* "Do you know where he works now?" She hit the speaker button and the receptionist's voice carried into the room.

"I'm not allowed to give out that information, ma'am."

"Can you tell me how to reach him?"

"I'm sorry, ma'am, I can't help you. Have a good day." The dial tone vibrated throughout the kitchen.

"Shit," said Paige, hitting the off button.

"Yeah," said Kate. "Shit."

"Do you have his home phone number?"

"No."

"His cell?"

"No."

"His fax?"

Kate stared at Paige. "Yes, Paige, he hid his home and cell phone numbers from me because he prefers to communicate solely by the new technology of what we like to call the 'Facsimile machine.' "

"Well, you don't need to get all snippy with me," pouted Paige.

"I'm sorry. I'm just so disappointed. I finally got my nerve up to call him and he's not even fucking there!"

"You know what you need, my snippy friend?"

"What?" asked Kate, her bottom lip thrust out in the universal sign for self-pity.

"You need a cup of coffee."

"*Coffee?*" she snapped. "I hardly need caffeine. The last thing in the world I need is—"

"A cup of coffee from the Starbucks in the Pacific Palisades?"

Kate let out a long "Oooooooooooooh!" as recognition dawned. "The Starbucks in the *Palisades*."

"Exactly," said Paige. "Shall I drive?"

"Yes, you shall," answered Kate, gathering her purse and doing a quick check in the mirror. "And drive quickly, please."

★   ★   ★

Michael sat at his computer, staring at a blank screen. Clearly, his right brain had called his left brain and told it that he had quit his job in a fit of misplaced integrity, thus successfully driving his creativity into hiding until he faced reality and got a real job again.

I won't do it, he told his right brain.

You have to. We'll starve, it answered.

So be it, Michael said firmly.

You're bluffing.

Try me.

I won't let you write, said his right brain, joining the conversation.

Really? he asked.

Really, it said confidently.

Well, then, how do you explain the fact that I am writing right now?

Curses! said his right brain.

"Ha ha!" he said aloud, relishing his victory over his own self-doubt.

"That is the worst fake laugh I've ever heard," said a voice behind him.

"I'm sorry. I tend to talk—"

"Out loud sometimes when you write? I know."

Time stopped for Michael. Could that really be Kate's voice? He desperately wanted to turn around and see if it was her, but he didn't know if he could stand the disappointment if it wasn't. Suddenly, she was in front of him, the vision of an angel.

"Hello, Michael," she said simply.

"Kate," he answered breathlessly, standing up so quickly that he knocked over his coffee, eliciting a "Damn it!" from his angry neighbor whose shoes got splashed. "Oh, shit, sorry," Michael sputtered. "Stay right there!" he told Kate firmly, adding, "Please?" as he ran to the condiment station to grab a handful of napkins, which he promptly threw at the lady with the damp shoes before planting himself in front of Kate. "I'm sorry," he said.

"It didn't even touch me," said Kate, gesturing to her dry feet.

"What?" asked Michael, confused.

"The coffee. It didn't get on me."

"The coffee? No, I wasn't saying I was sorry about the *coffee.* I mean, I am sorry about that, too, but—" He stopped abruptly in the middle of his nervous rant. He inhaled deeply, gently took both of Kate's hands in his, and looked her square in the eye. "I *am* sorry about spilling coffee near you." He almost melted when she smiled up at him but forced himself to continue. "But what I am really, *deeply* sorry about is lying to you. I don't know if it matters to you anymore, but I really am a full-time writer now, with no discernible income."

"No discernible income? That's your pitch?" asked Kate, grinning.

"Well, I do have interest income from the many years I spent selling my soul to the devil for a few gold coins—"

"Shhhh," whispered Kate, holding a finger up to his lips. "You had me at 'no income.' "

Michael smiled behind her finger and then reached up to pull her hand away. "I just can't believe you're here."

"Well, you know, a girl needs her coffee."

"Thank God for that," he whispered, tracing her cheek with his finger before reaching around to the back of her neck and pulling her face to his. When their lips were less than an inch apart he paused and asked, "You do know you're coming home with me today, don't you?" Kate managed a tiny nod before Michael's mouth was on hers, his lips warm, dry, and soft. The crowded coffeehouse was all but forgotten as Kate melted into Michael's embrace, losing herself in the wonderful solidity of his strong chest and arms and the gentle exploration of his tongue.

"*Gross,*" said Paige from her vantage point across the room, but her smile and the tears in her eyes exposed her for the sappy romantic she really was.

Acknowledgments

This book was a true labor of love, born out of the support of an amazing group of women. To Mary, Jean, Liz, Piper, and Chris: your keen interest in reading pages as quickly as I could write them motivated and inspired me. What you all lack in objectivity, you more than made up for in exaggerated enthusiasm. As for my mom's and my sister's endless protestations that their positive criticisms were completely unbiased: I didn't believe it for a second, although I thoroughly enjoyed every bit of inflated affirmation. I am beyond blessed to be surrounded by so much love from such smart, funny, loving women. And to my niece, Cassie, thank you for inspiring me with your own brilliantly funny stories.

Dad, thank you for your support and for bragging about your "daughter the author" to all who would listen. I expect very high sales numbers in Portola Valley.

I really need to thank my longtime theatrical agent, Joel Rudnick, for not laughing (at least not in front of me) at me when I told him I was writing a novel, and for introducing me to my wonderful literary agent, Lydia Wills. Lydia, your enthusiasm motivated me to keep writing, and your thoughtful notes on the pages I sent you kept me on track.

I am grateful to everyone at Broadway Books. Bill Thomas and Steve Rubin, I can never thank you enough for buying my manuscript based on a few pages and what must have been gut instinct. It would be impossible to say enough good things about my editor, Ann Campbell. Ann, you made me believe in myself as a writer, and your careful, insightful editing challenged and inspired me. *Outside In* is a much better book thanks to you. Laura Lee Mattingly, thank you for always being a friendly voice on the other end of the phone, and for being efficient and professional to boot. I also want to thank Michael Windsor for including me so graciously in the design of the cover art, and Susan Buckheit for her careful copy editing.

Thanks also need to go out to my longtime publicist, Jim Broutman, for his commitment and hard work in creating awareness for *Outside In*. Also, to the publicity and marketing teams at Broadway: David Drake, Tammy Blake, Andrea O'Brien, Julia Coblentz, and Julie Sills—I have felt your belief in my book from day one and I thank you for all of your hard work.

And finally, to my husband, Roger: it is no coincidence that I found the confidence to commit to my lifelong dream of writing a novel soon after meeting you. Your belief in me made me believe in myself. Thank you.